HOPE
AND A
FUTURE

HOPE
AND A
FUTURE

BETTY ARRIGOTTI

OakTara

WATERFORD, VIRGINIA

Hope and a Future

Published in the U.S. by:
OakTara Publishers
P.O. Box 8
Waterford, VA 20197

Visit OakTara at
www.oaktara.com

Cover design by www.yvonneparks.com
Cover image © www.shutterstock.com/horses awaiting storm, Peter Wey
Author photo © by George Arrigotti

Scripture taken from the HOLY BIBLE, NEW INTERNATIONAL VERSION®. NIV®. Copyright © 1973, 1978, 1984 by International Bible Society. Used by permission of Zondervan. All rights reserved.

ISBN: 978-1-60290-254-1

Hope and a Future is a work of fiction. References to real people, events, establishments, organizations, or locales are intended only to provide a sense of authenticity and are used fictitiously. All other characters, incidents, and dialogue are drawn from the author's imagination.

⌘ ⌘ ⌘

To George,
who bought me a beautiful pen when I graduated from college
and a laptop when I went back to school 25 years later.
Thank you for always supporting my writing.

Acknowledgments

Thank you to the fine therapists/researchers like John Gottman, Nan Silver, Terrence Real, David M Schnarch, and Bernie Zilbergeld, who provided my characters and readers tools to progress in their relationships. Wonderful Northwest writers and editors like Carol Craig, Jennie Shortridge, Miralee Ferrell, Randy Ingermanson, Nina Hoffman, and Nikki Arana, as well as online instructors like Mary Buckham, Laurie Schnebly Campbell, Gwen Shuster-Haynes, and Margie Lawson have encouraged and taught me along the way. All of the people who improve writing through their work at conferences earn my gratitude, especially the Oregon Writers Colony, Willamette Writers, Rose City Romance Writers, Pacific Northwest Writers Association, American Christian Fiction Writers, and Oregon Christian Writers. Jeff Nesbit, Ramona Tucker, and the staff at OakTara deserve special thanks for believing in this book.

However, even more instrumental in their support were my family: my husband, George, my daughters Melissa, Theresa, Kathleen, and Jennifer, my mother, Ruth, my brothers Bernie and Steve, and my mom-in-law, Marylu. My friends Brenda, Mary, Mary Jo, Mary Lou, Jennie, and Joan cheered me on while Word Women writers Debbie, Sue, Julie, Lynette, and Jen held me to high standards.

My thanks to you all, for helping me fulfill my heart's desire to be a writer.

Contents

Prologue

"All night long on my bed I looked for the one my heart loves;
I looked for him but did not find him."
SONG OF SOLOMON 3:1

Marjorie Gloriam accepted her husband's good night kiss and then turned her back to him, her mind on their younger daughter's college acceptance. As she nestled into her sleep position, her hand slid beneath her pillow and brushed against an envelope. She jumped and sat up, her heart heavy as she reached to turn on her bedside lamp.

"Oh, Michael, I forgot."

Her husband propped himself on an elbow and grinned, a dark cowlick of hair making him look as boyish as when they were newlyweds. "That's okay, dear. Our anniversary doesn't officially start for another hour."

Marjorie held the envelope in one hand, shaking her head. Not only had she forgotten to tuck the traditional card or gift under his pillow, she had completely forgotten their anniversary. How did March 15 sneak up on her unannounced? Her shoulders sagged under the weight of regret.

"Let's open our cards together tomorrow." She could squeeze in a shopping trip between her clients and marriage counseling classes.

"Nope, I'm too anxious. Tomorrow's fine to give me my card, but you have to open this tonight." Michael raised his pillow against the cherry headboard and sat upright against it. His eyes sparkled. "Go ahead."

When he rested his arm around her shoulder, she resisted the urge to shift away from him. She forced a smile but clenched her jaw as she tore open the envelope and removed a large, beautiful card with a cluster of lilies of the valley on the front. A white ribbon tied the stems together and laced through two interlocked wedding rings. Below the picture a verse from the Song of Solomon read:

My lover spoke and said to me,
"Arise, my darling, my beautiful one,
and come with me."

With foreboding, Marjorie opened the card. A United Airlines ticket folder covered whatever sweet saying had prompted Michael to choose it. She had never received such a gift; Michael disliked travel and only flew for occasional work assignments.

She slid two round-trip tickets out and murmured, "Italy." The smile took more effort to sustain.

Poor Michael. He was trying so hard to please her, yet all his efforts proved irritating. She pushed aside thoughts that Italy represented his heritage, not hers.

"Happy anniversary, dear." His voice was animated, but his words sounded rehearsed. "I know you've always wanted to go farther than our quick Oregon vacations. The dates aren't fixed in stone, but I'm hoping we can spend the whole summer away."

What he didn't say, but what she suspected he meant, was he hoped they could regain the joy their marriage had held for twenty-four years. Before this confounded restlessness set in and caused her to long for a change. Before the quirks of this kind, good man began to grate on her nerves.

"What's wrong? I thought you'd be thrilled." His eyes lost their light. She watched the muscles in his forehead contract into the confused expression she caused so frequently lately.

Marjorie took a deep breath and hoped he wouldn't see the effort it took to beam at him. "Of course I'm thrilled...and stunned. It's a wonderful gift."

She had always wanted to travel. However, she would have chosen Ireland, or even the East Coast. She'd love to see the monuments of the capital or the Statue of Liberty. Italy was his dream.

Pushing away her ungrateful thoughts, she leaned over to kiss his wrinkled brow. *Almighty Father,* she prayed, *forgive me for these feelings. Help this trip be the change I've been longing for. Help it bring back my love for Michael.*

⌘ ⌘ ⌘

The weeks flew past, fueled by the tasks necessary before leaving work, home, and daughters for three months. Already frazzled from the details of assigning clients to other counselors, she'd spent the last two weeks helping their daughter Colleen pack to move to Seattle and join her sister Sophie in an apartment near the university. Colleen had flown their nest yesterday, excited about her summer job and college life ahead. Now, after a final day at her office, Marjorie returned home and found Michael hurrying clothes into a garment bag. She tensed.

Michael glanced up from his packing. "I'm sorry, dear. Really sorry." His face confirmed his apology. "I have to make a quick trip to California."

Marjorie shook her head adamantly. "We leave for Europe in three days! You were supposed to start your vacation today so we'd get ready together."

"Jerry's wife went into premature labor. I told him I'd cover the client visit for him. I'll be back the day after tomorrow." He zipped the suit bag and drew her into his arms.

Marjorie stiffened. She knew she should understand. He was being the helpful, considerate person she fell in love with years ago. But it wasn't fair to leave her with all the packing and final preparations. Now even Colleen wasn't available to help.

Michael pulled back, obviously hurt by her rigidity. "I never seem to get it right for you anymore, do I?" His voice sounded tight and tinged with defeat.

Marjorie's heart sank as she looked up into his eyes. She would give anything not to be the cause of the pain she saw there. The dear man tried so hard. Her engineer always believed he could solve a problem, given the resources he needed. Yet she had no idea what those resources were, because she didn't know what was wrong. Only that she longed for a change, and a trip to Europe wasn't it.

She lifted up on her tiptoes and kissed him, a sad, apologetic kiss. He held her longer than usual, and she relaxed into his warmth. She did love him, she reminded herself. She always had and always would.

Then he was out the door on his way to the airport, and she remained a captive to the details of life, as well as an unrelenting irritation.

⌘ ⌘ ⌘

That night Marjorie dropped into bed, sick of luggage and lists. She replayed the moment of warmth in Michael's arms to remind herself that their love remained the enduring truth. The daydreams of independence that she hardly admitted into consciousness were fleeting feelings, meaningless in the long-term covenant of a committed marriage.

The phone rang. Eleven o'clock. The time Michael always called when he was away. She poured tenderness into her answer. "Hello, my dear."

"Mrs. Gloriam?"

One hand drew her robe closed over her chest as she sat up. "Oh, I thought you were my husband."

A pause and a soft throat clearing on the other end of the line caused the hair on the back of her neck to stand alert.

"I'm sorry, ma'am. This is Officer Drake with the California Highway Patrol. Your husband is Michael Gloriam?"

Marjorie's heart jolted as if lightning struck her chest. She looked at the clock again. She tried to swallow past a tight objection in her throat, but her mouth was too dry. Her mind began to intone *no, no, no,* keeping time with her increasing heart rate. She could barely pry out the word, "Yes?"

"Mrs. Gloriam, are you alone? Is there someone you can call to be with you?"

She grasped the phone with both hands, holding on as if to a badly fraying rope. "What's wrong? What happened?"

In an incoherent moment of terrifying finality—"car accident...heart attack...deepest sympathies"—daydream became nightmare.

Michael was gone. Marjorie was alone.

⌘ ⌘ ⌘

After time that could have been seconds or hours, Marjorie emerged from a void and replaced the phone receiver. The closest she had come to this disembodied sensation was after having her wisdom teeth removed. Then the anesthesia had left her in a suspended state, but she could force herself out of it to answer questions and move from wheelchair to car and again to her bed. This void loomed more menacing and required more of a struggle to focus her attention.

Her empty arms longed to hold Michael. Her words to grieving clients came to mind and rang as hollow as she felt. *"One day at a time."*

But how do I survive the nights?

At the realization that Michael wouldn't lie on his side of the bed—or hers—ever again, she began to shiver. The sheets and blanket held no warmth or comfort. She stood. Her shaking worsened.

She knew she should call her daughters, but how could she inflict this intolerable pain on them?

She curled into the bedroom chair and imagined her head on Michael's shoulder. *Michael, my love, I'm so sorry. I wish I'd been happier for you these last few months.*

She felt small and abandoned. Her mind slipped back to the void but wouldn't stay. Prayer moaned behind clenched, chattering teeth.

Almighty Father, make it not true! Is this Your punishment? Did I cause this by wishing for something new? Why couldn't I have been satisfied?

Marjorie pulled the afghan that lay folded across the back of the chair around her. She covered her head with it and squeezed her eyes tight, but she could not stop the tears.

One

Change is frightening
but calls us to growth.

M arjorie lay stunned. Cold mud began oozing through her shirt and jeans, the smell of horse muck overwhelming her senses. Afraid to move enough to assess the damage, she scanned what she could see without moving her head. The arena fence rail blocked most of her view of the unseasonable gray Oregon sky. She could hear Oasis' hooves as the horse began to slow its flight. The explosion of pheasant wings that caused the horse to rear had fallen silent, but a red-winged blackbird trilled for its lost mate. The sound of the lonely bird connected the pain of her body to the unrelenting ache in her heart.

A car door slammed, and she heard steps running toward her. A slight Irish brogue called, "Saints, preserve us! Don't move!" Even in her predicament, something about the sound of his voice stirred a reaction that touched ancestral roots.

Gingerly she turned her head. Her would-be rescuer looked as if he could be hurrying from an Irish Spring soap commercial, complete with the kind of white cable-knit sweater that had always made her want to take up knitting.

"I'm okay." She raised her chin to test her claim. "I think the helmet took the brunt of the fall. I'll let my head clear before I stand." As the man helped her sit, Marjorie could feel his arm shaking against her back. Her worry shifted from the manure ruining his knit sleeve to his well-being.

"I'm sorry I frightened you," she said. "Are you all right?"

He glanced at the horse, which now approached them, head lowered and ears drooped, giving Marjorie only a quick moment to notice his strong Gaelic jaw line before he turned back to her. The Irishman appeared to force himself to focus only on Marjorie. "Can you walk at all, at all?"

She nodded, and he helped her stand. As they made their way across the arena to the gate, he kept her hand enveloped in the warmth of his while his arm firmly braced her back. The horse followed them, but he didn't look at it again.

Marjorie noticed one of the teenage girls who, like her, rented stall space at the stable, loading a wheelbarrow from a mound of woodchips. "Jenny," she called to her, "I've taken a bit of a spill. Could you walk Oasis until she calms down and then get her settled in her stall?"

"Sure thing, Mrs. Gloriam. Happy to."

The man glanced down at the wedding ring on her finger as he heard her name. "Ah, you're married."

"Yes...no..."

She could see his confusion but was there a bit of disappointment, too?

"May I call your husband?"

"I'm..." She hesitated. The word *widow* still made her think of a black spider. She repressed the familiar spark of guilt shackled to her loss. "He died. Fifteen months ago." She heard the pain in her voice and hurried to fend off any pity. "Thank you, but I'm sure I'll be fine."

The gentleman's voice held only sincerity. "I'm very sorry. May I at least get you a cup of tea?"

"That sounds wonderful, but there's none to be had around here, I'm afraid. There's a coffee machine in the indoor arena, but it's worse than nothing at all." *"At all, at all,"* she added silently, repeating the lilt of his words.

"I've a thermos in the car. Sit here and I'll be right back with it."

She eased herself onto the arena bleachers and watched him hurry away, giving Jenny and the horse wide berth when they passed him.

What kind of man dresses like that at a horse stable? It was chilly for August, but a sweatshirt or jacket would be more appropriate than that handsome sweater.

She caught herself stroking her wedding ring. She supposed she should quit wearing it at some point. An involuntary shudder escaped her heart and made her shoulders quiver at the thought of removing the ring. She raised her eyes to the sky. *Seems like both yesterday and forever ago. Almighty Father, help me. Forgive me for not being more grateful for Michael.*

As the Irishman returned to her with the tea, he grinned and his whole face brightened. Marjorie figured he was about her age, in his forties. His hair was dark brown, but copper highlighted his eyebrows and trim sideburns. His green eyes still showed his concern and held hers a moment too long. Marjorie's pulse raced as she shifted her gaze to the tea he poured, but she attributed it to her fall.

"It may be a wee bit strong. I left the bags in."

"Bags?"

"Four. One for each cup."

Marjorie, who loved tea but usually preferred hers rather weak, sipped the bitterest tea she had ever tasted. However, she felt it begin to soothe, more from the comfort of a familiar ritual than from the strong brew. As the man wiped his forehead with a pristine but shaking handkerchief, she realized he could use a bit of bracing, himself. She offered him the half-full cup. He smiled and drank the rest, but when he refilled the cup and returned it to her, the tea rippled with the tremor of his hand.

"'Tis dead scared of horses, I am," he blurted, and then Marjorie joined him in laughter that began from simple relief that they were both relatively unharmed but continued into an embarrassing giddiness.

She took a deep breath to regain her composure. "I'm Marjorie. Thank you for your help and for the tea." Then she saw the dirty hand she had offered him, pulled it back, and surrendered into giggles. Marjorie's sides hurt more from the laughter than from her fall.

He took her hand in his, and Marjorie was again struck with the heat of his palm against her mud-chilled skin.

"Colm McCloskey. Thank you, Marjorie, for your brilliant way of helping me confront my horse-terror."

Marjorie squeezed his hand and released it, then shook her head in disbelief. "What in the world are you doing at a stable if horses frighten you so?"

"They were next in line on the list of fears I'm facing," Colm answered matter-of-factly. "I started on the easiest and am working up to the hardest." He paused and straightened, as if drawing courage for some new challenge. "Would you forgive the forwardness of a stranger and allow me to take you to dinner to show my appreciation?"

"Oh, no, I couldn't." She hadn't dated since Michael died. The mere possibility flooded her with guilt.

She softened her voice when she saw his disappointment. "I assume you're from Ireland, and I'd love to learn more about your country but my daughters are coming for the weekend. Not to mention that I'm covered in mud and reek of Oasis."

"Oasis?"

"The horse."

"Ah, of course. You should soak in hot water before your muscles realize what that beastie has done to them. Perhaps after your daughters have visited, call me—I'll give you my card—and tell me a time and place. I'd be delighted to see you again."

As they walked toward their cars, he asked, "You're well enough to drive?"

She nodded. "I live just two exits back toward Portland."

"Good, then I'll be going your direction and can keep an eye on you until you're off the highway." He took her hand, and for a moment Marjorie imagined he might bend to kiss it, but he simply covered it momentarily with his other. His eyes, however, held hers captive as he said, "I'll look forward to your call."

Marjorie broke the gaze and dipped her head. "Thank you, Colm."

"And you, Marjorie." His accent diminished when he relaxed and Marjorie realized she missed his brogue.

Down the muddy road and on the highway, she watched his car in her rearview mirror until she exited. *Such a long time since someone other than the Almighty looked out for me.* The realization caused her forehead to tighten and her hands to clench the wheel.

It doesn't seem right for it not to be Michael.

⌘ ⌘ ⌘

Once at home, Marjorie set Colm's card next to the phone on her nightstand. As she did, the framed photograph of Michael caught her attention. A sympathy card next to the picture quoted St. John Chrysostom:

> He whom we love and lose
> is no longer where he was before.
> He is now wherever we are.

Her eyes rested on Michael's pillow. After more than a year without him, she still found comfort in having it on the bed next to hers. She looked around the room and remembered him standing the last anniversary card on their dresser, before sliding the previous birthday card into the drawer where he kept all her greetings from over the years. She turned to the overstuffed chair and could almost feel him pulling her onto his lap, almost smell his Old Spice aftershave. She raised her eyes to the mirror and recalled the countless times he came up behind her to give her a kiss and help her fasten a necklace.

She opened the nightstand drawer and dropped Colm's card in, saying to herself, *Nobody could ever take Michael's place.* She closed the drawer, but her hand rested a bit longer on the wood.

⌘ ⌘ ⌘

Marjorie had finished her shower and stepped into her favorite turquoise summer dress when she heard the front door open. Her beagle Nutmeg barked, and she listened to the dog's toenails dance as the girls called, "Mom, we're home! Happy birthday weekend!"

Marjorie grabbed a sweater and her overnight bag. Though careful not to jolt her sore back, she hurried down the stairs to greet them with a three-way hug. She looked up into their merry eyes. Both stood taller than she did, but beyond that, their similarity ended. Sophie had the dark coloring, wavy hair, and chiseled features of Michael's Italian side and led with her head. She wore khaki slacks and a fitted black weskit shirt. Colleen favored their mother's Irish ancestry with red corkscrew curls, freckles, and delicate features. She led with her heart. Normally comfortable in her ever-present jeans, today she wore a soft skirt, presumably to honor the occasion.

"Good to see you two! I've really been looking forward to Ladies' Day Out."

"We wouldn't miss it, Mom, even though it meant listening to jazz all the way from Seattle." Sophie rolled her eyes at Colleen, who, though colored like her mother, had her father's taste in music.

"Which somehow is worse than three hours of country on our way back?" her sister retorted.

"That must mean it's my choice from here to the restaurant." Marjorie grabbed her keys, and both girls groaned as they followed her to the garage.

In the car, they covered the typical updates. Sophie's job as an engineer for a software company in Seattle was going well. A sophomore in college, Colleen's summer school classes and work kept her sleep-deprived but happy. Yes, they still skirmished like teenagers in their shared apartment but often managed moments of peace. No, they weren't so busy that they needed to skip their Ladies' Day Out.

Their visit was part of a plan the girls had devised to ease their mother's loneliness. Since their father died, on the Saturdays closest to Marjorie's anniversary and birthday the girls arrived in time to take their mother to dinner and a movie. The three would check in to a downtown hotel and update each other on the news in their lives, make fun of women's magazines, and usually laugh late into the night. On Sunday, they would attend church together and follow it with a breakfast feast. Last August, they had wandered through Saturday Market browsing the outdoor craft booths. In March they commemorated her first anniversary alone with a trip to one of Portland's many gardens to admire spring blossoms. This August Marjorie considered the birthday visit the official end to the year she had taken off work to adjust to her loss, a final weekend before returning to her work as a professor of counseling.

Their conversation over dinner turned to current young men in the girls' lives. Sophie talked about Niko, a software designer she had met earlier in the summer. Marjorie congratulated herself on only raising an eyebrow but holding her tongue when Sophie mentioned he was an atheist. Colleen declared she was too busy for boyfriends, for the time being, but teased, "What about you, Mom? Any men in your life that we should know about?"

Water splashed out of Marjorie's glass as she set it back down on the table without taking a drink. She felt her cheeks warm. "Interesting you should ask. I fell for a man just today," she said, and then told them about Colm McCloskey.

Colleen's eyes opened wide. "Cool, Mom, call him! I'd love to see you happy with someone again."

Marjorie's breath caught in her throat. The idea of replacing Michael was unthinkable. She had loved him and loved him still. But why had she been so restless those months before his death?

Sophie's chin shifted slightly forward and reminded Marjorie of the days before Sophie learned to prioritize thinking over feeling, when that pout used to accompany angry crossed arms.

Colleen glanced at her sister and then admitted, "It would be weird for it not to be Daddy, but you have great taste in men. I'm sure you'd find someone we'd all love."

"No, my dears." Marjorie shook her head and steeled her heart against the onslaught of guilt. "I couldn't ever replace your dad. My work is my life now. Helping other people overcome their loneliness."

After the visit ended and the girls left for Seattle, their opposite reactions to the mention of Colm stayed with Marjorie. Strange how perfectly Colleen's excitement and Sophie's disapproval portrayed her own mixed feelings.

Two

Love needs maintenance, man.

Tessa Bernette showered after dinner while her husband, Joe, dropped off their children, Amy and Stephen, at friends' houses to spend the last Friday night of summer vacation. Tessa didn't wash her hair, not wanting it to be wet, but carefully curled it like years ago when she and Joe were dating. Alone in the house, she walked naked to her closet and chose a white lace negligee, cut low in front. She spritzed and then walked into a mist of cologne she had chosen at the mall, a blend of clove and vanilla. She inhaled and smiled, uncovered the bed pillows, and sprayed them lightly, too.

Tessa glanced around the fern-green walls and wished she had been brave enough to choose the scarlet paint that had caught her eye recently. She imagined Joe's surprise when he came home to find her ready for bed so early. It had been a long time since they had a night alone together. She carried candles to both sides of the bed and lit them, guessing that Joe would return any minute.

An hour later, Joe honked the horn as he drove into the garage, their signal that the driver needed help unloading the car. Tessa, in frustration and disappointment, considered going to the garage in her white lace to show Joe what he had missed. Afraid he might not be alone for some reason, she grabbed a robe and tugged it on as she stomped to the door.

"Hi, Hon. Were you in bed already?" Joe brushed against her as he passed with bags of hardware filling his arms. The aroma of fresh cut pine followed him and she couldn't help but inhale deeply.

"Stephen's friend lives right near Home Depot, so I stopped to buy the shelves we talked about putting up in the kids' rooms. I figure with a couple of hours before bed we could maybe have them in by the time they get home tomorrow. Won't they be surprised?"

When Tessa didn't answer, Joe stopped and looked at her. "What's wrong?"

Unable to put into words, even to herself, everything that seemed wrong, Tessa turned, walked back to her room, and closed the door behind her. Tessa curled in a tight ball under the blankets, her back to the door. She could hear Joe unload the shelving material from the car into Stephen's and Amy's rooms. She listened to him wash his hands and then, as he opened the door with a sigh, venture into the dark bedroom.

Joe sat on his side of the bed and tried again. "Tessa, what's up? Are you sick? Did someone call with bad news?"

Tessa wiped her eyes and climbed out of the bed, still wearing her white lace nightie. Without looking at Joe, she lit her nightstand lamp, walked to the closet, and changed into a flannel nightgown. Then she returned to the bed and settled into it, her back to Joe.

"Oh." A full minute passed while Tessa let Joe take in the burned-out candles, the moist feel to the air from the recent shower and the spicy aroma. "Oh."

Still Tessa didn't turn to him, and she felt completely justified. He had rejected her so many times lately. Now he could feel what she had felt: the aloneness, the sadness. However, a melody played in Tessa's mind. She couldn't shake it. Words about turning back and bending to others' needs insisted their way into the tune. This chapel song, her favorite while she and Joe were in college, softened her heart.

Joe rose and approached her side of the bed. She straightened her legs to make room for him to sit on the edge.

"I'm sorry, Tessa. I guess we both saw the kids being gone as an opportunity. I imagined the fun of us working together to surprise them both. I didn't know you were planning this. I would have come right home if I had. Guess you've been waiting quite awhile, huh?"

Tessa sniffed.

"Don't suppose you're still in the mood?"

"No."

"Didn't think so." He hung his head, then raised it suddenly. "You know, we could compromise. You could wear your white lace while you help me build shelves."

Tessa couldn't keep back a tiny smile at the mental image.

Encouraged, Joe ventured, "And you could wear my tool belt."

Now the picture in Tessa's mind became ridiculous. "Oh, Joe, no fair trying to make me laugh when I want to be mad at you." Tessa swung her legs back out of bed and sat up but avoided Joe, who had leaned over to kiss her. "No way, I'm still too upset for that. Let me get some jeans on and pull myself together. I'll come to help in a few minutes."

As Tessa went to the closet to change for the third time that evening, she tried to talk herself into a better mood. *Making love isn't everything. There's building love, too. Maybe one bookshelf at a time.*

When Tessa joined Joe in Amy's room, he asked her to hold the brackets while he screwed them to the wall with his electric drill. They installed four brackets and were trying to fit the shelf supports into them when they realized they had mounted all four upside down.

When they had at last installed the shelves correctly in Amy's room, they discussed whether to go to bed or to tackle Stephen's room. Figuring the second set would go much more quickly, they kept working. At 2 a.m. they finally stood back and admired the four new shelves in their son's room. Joe took his tools back to the garage while Tessa lugged out the vacuum to clean the drywall dust off the floors.

Joe had finished getting ready for bed by the time Tessa put the vacuum away. While she washed her face, she tried to decide what to wear for the night. Looking for a clue, she peeked out at the bed and heard the too-familiar snore. "Well, it is awfully late." She exhaled slowly and took the flannel gown off its hook.

Lying in bed, Tessa felt like the rumbled breathing next to her came from the opposite rim of the Grand Canyon. A decision became clear. When she registered for graduate school courses, she would take Marjorie Gloriam's Couples' Counseling class. One way or another she had to learn how to bridge this chasm between them.

Three

Knowledge will
help us heal.

Tessa awoke the Thursday after Labor Day to the familiar sadness. Joe had already left for work after a quick kiss on her nose that barely brought her to consciousness.

Maybe I should be getting up with him and seeing him off, she thought. *At night, he's so tired, and in the morning, I'm sleepy. We need more rest. Or more exercise? Maybe if we were in better shape, the spark would return.*

She sighed and slid her feet out from under the covers and into slippers. She remembered that tonight she'd begin her Couples' Counseling class.

Dear Lord, let me learn something that will help.

⌘ ⌘ ⌘

Across town, Gwen O'Connell opened her eyes facing her bedroom window and felt betrayed by the blue sky and sunshine. Sympathetic weather would have wept with her. Afraid turning over would confirm her fears, she listened past the plaintive mourning dove and with relief heard Brian's quiet breath.

What makes me think I can learn to be a marriage counselor when I can't even keep my husband coming to bed with me at night?

⌘ ⌘ ⌘

In a suburb apartment, Hank Glenn eyed his unmade bed and wished he could sleep. Instead, he showered and ate a bowl of cereal before hurrying off to a volunteer's meeting at the Portland Youth Club, where he would spend the afternoon with children whose childhoods reflected the emptiness he still felt from his own early years.

⌘ ⌘ ⌘

Marjorie lay savoring the comforting weight of Michael's arm across her shoulder. She felt him draw her to him, and she snuggled back in the bed to enjoy the warmth of his chest against her....

But then the alarm sounded, and Marjorie awoke to the empty pillow and the sheet still neatly folded down over the blanket on Michael's side of the bed, as it had been every morning since he died. She closed her eyes, breathed in, but failed to recapture the fleeting feeling of Michael's arm around her. She exhaled and forced her attention to the day.

September. A new semester; a new group of future counselors. Time for me to return to my life.

A new quirk since living alone, she said her quick prayers aloud. "Almighty Father, bless my new students. Help me be a tool for You, so they'll build stronger relationships for themselves and learn how to help their future clients do the same."

⌘ ⌘ ⌘

Late that afternoon, Marjorie was determined to put the memory of Michael's touch out of her mind as she watched the new crop of graduate students choose desks among the circled seats of her classroom. At least a third were nontraditional students, usually middle-aged men and women changing careers or, in some cases, entering their first career after raising a family. The remainders were "twenty-somethings." Some came fresh out of college to make a bachelor degree in psychology more employable. Others had begun work in the field but wanted to add to their credentials and knowledge.

A few were passing through her Couples' Counseling class on their way to becoming doctors of psychology.

Couples' Counseling wasn't a required course, though in Marjorie's mind it should be, so why the students chose this course as one of their few electives always interested her. She suspected most hoped to understand their personal relationships better. She sighed. If only she'd understood herself better before Michael had died.

She took a deep breath, focusing on the fresh floor-polish smell rather than her thoughts. She glanced at the clock; time to begin.

"Welcome." She smiled as she stood. "I'm Marjorie Gloriam, and this is Counseling Psych 560, Couples' Counseling." She paused to make sure everyone really did mean to be in this class and then continued. "We used to call the class Marriage Counseling, before we realized that, although all people in marriages can use help—" Her stomach tightened. She, of all people, was well aware of the truth behind those words. She forced herself on—"not all people who could use some help are in marriages."

Polite smiles. Okay, they're listening.

"I chose working with relationships because it seems to me that most individual counseling revolves around people's difficulties dealing with other people. Much child and adolescent counseling is required because of the unhealthy adult relationships they are subjected to. So, I see couples' counseling as working with the root of the problem. That's my excuse. Now I'd like to know what brought each of you here."

Pause. Eye contact. Time to think. A few hands went up. *Good. I can always count on the nontraditional students to start the discussion.*

A woman with graying temples said, "I'm newly divorced and wish I understood what went wrong. I guess I'm mostly here for myself."

"I'm glad you're here," Marjorie answered. "The better we understand ourselves, the better we can help those we counsel."

The woman's admission opened the way for the other students to be honest about their reasons for choosing the class.

"I keep dating the same kind of guy."

"My parents' marriage is falling apart, and I need to help them fall in love again."

"I work with abused women and want to guide them toward

healthier future relationships."

"My husband drives me crazy."

Everyone laughed, but Marjorie's heart ached anew, remembering the restlessness that made her feel the same way before Michael died. She forced a smile and wished her clients and students could realize their blessings. If she could have her husband back, she would never complain about him again. She tugged her attention back to the task at hand, refusing to submit to the loneliness of knowing she would never be able to feel his fingers intertwine with hers, to relax under the weight of his arm around her, or to hear the tender words "I love you."

"Okay," she said, pushing away her self-pity. "Then let's get started."

Marjorie handed out the syllabus that would normally summarize the theories to be studied, the necessary reading and assignments, and how the grade would be figured. Her syllabus listed two-dozen books written about relationships, with short summaries. As soon as the students saw the long list of books, they looked at Marjorie with wide eyes.

"Don't worry," she reassured them, "these aren't all required reading. Glance at a few in the library. I want you to keep a journal about the deepest current relationship in your life and choose one of these books' theories to apply to that relationship.

"You'll meet in groups of three for the first hour of each class to discuss your chosen theory and as much about the development of your relationships as you're comfortable sharing. Again, don't worry. You do have to discuss the theory, but you don't have to talk about any private issues that would make you uncomfortable.

"During the week, apply what you are learning, journal to record your relationship's progress, and turn in the pages at the beginning of the next class. I'll read and return them the following week, with written comments or suggestions. At the end of the semester, draw from your journal to write a paper that summarizes what steps you took to help your own relationship and what effect your efforts had on your lives. We'll start the assignment right now. Please write about yourself and why you are taking the class. What relationship will you be improving?"

As papers rustled, Marjorie settled behind her desk and felt separated from her students by more than furniture.

What about me, Father? What intimate relationship is left for me to improve?

Four

We are survivors!

Saturday morning, Tessa mulled over the couples' course requirements as she drove east on the Sunset Highway. Marjorie seemed to be a good teacher, but Tessa didn't know if she could do what Marjorie had asked. She didn't want to infringe on Joe's privacy by talking about their relationship. On the other hand, she sure could use some way to work through their trouble. She couldn't talk to family or friends about something so personal.

As she emerged from the West Hills tunnel into downtown, Tessa considered the last few weeks. A month ago, a cold left her exhausted, so they hadn't made love for at least a week. She had to admit, she felt relieved that Joe didn't seem in the mood either. But then she'd felt better and had missed him and wanted him.

She guessed that was when she realized Joe hadn't initiated in a long time. She'd been starting things for quite a while and got it into her head to wait and see how long Joe would go before he missed their lovemaking.

Maybe she shouldn't have done that. Better oblivious than miserable. It had been two weeks since then, and he still hadn't made a move, even after that white lace fiasco when they'd ended up building shelves. Tessa laughed at the picture in her mind of white lace and a tool belt. *Am I being stupid? Should I just let him know what I need?* She didn't want to embarrass him. Hard stuff to talk about. She circled a block, hoping to find street parking.

How long had their love life been slipping? More than a few weeks. She couldn't even remember the last time it was his idea. Months ago, maybe?

She'd wear a sexy nightie, or kiss him passionately, or caress him the way he liked, but even that didn't work anymore. Like last night. She'd given up waiting for him again, had put on the most revealing of her nightgowns, and he didn't even notice. He kissed her after they got in bed together, said, "Sweet dreams, honey, God bless," and rolled over to go to sleep.

The car seemed suddenly too warm, so Tessa rolled down her window a few inches. The moist, fresh air blowing off the river cooled her face.

Before, she would have said they didn't have much that needed working on, but now she was worried. Joe's disinterest was always on her mind. Maybe she was obsessing, probably making a lot more out of this than she should. *Joe's a wonderful husband. Good with the kids. I know he loves me.*

Tessa squared her shoulders and tried to think of something else. She waited behind a car that was signaling to pull out of a space, and a new possibility pushed itself to her consciousness as she parked. Could this have been going on since her breast cancer? Chilled, Tessa closed the car window.

Could it be that long? No, she remembered after the chemo, when her hair grew back, it brought new life into their relationship. Joe seemed delighted and relieved. They'd make love, and he'd run his fingers through her new short curls. *No, he definitely enjoyed lovemaking then.*

Tessa glanced into the rearview mirror as she backed into the space and caught her own smile. Reminiscence about her recovery and Joe's tenderness brightened her mood. She reached into the backseat for her personal symbol of survival, the bright pink paddle.

After her cancer treatments, Tessa had forced a positive, confident attitude. Up to that point in her life, she had seen herself as intelligent and in control. However, the possibility of dying and leaving Joe alone to raise their children had truly frightened her and left her feeling powerless.

She had been brooding in her kitchen, overcome with a sense of helplessness when, on a day she looked back to as the beginning of her emotional recovery, her neighbor Gayle visited. Normally, Tessa would have smiled and said she was doing well, but Gayle had also fought breast cancer, so Tessa felt free to admit her sadness. Gayle's words changed her life: "Why don't you find out about the Pink Phoenix? You know, that dragon boat team made up of survivors of breast cancer."

Now, two years later, Tessa hurried to join her Pink Phoenix friends for their Saturday practice. After shared hugs and a few stretching exercises, she balanced in one of the long, narrow boats with fifteen other women, each wearing a hot pink life jacket and holding a pink paddle. They sat in pairs and faced the same direction as a giant dragonhead, which formed the prow of the boat. Behind them, the dragontail stern rose as high as the head. They pushed off and then leaned into their strokes, which, in unison, shot the boat forward. Tessa's heart soared, but she resisted a grin in order to keep the splashing river water from getting into her mouth.

The women ranged in age from late twenties to mid-sixties. Separately, they had each battled cancer and survived. Together, they encouraged each other in a new affirmation of their resilience, symbolized by their namesake, the mythical bird, said to be consumed in flames and then reborn from its own ashes.

From February through Portland's Rose Festival races in June, the Pink Phoenix practiced several times each week. In the fall, the limited daylight and women's working schedules limited their practices to Saturdays. Though many were still recuperating, and some had restricted upper body movement, they grew in strength and determination. Tessa remembered her pride the first time her team succeeded in propelling the boat diagonally across the Willamette River, from the starting point to the finish line, then turning and paddling back to do it again. They grew closer, too, as they cheered one another in their recovery or encouraged the friends whose cancer returned.

As she drew the paddle through the water, Tessa recalled Race Day of her first year. The women competed against other breast cancer survivors and came in fourth. The next year they placed second. The memory of how close the race had been stirred Tessa's determination as she bent into each stroke. "First place next June!" she yelled to her teammates but stifled the laughter that bubbled inside as the paddle in front of her cut into the water at the wrong angle and sent freezing spray her way. The cold sobered her, and soon her dampened spirits brought back the nagging worries about her marriage.

Should she talk to her pink life-jacketed friends about her marriage? They had shared so many concerns with each other, but she rejected that idea quickly. These women's worries dealt with life and death.

With proper perspective regained, she admitted a marriage counseling class provided a better place to look for answers. She still couldn't discuss it in her small group, but maybe she could journal to Dr. Gloriam.

She looked at the straining backs of the women in front of her. *Whatever the problem, Joe and I can work it out. I'm a survivor.*

⌘ ⌘ ⌘

That afternoon, Tessa scanned several chapters of *The New Male Sexuality* by Bernie Zilbergeld and decided to talk to Joe. After dinner, while the children washed dishes, she invited him out for a drive. He agreed but grumbled, commenting on the length of his to-do list.

Back when they had been dating, most drives ended with them snuggling in the car, enjoying the nearness of each other, and postponing the time when Tessa would give Joe a final slow kiss and go inside. Lately, they dashed from one commitment to another and rushed out the door with barely a quick kiss and a good-bye. More than anything, Tessa wanted to go back to that other lifetime when they had cuddled and lingered, enjoying the companionship.

Tessa parked near a fountain that served as a focal point for a commercial park. Paths along the grass and ponds gave employees a place to walk or jog at noon to refresh themselves. *Lord, please let this be a chance to refresh our relationship,* Tessa prayed.

"Joe," she ventured, "I love you so much, and I feel blessed to be your wife."

She paused to consider her husband. His eyebrows were pinched over his hazel eyes, and he seemed to be clenching his jaw. His dark hair still fended off any gray, but when did he start looking so tired?

Tessa reached over and took his hand. "I love you," she repeated, "and our relationship is too important to me not to talk to you when I'm worried."

He looked scared. This was going to be harder than she'd thought. *What kind of counselor will I be if I can't even talk about difficult things with my husband?*

"Joe, do you realize it's been two weeks since we've made love?"

His shoulders dropped in relief. "Oh, that's what this is all about." Joe sighed. "You had me worried. I've just been tired lately. Maybe when the stress at work lets up, things will go back to normal."

"But it isn't only the last few weeks that concern me. Before that, we were only making love when I made the first move. I stopped initiating two weeks ago to see if you'd get interested again. You didn't. Even when I wear sexy nighties, you don't notice. I miss having you touch me and want me." Tessa's voice gave way, and although she had promised herself she wouldn't cry, she did.

"Aw, Tessa, honey." Joe reached over and stroked her cheek. "I love you. I never want to hurt you. I'm sorry. I didn't realize. I'll try harder."

She jerked back. "But you shouldn't have to try harder. Wanting to touch me and hold me and love me shouldn't be an effort. What's wrong with us?"

Joe shook his head. "Nothing's wrong. It's probably that we've been together so long, we're mellowing or something. We see each other naked getting in and out of the shower. We hardly even notice because we've gotten used to the everydayness of it. There isn't that newness or excitement that we had before."

"I've been afraid that since the breast surgery, I'm not attractive to you anymore. Or maybe you want someone else." Tessa felt another tear roll down her cheek. She had admitted her deepest fear.

Joe took her hand in his. "Honey, I swear there's no one else. You're the only one for me and always will be, I promise. I'm just tired at night, and there are mountains of things waiting for me to do each day. I usually wake up feeling as exhausted as when I went to bed the night before. Listen, we'll try to get to bed earlier, starting tonight.

Maybe that will help."

"I hope so." She paused to give herself time to figure out how to approach the subject. "I'm reading a book about male sexuality for my class. You know, sometimes when we do try to make love, well—" she raised one shoulder—"things don't go well. You could read this book with me, and maybe we could find some answers. They used to think sexual problems were psychological most of the time, but now they believe they're usually physical."

He released her hand and turned to stare out the windshield. "I don't know, hon. Let's try getting more sleep and see how that goes. I don't think anything's really wrong with me. I'm just tired."

Tessa heard the "case closed" in Joe's voice and watched him withdraw.

"Okay, we'll try more sleep," Tessa conceded, but her hands were trembling as she started the car, and she felt as afraid as before. *Fine. If you're tired of seeing me naked, then you won't see me naked anymore.*

Still, maybe it was something physical. The book she'd read said lack of interest could come from medication or from heart trouble or diabetes. They'd try more rest, but if that didn't work, she was going to call the doctor and schedule an appointment.

⌘ ⌘ ⌘

Back at home, Tessa tucked her feet under her in the easy chair to begin reading for her classes, while Joe retreated to the office to pay bills. She imagined his thoughts as he sat at his desk.

So, Tessa keeps track of how often we make love, and it isn't enough. Her period. That's it. I bet her period starts tomorrow.

Tessa fumed at her own conjecture, sure that now Joe felt better and had easily shifted focus to the bills. With an effort, she distracted herself with homework.

Before she realized it, the clock struck eleven. Neither of them had made the move to prepare for bed earlier than usual.

"Sorry," Joe said as they both headed to the bedroom. "I lost track of the time. So many bills to pay."

"It's all right. I got absorbed in my studying, too. We'll try again tomorrow. How about if we set an alarm to go off at 10:00 to remind us to get ready for bed?" Those were the words she forced herself to say, but her thoughts were less forgiving. *Am I going to have to nag him? Why doesn't he look forward to going to bed with me?*

Tessa looked at herself in the full-length mirror of their walk-in closet. Her short, dark hair curled softly around her heart-shaped face. The cut was pert and flattering. She smiled, appreciating her hair more now than before it had fallen out from chemotherapy. Her attention moved down as she examined her body critically. The scar on her breast had faded to a silver line. She traced it with a finger and then her assessment continued. She had accepted her soft curves early in her marriage, when she learned how much Joe appreciated them. Still, she struggled constantly to be in control of her size. She felt heavier now than she had for several years. *Is Joe reacting to my weight?* Her sigh sounded as pathetic as she felt.

Now what was she going to wear? If she put on a pretty nightie, would he feel pressured for romance even though he was tired? Would he even notice? No, now she'd feel too needy if she dressed like that. Maybe she *was* too needy. She'd put on her regular nightgown, but she'd do it in the closet. She'd make sure he didn't see her change for a while.

When Tessa came out of the closet, Joe was already brushing his teeth in the bathroom. She joined him, hoping for him to meet her eyes in the mirror and smile. She needed some reassurance after their talk in the car. But Joe read a magazine while he brushed. She finished washing her face and was already in bed when he came out of the bathroom and climbed in beside her.

"Let me give you a backrub," she offered, hoping the soothing touch would relax them both and perhaps lead to more.

"Great." Joe turned on to his stomach and rumbled appreciation while she kneaded his tense muscles.

Tessa talked about her new class and some of the interesting books on the reading list. "You were really tight tonight," she ventured after a few minutes of rubbing, but Joe barely mumbled a reply and his breathing slowed. Discouraged, Tessa lay back, feeling the familiar emptiness as she wiped away her tears before they reached the pillow.

Dear Lord, this hurts so much. Please show me what to do so that we feel close again.

When the alarm went off the next morning, Joe groaned and hit the snooze button. When it sounded once more, he rolled over to nestle against Tessa's back. "Good morning, honey. I love you." He drew her close and kissed her cheek.

Tessa opened her eyes and smiled, then turned to see him better and return his hug. She couldn't decide which position she loved more, having his chest against her back with knees behind her knees and arm around her protectively, or face-to-face and chests together, arms drawing each other closer.

Oh Lord, I love this man. Thank You for bringing us together.

"Gotta go." Joe gave her a quick kiss on the tip of the nose and lumbered out of bed.

Tessa's loneliness from the night before hit her again. *We're definitely going to bed early tonight,* she thought as she swung her legs out of the bed.

Five

Even in a relationship,
we often feel alone.

Marjorie rose early Saturday morning, hoping, but doubting that reading her students' introductions of themselves and their relationships would distract her from her loneliness. September was Michael's birthday month, and even though missing him dominated her attention, she struggled to carry on with her responsibilities. She brewed a pot of decaffeinated orange-spice tea and then balanced the pot, a large mug, and two slices of cinnamon toast on her way to her kitchen nook.

Piles of papers had to be scooted to clear room for her breakfast. Though she had disciplined herself to keep the living room tidy for unexpected guests, textbooks, novels, and bestsellers adorned the family room and her bedroom. Only a few days into the school year, her dining room already overflowed with student papers and reference sources. Without family meals, even the kitchen table supported wobbly piles.

Michael wouldn't have been able to stand the mess. She had relaxed her housekeeping considerably since he'd been gone. *I shouldn't have resented his need for order. I shouldn't have longed for change.* Sorrow shrouded her heart like a Montana snowfall.

Resolute, Marjorie reminded herself of her blessings: the sun warm on her back, the orange-spice aroma, and the window open to hear the birds. She pushed a stack of books, as well as her self-critical thoughts, out of her way and drew the first student paper closer.

I'm a newlywed, so of course my marriage is my most important relationship. In fact, we've only been back home from our honeymoon for a week now, and we're still getting settled into our apartment and trying to find places to put away wedding presents.

We had so much fun on our cruise, but now my husband is back to work, and I need to settle in to my studies. He's so distracting; it's hard to stay focused. I took this class partly because I want our marriage to be perfect. I want to know what we can do to make it strong right from the start so we avoid the problems that ruin so many marriages.

Marjorie closed her eyes and inhaled deeply as she recalled the glowing euphoria of the first idyllic days of her marriage. They had agreed to keep their wedding and honeymoon simple, in order to save money toward a house. She could almost smell the pine trees and wood smoke of their honeymoon campsite. She smiled at the snatches of memory: the softness of Michael's lips against her ankle when he noticed her limping on a hike and discovered the blister she had tried to hide; his eyes wide in a face bronzed by both the campfire and the flaming marshmallow that he drew close to blow out; his heartbeat against her back as they sat together in front of their tent in the silver-blue light of the rising moon. Her chest ached with longing.

She straightened her shoulders and forced her attention back to the paper, refusing to surrender to the tide that threatened to rise every time she thought of Michael. "Well, newlywed, your rose-colored honeymoon glasses may be a bit new for you to think your relationship needs improving," Marjorie said aloud.

Her beagle Nutmeg lifted her head, cocked it to one side, and beat her tail on the floor.

"Let's take the focus off your marriage and look at the marriages of your parents." She wrote a few suggestions on the paper and concluded:

Consider spending some time talking to your husband about what you like in your parents' marriages and what you'd like to do differently in your own.

Marjorie's thoughts bounced back to her own first year of marriage and then to other young couples she had counseled. This year would set the stage for the new bride's marriage: expectations to discover, options to discuss, and agreements to reach. This was the year for them to start thinking of themselves as their primary family. Boundaries would need to be established so their extended families saw them as a couple and respected their relationship.

She recalled the dismay of Michael's parents when he told them he planned to convert to his new wife's religion. It still hurt to remember his mother's tears and his father's scowl. They didn't attend the ceremony when he joined her church, but Michael patiently won them over. Marjorie smiled at the memory of them sitting proudly in the front row of the church at Sophie's christening.

She hoped this student and her husband would learn to put each other first. Too many newlywed couples complained to their respective families. Their greatest loyalty had to be to one another now.

From those bouncy pages, Marjorie turned to read what Gwen O'Connell had written:

I took this class to try to save my marriage.

"Oh dear." Marjorie's stomach clenched as it did whenever she encountered a family in crisis. This time Nutmeg only raised her ears at Marjorie's voice. "Almighty Father, give me wisdom and Your words to help my students. Give us all encouragement."

She pictured Gwen as she remembered her from class—blond hair in a ponytail, a runner's build, and a competitor's passion in her dark blue eyes. She had struck Marjorie as both intelligent and intense, with an energy that kept her foot almost constantly jiggling.

She read on.

Lately, my husband doesn't even come to bed until long after I'm asleep. If I told him how sad that makes me, he'd complain about me not being fun anymore. It's true; I'm not. I'm busy with our three little boys, the house, laundry, meals, and then studying. And I think I might be losing him to someone else. I'd do anything not to lose him!

Again, Marjorie's thoughts strayed to her own marriage. She, too, had felt precarious during those last months when she would awaken in the night and pace restlessly in the hallway. Then Michael would come to her and hold her, trying to understand her frustration, the angst that she couldn't understand herself. He thought perhaps it was her recurring fear of abandonment. He had spent years convincing her he wouldn't leave her, but in those last months, desertion by Michael wasn't her fear. She was terrified by her own need for space. Then cruelly, ironically, he did leave her, though not intentionally. A shiver up her spine shook her back to the present.

On Gwen's paper Marjorie wrote:

It's hard to juggle being a mother, a student, and a wife.

Marjorie turned her mind to the advice she'd like to give every mother. Children need their parents' relationship to be happy. They can do without a great deal if they have the security of parents who love each other.

Michael had taught her that. One night when the girls were little, she had arrived home harried and stressed about the research she needed to do, the dinner she hadn't planned, and where she would find the energy for another night of rushed baths and bedtime stories. Then she opened the front door to find a babysitter reading to the girls, a pizza ordered, and Michael waiting to take her to dinner. "I miss you," he had said in explanation. The old familiar knot formed in her throat.

I will not cry!

Some counselor she was. She turned her attention back to her student. She knew she should draw some ideas for action from Gwen herself. Marjorie wrote:

What could you do this week that would nourish you, so that indirectly your husband and children can benefit?

She hoped Gwen would do something fun for herself, for even a few minutes. Then go out with her husband, without the boys. Maybe trade with another couple to take their kids for an evening. People needed time to be a couple so that together they'd have the strength and energy to be parents.

She imagined Gwen walking hand in hand with her husband. The thought made Marjorie's chest tighten with an ache to feel Michael's fingers interweave with hers.

She gave her head a shake and wrote:

Take a look at the books by David Schnarch or John Gottman on your reading list. And know I'll be praying for you and your marriage.

Marjorie turned to the next paper.

I've been trying to figure out what went wrong. I know it takes two to ruin a relationship. What could I have done better? I tried to anticipate his needs, to please him in any way I could. I wore my hair the way he liked, dressed the way he wanted, made his favorite foods. I put on a cheerful face around him, even when my heart ached. Then one day he announced he'd found someone new and had fallen in love with her. How could he love anyone more than me? I'd let him mold me into whatever he wanted.

I know you said we should write about a current relationship, but I need to figure out this one and learn from it. I don't want to make the same mistake again and go through this much pain.

Years ago, losing Michael to another woman was the worst fate Marjorie could have imagined. If he had lived longer, might she have found herself in this woman's place? Temptation could have taken hold at points in their marriage, but no, Michael had never given her any reason to doubt his faithfulness. Even when one of them struggled, like in their last few months, the other's steadfast love would pull them through. Maybe Michael's plan to travel to Europe would have been what she needed….

Marjorie wrote:

I have to disagree that it always takes two to ruin a relationship. Sometimes one person can do it all alone. But it does take two to keep a marriage strong and healthy or to rebuild a troubled relationship. One person can't do that all by herself. Even if you did all you could to save your marriage, sometimes it isn't enough.

Again, Marjorie tried to resist the impulse to give advice, to counsel rather than teach. She wanted to say, "Stop blaming yourself for what you have no control over. Since trying to please him in every way didn't work, discover what pleases you. Wear your hair the way you like. Dress the way that makes you feel most attractive. Remind yourself every day what you like about you. Try to enjoy your new independence, and use it to rediscover who you are. Then later, when you're ready to share yourself, it will be the real you, not what anyone else wants to make you."

Will I eventually be ready to share myself again?

She and Michael had so much history. As if turning pages of their photo album, she saw him grinning at the front of the chapel as he waited to become her husband. Then holding newborn Sophie with tender pride shining on his face. Bending to hold Colleen's hands as he rollerskated backwards to guide her forward. Playing guitar as they sang campfire songs. Grinning up at her when she'd distract him from his deskwork. Plaguing them all with his new video camera. Returning pale-faced from the girls' driving lessons. Reaching out to hug Colleen in her high school graduation gown. Smiling and waving as he drove off for his last business trip.

Marjorie recoiled from that final memory. She couldn't survive losing someone else that she loved.

Shaken, she took a drink of her tea and returned to teacher mode. She wrote:

> What would you tell a client in your situation? How would you help her validate herself? Can you take your own advice?

With relief, she saw that the next paper in the stack displayed a strong, masculine print. She didn't want to identify with any more women, for the moment. Marjorie read Hank Glenn's words:

> I work nights at a local hospital as a physician assistant. I got my training in the service and really like my job, but I'm in this program because I'm interested in helping people with their emotional wounds as well as the physical ones. I volunteer at the Youth Club, where I hang out with kids whose futures are at risk. I started there

as a health education resource, but mostly I just spend time with the kids. I believe a lot of healing happens from being listened to.

So, why am I in your couples' class? And what relationship can I work on? Good questions. When kids ask my advice about their girlfriends or boyfriends, I never know what to tell them. I guess I'm here to find out about normal couples and their relationships. I haven't ever gone beyond a few dates with anyone. I've never really had a romantic relationship, and I wonder why. It would be great if I could figure that out and maybe do what I need to do to become part of a couple.

Marjorie pushed away from the table, giving up. Maybe housework would keep her too busy to be reminded constantly of her own loneliness. Or maybe nothing would ever cure the emptiness she felt.

⌘ ⌘ ⌘

On Tuesday afternoon, Marjorie hurried along the path from the parking lot to her campus office, distracted by the aroma of wood smoke. Someone nearby was taking the edge off the crisp morning with a fire in their fireplace. Leaves would be turning color soon, she realized. But after a brief glance above her to appreciate the varying greens of maple and oak leaves that permitted only glimpses of blue sky, she returned to her calculations of minutes available during the day. She hoped to finish grading papers in time to return them to her Advanced Family Counseling class that evening.

As she passed the campus chapel, she slowed her steps. Several days had passed since she stopped in for a visit. Resolving to read faster in order to make up the time, she slipped into the chapel and settled into a seat near the back.

She loved the little circular building. The floors and walls were oak, the ceiling cedar, and the seats and altar hewn from maple. High stained-glass windows filtered soft light and added color to the room.

She heard a sniff and, as her eyes became accustomed to the shadows, she saw a hunched figure sitting against the curved wall to her left. Marjorie bowed her head and said a quick prayer for her chapel companion.

The ragged inhale that follows a long cry accompanied another sniff. Marjorie's mind turned from her students—they would survive one more class period without their papers returned—and her heart turned toward the grief-stricken figure. She rose and walked quietly to a young woman in jeans and a sweatshirt sitting on the floor, her arms folded across raised knees and supporting her head.

"Are you okay?" Marjorie asked, causing the girl to jump and look up at her.

Her brown ponytail bounced as she nodded yes; then when she looked into Marjorie's eyes, she slowly shook her head no.

Marjorie remembered the same look in her own daughters' eyes and took a seat facing her. "Need someone to talk to? I'm Dr. Gloriam. I teach counseling here, so I'm a pretty good listener."

The girl wiped her cheeks on the sleeve of her sweatshirt and gave Marjorie a shaky smile. "I'm Trish. I'm a new freshman and I'm okay, really. Just missing my family."

Marjorie had noticed before that freshmen looked younger every year, but this girl surely couldn't be eighteen yet. Her ponytail and freckles accentuated her youth, but even taking that into account, Marjorie would have guessed her to be sixteen at the most. Rather than ask her age, however, she took a more tactful route.

"Where do they live?"

"Montana."

That made the girl seem like family. "I'm from Montana, too. What part?"

"Bozeman. They wanted me to go to school there, but I was anxious to be independent. I promised myself I wouldn't call more than once a week, and I wouldn't go home before Thanksgiving. I have to make the break, you know? But I've never been away from them for more than two weeks. And I'm really homesick."

Marjorie nodded. Yes, she knew all about the need to make the break. Her daughters both went through a period when they thought limiting communication showed maturity. Marjorie remembered the pain of that distance, which had seemed so unnecessary to her. She smiled sadly at the thought.

"You know, Trish, it might be kinder of you to call home more often for a while. At least until your family adjusts to you being so far away."

The freckled face brightened. "You think so? I mean, if it would be good for them, of course."

Marjorie laid her hand on Trish's arm. "Go make the call."

As Trish stood, hoisted her backpack onto her shoulder, and thanked Marjorie, the image of Colm's business card in her drawer settled into Marjorie's mind. She allowed her thoughts to wander to the twinkle in his green eyes as he smiled. Her heart danced a quick moment to the echo of her last few words before she remembered the papers and hastened to follow Trish out the door.

Six

All relationships contain conflict.

Thursday, Tessa found Marjorie had assigned her to a group with Hank and Gwen. They were asked to describe the relationship theories they were studying and to talk about how they were applying what they learned. She and Gwen chatted in an effort to get to know each other, but Hank made Tessa uncomfortable. He would answer any questions they asked him, but then didn't offer more information or ask them anything.

After a few stumbling attempts to draw him out, Tessa said, "I guess we should start talking about the book we've chosen. Does that sound okay?" Their nods encouraged her.

However, as she tried to report on the book, *The New Male Sexuality,* her heart accelerated, and her mouth went dry. She couldn't do it. She didn't know these people and couldn't imagine herself talking with them casually about the issue that felt so intimate and crucial to her life.

She decided to take a safer route. "In the library I read a little bit from several of the books on the list to try to decide which to base this project on. I haven't settled on one yet, but something interested me in John Gottman's *Why Marriages Succeed or Fail: and How You Can Make Yours Last.* He makes a point that grabbed my attention. He says one person in a couple, usually the man, has more trouble dealing with conflict than the other one."

She glanced at Hank, who flushed and looked down as she continued. "Typically a man reacts to any discussion of relationship trouble with an increased heart rate and a sense of panic. Rather than soothing himself with reassurances like most women do, he convinces himself he's experiencing a catastrophe. Between his frightening thoughts and his racing heart, he becomes overwhelmed and needs to shut down in order to protect himself. Gottman thinks that this anxiety causes most men to try to avoid discussing problems in a relationship, while most women have grown up talking through problems and have learned how to do it without feeling overwhelmed."

Tessa remembered Joe's withdrawal in the car and shook her head at her earlier irritation with him. She wished she had read this book before that night.

"This helped me understand a talk I tried to have with my husband a few days ago," she said, noting Hank's darkening blush and hoping she wasn't its cause. "For me, talking about it was the first step to improving the situation. But maybe for him, talking about it was his first realization of a problem. So what encouraged me threatened him."

Hank shifted his long legs and cleared his throat before saying, "That might explain why I'm feeling overwhelmed just thinking about this project."

They laughed, but Tessa could see the courage it took for Hank to talk. She wondered if he was always so quiet, as if afraid to do the wrong thing.

"I'm reading *I Don't Want to Talk About It,* by Terrence Real."

Tessa couldn't imagine a more appropriate title for Hank to read. With a smile, she encouraged him to continue.

He offered back a timid grin. "It caught my eye on the list because it seemed male-oriented. It's about men and how being raised in our society damages men from the time they're little boys. We're supposed to distance ourselves from our mothers, who've been our source of love and safety until we reach three or four. Then, suddenly, we're made to feel weak if we want to be with them or if we look for their attention. Our dads, if they're around, try to teach us we're supposed to be tough and strong and not have feelings."

He paused, and Tessa wondered if society had hurt her Joe. Had his father taught him not to feel? Not to love? She frowned at the thought.

Hank paused to push his hands into his pockets. "Unfortunately, according to this book, we succeed at stuffing our feelings down until we don't even know they're there. Then we become adults, and two things happen. On the one hand, women suddenly want us to be in touch with feelings that we've disowned for twenty-some years." He looked at both women and shrugged with a quick smile.

Tessa felt strangely guilty. Didn't she often complain about Joe not expressing his feelings?

"On the other hand, the book says the only feeling we seem to be able to produce in times of stress is anger. It's as if we traded all the range of emotions—tenderness, love, frustration, fear—and we're only left with anger." Hank fell silent.

Tessa studied his face and decided he didn't look like he only knew anger; his face spoke of sadness instead. Then she wondered if Joe, too, experienced fewer feelings than she did, and if his primary feeling was sadness. Hank's face blurred until she blinked away the tears that welled. She prayed she would find an answer to these unsettling questions.

⌘ ⌘ ⌘

Marjorie had been walking between groups listening to their discussions. Hank's face caught her eye. His discomfort showed in the color that had risen from his throat, past his cheeks, right up to his red hair. What struck her most however, were his dark eyes that spoke of sorrow long endured. His sadness stirred feelings in her that reaffirmed her choice to counsel and teach. She was driven by a passion to help people overcome their pain and loneliness. *Ironic,* she thought. *Physician, heal thyself.*

Marjorie didn't miss the tears in Tessa's eyes and blinked reflexively as Tessa responded to Hank. "Your book could help a lot of people."

"It makes me want to be a better mom to my boys," said Gwen. "I have three, so I think I'd better read that book. I don't want to do anything to make growing up harder on them than it already is."

Marjorie sighed in agreement. Growing up was never easy, and it didn't stop when a person turned eighteen. Marjorie was still growing, still fighting daily battles that prepared her for life. Or love? How could she ever love, when love brought such sorrow? *And happiness,* she reminded herself. *Incredible, unforgettable happiness.* Not wanting to be alone with her thoughts, she lingered while Gwen took her turn to talk about her book.

"I've been reading John Gottman, too, about his"—Gwen made little quotation marks with her fingers—"'Four Horsemen of the Apocalypse.' That's what he calls the four practices that destroy a marriage little by little." She took a deep breath as though gathering her courage. "My own marriage isn't going so well, and when I read his book, I realized that we suffer from all four. It's the first time I've admitted that I might be partly to blame for our trouble." She bit her lip and broke eye contact.

"What are the four problems?" asked Marjorie, laying a hand on Gwen's shoulder. She met Marjorie's gaze.

Shame shadowed Gwen's features. "Criticism, contempt, defensiveness, and stonewalling. I'm personally familiar with all of them." She let out a small, derisive laugh. "Criticism is different than complaining. When I gripe at Brian because he didn't put his socks in the hamper, that's a complaint, and complaints are all right. They're specific and about just one event. But I go beyond that and criticize him by generalizing, like when I say, 'Brian, don't you ever pick up after yourself?'"

Marjorie sagged inwardly. *Criticism.* In the months before Michael died, criticism had rooted into her thoughts, sprouted into her conversations with him, and bloomed into fantasies of "what if." In the throes of midlife doldrums, she had begun to feel stifled. Michael's stability and calm, as well as his contentment, irritated her. The familiar pang of guilt struck as she remembered wishing for change in her life. She retreated to her desk to sit and busy herself with papers but kept listening to Gwen.

"If I'm particularly grouchy, I'm likely to really attack him with a put-down like, 'You're such a slob!' That's an example of contempt. But there are more subtle forms of contempt, like when he rolls his eyes at me." Gwen's eyes mimicked looking to heaven for sympathy.

Marjorie took comfort in knowing she had never felt contempt for Michael. She had loved him dearly and respected him. She had just wanted…more.

"Defensiveness describes how we both behave when we've been attacked," Gwen went on. "We put on the innocent victim role. He might say, 'Give me a break; you're always on my back.' I'll respond, 'My life would be so much easier if you weren't a *fourth* little boy to take care of.' Actually, that jab might be both defensive and charged with contempt. If we've had enough bickering, either one of us might stonewall. That's when you pull back, withdraw, and ignore the other one."

Marjorie's thoughts tormented her. Michael hadn't become defensive. He never stormed off or withdrew. Instead, he reached out to Marjorie and loved her more. He even tried to be more spontaneous, planned the trip to Italy….

Marjorie couldn't listen to Gwen any longer. She couldn't dwell on the past or she wouldn't be able to teach. She'd become imprisoned in the vault of emotions she'd carefully locked away to be opened at a future date. But that vault had been setting off alarms recently. Maybe God was telling her it was time to wake up, to open the heart that she had bolted closed the day she'd buried Michael.

No longer able to be alone with her thoughts, she stood suddenly. The noise of her scraping chair startled the room to silent attention. Marjorie braced herself with a deep breath and pushed away her pain.

"Let's gather into one group, everybody. I want to talk about some basic building blocks of relationships." Marjorie picked up a dry-erase marker. "What do you look for in a relationship?"

The students dragged their desks back into a circle as they called out answers. She hurried to capture their responses, relieved to face the board and gather her composure.

"Fun."

"Trust."

"Sharing."

Marjorie wrote quickly as they answered: *Love, friendship, intelligent conversation, mutuality, intimacy, respect, companionship, security, stimulation, relaxation, challenge, guidance, honesty.* She felt her confidence return with the safety of the subject matter.

She turned around to face the class. "The list can go on and on.

How about some of your worst dates? What did they seem to be looking for in a relationship?"

"Sex!"

"Control!"

Marjorie again recorded their answers: *Power, free meals, adoration.*

"That list could grow long, too, unfortunately." She snapped the lid back on the marker and set it down. "Some folks say that all we need is love and respect. That's it. If we have those, we're happy. I'd certainly agree that if we don't have love and respect in an intimate relationship, we won't be happy. But how do we find those relationships? And what do people do to keep them going?"

Marjorie noticed how attentive Hank had become. She hoped he would benefit from this lecture. She had a feeling he could overcome his loneliness if he would reach out. *Of course, opening a heart to a relationship is easier said than done.*

"John Gottman talks about bids for emotional connection. He says we all make verbal and nonverbal attempts at contact. They range from meeting someone's eyes and smiling, to asking how their day went, or simply a statement like, 'Man, it's cold out there.' Once we've made a bid, it can be received three ways: accepted, such as with a smile or some verbal acknowledgment; rejected, often with a hurtful response; or simply ignored."

Confused looks prompted her to give an example.

"Picture a fifteen-year-old coming home. His mom asks, 'How was your day?' On a good day he might shrug and smile. Bid accepted. But on a bad day, he growls, 'What do you care?' Or, 'Get off my back.' Bid rejected. Surprisingly, Gottman found that, as bad as this rejection can be, the bids that are ignored do the most damage. It would be worse if that fifteen-year-old just glared at his mother and turned his back.

"Gottman found that people tend to try a bid again only 20 percent of the time if that happens. If you get ignored enough, you quit trying. In a marriage, the ignored bids are also the most destructive. They predict a sooner end to a marriage than even the snarled rejection of attempts to connect. People just give up and withdraw."

An image of the Irishman's card sitting in the darkness of her nightstand drawer flashed into Marjorie's mind, and she immediately felt guilty. She had ignored his kind offer of dinner. She faltered and struggled to regain her concentration.

"On the other hand, bids that are accepted and acknowledged become an insurance policy against hard times. People who routinely make successful emotional contact, who listen and react to the emotions of those around them protect their relationship against those times when, out of distraction or bad moods, they ignore or reject a bid from someone."

Marjorie checked the clock, surprised at how fast the time had gone.

"This emotional bidding happens in marriages, friendships, and even in the workplace. This week, be aware of turning toward people with either a bid for connection or a response to their attempts. Notice when you turn away or when someone ignores you. How do you feel? What could you have changed?"

As the students gathered their backpacks and left the room, Marjorie considered the range of emotions she had witnessed during the class: Hank's sadness, Tessa's empathy, and Gwen's frank honesty. She knew each was fighting their own type of loneliness, and she hoped her class would give them tools to overcome their isolation.

She reflected on her own swing through regret, loneliness, and guilt during the evening. If only someone waited for her at home to share the emotional burden of her days. But she had enjoyed that companionship once before, wished it away, and vowed she would never again be ungrateful enough to yearn for her life to change.

Changes carry so much hurt. Could she ever risk such pain again?

Seven

Grief stifled burns on.

After class, Hank drove to work at the hospital for a double shift, and then to the Youth Club for his afternoon volunteering. All through the long night and day, his spare thoughts mulled over why he couldn't manage to form relationships with people. He was no closer to an answer, but dangerously close to nodding off, when Teesha, a seven-year-old with a multitude of tiny black braids, peeked into the small room set aside for him in case any of the children wanted privacy to ask him medical questions.

"Pa Hank?" He was still amused at the children's interpretation of his volunteer ID badge, which read P.A. HANK GLENN, the P.A. for Physician Assistant.

"Hey, Teesha, what's up?"

"Miss Crow ain't here yet, and she usually holds an end so we can jump rope. Can you come turn?"

"Sure thing." Hank followed her into the gym with an amused smile. Teesha had a reputation for trying to fix people's problems, whether the help was wanted or not. He wondered what conspiracy she planned now.

"Pa Hank, you got a girlfriend?"

So that was it. The child was uncanny.

He hedged. "I have some new friends who are ladies."

"What do they look like?"

Hank thought more about the women in his small group. How would he describe them? A picture of a Chihuahua and a black Labrador puppy jumped into his mind, and he chuckled. Hank had spent long hours researching types of dogs as a child when he had tried in vain to convince his father to let him have one. Now, living alone, he kept himself from fulfilling that dream. As much as he would like to own a dog, he figured he didn't spend enough time at home to be fair to the animal. However, he still liked to compare the breeds' characteristics and plan which type he would have some day. As a result, he often classified people according to dog breed. He decided Teesha would approve of his descriptions.

"Gwen's like a Chihuahua, with blond hair and a pointy little nose." He mentally added that she was full of energy and spunk, quite vocal, and often on the defensive. "Tessa's like a Labrador puppy, with deep brown eyes, short dark hair, and a desire to please everyone." He considered how her curves gave an impression of gentle softness.

Enjoying the fun of these associations, Hank wondered which breed their professor would be, given her temperament. Her reddish hair caused him to think of an Irish setter, but he rejected the idea quickly. Dr. Gloriam was petite and, frankly, more intelligent than the big, red hunting dog. He considered a fox but decided she wasn't smart in a cunning way, as much as intellectual. *But not one of the snooty breeds. How about a Sheltie Collie? A herding dog, as prized for its loyalty and intelligence as its appearance. Perfect.* He smiled, satisfied with his decision.

He was startled back to the moment when Teesha, who regarded him seriously as she held out the long rope's end, asked, "Which one are you going to make your girlfriend?"

"Oh, no, Teesha, they're already married." He felt his face warm and wished as always that he had descended from a long line of dark-complected ancestors.

"Well," Teesha replied as she smoothly jumped into the rope that Hank and a smaller girl were turning, "you need a girlfriend, and I'm still too little." The other rope turner giggled.

"Here's Miss Crow, how about her? Miss Crow, you want to be Pa Hank's girlfriend?"

Where his face had been warm before, now it burned. Kaya Crow took the end of the rope from Hank without changing the rhythm of its circling and looked at him with a smile that showed she understood his embarrassment. "Sorry, Teesha, but Pa Hank's too late. I tried to get his attention for a long time, then I gave up and found another boyfriend."

Hank stood empty-handed, caught by surprise. What did she mean she'd tried? How had he not known? Kaya and Teesha looked at him expectantly, as though wanting something from him. He had no idea what. He nodded to Kaya and escaped to his office as Teesha called between jumps, "Don't worry...Pa Hank...I'll keep...looking."

Back behind his desk, his emotions and his lack of sleep combined to keep thoughts from being more than quick mental images. He saw pretty Kaya smiling at him as he put his arm around her shoulder. He pictured them sitting together holding hands at a movie. The scene changed to another man holding her hand while he sat alone, watching them instead of the movie. Why hadn't he done something sooner? And how had he missed Kaya's cues?

Exhausted and shaken, Hank stood to leave early when Manny, a thirteen-year-old whom he had played basketball with two days earlier, came into his office, checking behind him like he hoped he hadn't been seen.

Hank settled back in his chair. "Hey, Manny, what's new?"

"I need to ask you some questions. I hear things from the guys, but I want to check them out with you."

Hank nodded. He had noticed before that Manny didn't follow anyone blindly but liked to make sure of his facts. He waited while Manny spun a basketball on his fingertips and collected his thoughts.

"About girls getting pregnant. Is it true it can't happen the first time? Or standing up?"

Hank relaxed. This he could handle. Medical questions he could answer. He spent the next few minutes assuring Manny that "the guys" were definitely and dangerously misinformed. He was glad to see that Manny wasn't worried by Hank's information. He must still be in the information-gathering stage and not yet sexually active. Hank kept the conversation light but emphasized respect for girls and encouraged Manny to come back anytime to talk more.

As Manny started to leave, he turned back to look at Hank. "Thanks, Pa Hank, that's what I like about you. You're full of information, but you don't ask questions."

The intended compliment stunned Hank and sent him back to his childhood. He could hear his father's voice. Though lacking expression and quiet most of the time, the voice was always strong and always frightening when it boomed, "Don't ask questions!"

With every nerve in his body calling for sleep and escape, Hank forced himself to seek out Kaya. When he found her helping some middleschoolers with their homework, he asked to speak to her alone. The two stepped outside. The way the breeze played with Kaya's long black hair and the hint of perfume it carried made him wish again that he had noticed her interest.

"Sorry about Teesha," she offered.

"Kaya, you said earlier you tried to get my attention. I'm really dense. Can you tell me what you did that I should have noticed?"

Kaya looked down. "It doesn't matter now, Hank. I've found someone else."

Hank persisted. "It matters to me. I'm sorry if I hurt you by ignoring you. I just wasn't aware. But I'd like to learn so that next time someone as nice as you is interested, I won't miss an opportunity."

She met his eyes. "Just little things, really, like initiating conversation, asking how your weekend went, longer eye contact maybe." She shrugged.

"Bids for connection," he said.

"What? Yeah, I guess so."

Hank decided to make the most of Kaya's helpfulness. "One of the boys told me he likes that I don't ask questions. Is that a good thing?"

She thought for a minute. "Depends. These kids have hard lives. The last thing they need is for us to cross the boundaries they put up to protect themselves. But sometimes we need to probe if we think they're being hurt or might hurt someone."

"I learned to ask questions of patients so I could diagnose correctly."

She nodded. "Guess it's like that. You have to know when to ask."

Kaya seemed to consider and then decide to speak up. "Hank, questions keep a conversation going. They show people you're interested in them and make it possible to get to know them better." She shrugged. "I gave up waiting for you to ever ask how my weekend went."

For a moment, he was stunned into silence. He'd been so self-absorbed; he hadn't even thought to ask about her. He could feel his cheeks warm, and wished again that his Scottish heritage didn't give him away.

"I'm sorry, Kaya. I really missed out." Hank thought how good life could have been with someone as kind as Kaya.

"Hope you find what you're looking for," she said, then went back indoors.

Hank headed to his Jeep Wrangler, his thoughts muddled by lack of sleep.

Once he was home, he headed straight for his bed. An imposing sadness settled over him. He tugged the covers over his shoulders and drew his knees close to his chest. He felt vulnerable and lonely.

With his eyes closed, the dark room of a three-year-old boy surrounded him. He flung open his eyes and stretched out to his full six feet, two inches. But even so, he became again the child he'd once been. His father sat down with him at the dinner table. In a matter-of-fact voice he said, "Your mom's dead."

Hank relived his confusion from that night. His father had seemed angry. Hank was afraid he had done something wrong—that he might be spanked. But his dad hoisted him into his lap and gave him a hard hug. Hank's nose hurt from being squished into his dad's shirt button.

"What happened?" Hank asked.

His father set him down firmly and growled, "Don't ask questions."

So Hank had stopped asking for fear of the answers. Now the sleep Hank desperately needed refused to come.

Eight

Our past haunts the present,
but the future depends on our choice today.

Marjorie used to love Saturdays and was determined to enjoy them again. She supposed some of their old delight lingered from childhood, when Saturday brought a few chores in the morning followed by a whole day of play. She had lived in a neighborhood full of children, with friends always ready for kickball, races, or hide-and-go-seek. She still filled her Saturday mornings with the housework that accumulated all week, but Saturday afternoons, even now, called for playtime. They had kept the same pattern when her husband Michael had been alive. Sometimes they would work together in the house. Other times he might be out in the garage while she weeded, but the afternoon always found them together, ready for pure enjoyment.

When she had first moved to Oregon, Michael had to convince her that she couldn't be a true Oregonian if rain kept her indoors. "Liquid sunshine," he had called it, and soon she appreciated a "bright gray day" without pining for the faithful blue sky of her Montana youth. She developed the Oregon squint that greeted the occasional sunny winter day while her cloud-comfortable eyes adjusted to the surprising light. She had been an Oregonian for twenty-five years, and her car always carried both sunglasses and an umbrella, ready for any outing with Michael.

The memory squeezed her heart.

She still longed for him. She missed him the most at night and on Saturday afternoons, but the ache of it throbbed less frequently now. More often, missing him shadowed her like a quiet, melancholy companion. Throughout the first year, Michael's death had darkened her affection for Saturdays. At the end of that mournful twelve months, she realized how deeply she needed a companion, but how disloyal she would feel to grow close to any person other than Michael. As an almost desperate alternative, she had leased half-ownership in the pretty, affectionate Appaloosa, Oasis.

She paid half of the horse's expenses and, in return, could ride her every Saturday, as well as Tuesdays and Thursdays. Suzanne Price-Hampton, the other half-owner, worked to improve the horse's performance, but Marjorie rode for the love of riding. Though she ached to be wrapped in an embrace or cuddled at night, she could talk to the horse about her sadness or loneliness and always seemed to receive empathy from those huge brown eyes or soft muzzle.

The previous night's rain had cooled the overcast September day and, as Marjorie walked to the stable from her car, she anticipated the fresh, damp smell of the wooded path. Approaching Oasis' stall, she could see a white envelope push-pinned to the wall, well out of reach of the gentle horse. The envelope had her name on it, so she opened it and read:

Dear Marjorie,

I hope you don't find me too forward. When I didn't hear from you, I began to worry that perhaps you were seriously injured. I pray that is not the case.

I thoroughly enjoyed making your acquaintance. Our shared laughter lifted my heart, and I smile now each time it comes to mind. Please permit me to be so bold as to repeat my dinner invitation, if you have recovered from your time "off Oasis." My card is enclosed in the event the other has been misplaced.

Sincerely,

Colm McCloskey

"Oh dear," Marjorie said aloud. She felt a flutter of excitement from Colm's letter, but also dismay. She'd been rude not to let him know she was fine. And with his fear of horses, it must have cost him dearly to bring this letter into the stable. What a nice gesture. She fanned herself with the letter and smiled, then immediately felt a twinge of guilt and pushed it into her pocket. She certainly didn't want a relationship with Colm—or any man. How could she even consider betraying Michael's memory? The dull heartache returned, and she rubbed at the pain in her chest.

She pondered how to respond to Colm while she saddled the horse, but her thoughts kept returning to Michael. To ease the burden of her feelings, she turned Oasis toward the trail and turned her mind to her classes.

Almighty Father, help me teach them well and be an encourager for their futures. But how could she give them what they needed when she couldn't even help herself? She felt humbled by the trust they placed in her, allowing her to read their words of insecurity, and sharing their intimate thoughts with her. *Keep me from hurting them in any way. The way I hurt Michael.*

As she ducked under a low branch of a Douglas fir, her thoughts moved to Tessa. From her journal, it sounded like her husband was a good man. She hoped they could solve this sexual trouble. *Please make their challenges pull them together instead of apart. And Hank, please heal his loneliness.* He was a sensitive man and would make a wonderful husband and father if he could rise above whatever was keeping him from reaching out.

Be with Gwen in her struggles. Please renew her marriage, and let it grow. If they do go their separate ways, give her strength and comfort. As she adjusted to the rhythm of the horse's stride, she continued to bring her students to mind and prayed that their needs be met. By the end of the ride, she felt less burdened by their struggles and more grateful for God's providence.

Thank you, Mighty Father, for this time in Your beautiful forest together. Keep me on Your path during the week, and remind me to appreciate the beauty of the people around me. Help me to trust Your work for goodness in each of our lives. Her favorite passage in Jeremiah came to mind, one she had often claimed for herself, her girls, and her students. *"I have plans for you, plans to prosper you and not to harm you, plans to give you hope and a future."*

Is that what Colm could be—hope and a future? But immediately she thought of Michael, and remorse replaced any thought of happiness.

As soon as Marjorie arrived home, she wrote to the Irishman:

Dear Colm,

I'm so sorry for not calling or writing you sooner. It was very impolite, especially after your kindness to me. I ached for a few days after my fall, but I'm fine now.

To be completely honest, I didn't call because I'm still married in my heart, even though my husband's been gone for many months. Driving home I looked forward to dinner and getting to know you better, but once I stood in my house surrounded by memories of Michael, I knew I wasn't ready to sit across the table from a man, share a meal, and not have it be him. The thought of it makes me need to blink away tears.

I considered writing other excuses to you, that the beginning of a school year is so busy, or that I don't date, both of which are true, but you deserved a better reply.

I know how difficult it must have been for you to deliver your note to Oasis' stall. Your courage in facing your fears is inspiring. I'm sorry I'm not ready to face my own.

Sincerely,

Marjorie

⌘ ⌘ ⌘

Sunday morning, Hank rose with the sun to clear skies, slid on his jeans and boots, and treated himself to bacon, eggs, and a stack of toast. He made a lunch and wished again that he had a good dog to accompany him for the day. *Wouldn't be fair to the dog,* he reminded himself. *I'm not home enough. It'd be too lonely.*

As he dumped his books out of his backpack to load it with his lunch, water, and a jacket, he noticed his journal for Dr. Gloriam. He had read her comments as soon as she returned his self-introduction but had pushed her suggestion to the back of his mind, uncomfortable with the idea.

Now he opened to her comment page and read again:

Hank, welcome to the class. How interesting that you are already busy healing people's bodies and now studying to help heal their hearts. Your volunteer time at the Youth Club will be wonderful experience for you as a counselor. Good for you.

Where Hank had written of his own confusion about the reasons for taking the class and his lack of relationships, she had responded:

Maybe you will know what brought you to this class as the semester progresses. In the meantime, you could work to understand a relationship from your past, either from your childhood, or as an adolescent. You could spend some time this week thinking about your interaction with your parents. As memories come forward, ask yourself how you *felt* at the time, apart from what you thought. Write about your discoveries.

Hank resisted. His past couldn't be called a happy one. Why would he want to waste a day thinking about it? He did much better living in the present. However, it sounded like an assignment, so he stuffed the journal into his backpack with his lunch, hoping he'd figure a way around her expectation as he headed out for his weekly trek through the woods.

Portland offered many options to someone who liked to take frequent hikes. Less than an hour's drive in nearly any direction Hank had his choice of trailheads. Today he selected a familiar destination, Ramona Falls. By lunchtime, he would be at the falls and could enjoy his sandwiches in front of the mossy cascade.

The walk wasn't strenuous or challenging, so his mind wandered. He didn't like thinking about his childhood and avoided it most of the time but reading the journal comments had loosened unbidden—and unwanted—memories.

He remembered someone—his mother before she died?—helping him to hold up three fingers to show his age. He had struggled to catch his little finger with his thumb, but she taught him an easier way, catching the finger next to the thumb. Proud of learning the trick, he had showed a large, older woman. She wiped her eyes and said, "Poor lamb, to be three and have lost your mum."

Who was that lady? A realtor? She'd let them into their house. It was empty in the memory, without a single piece of furniture. They must have moved there after his mom died.

Another memory surfaced of a daycare center and he clenched his teeth against the associated emotions. He had found a building set and started constructing a tower. A little girl came by and said, "You can't make that; you have to make a house so you can be the daddy and I can be the mommy. Here, like this." She'd knocked his tower down to start a house, and then someone called them away to join the group for a snack.

Even now, he could feel himself blush. He hadn't known the first thing about mothers and fathers. He still didn't. *What makes me think I could be part of a normal family?* He pulled the journal from his backpack, sat on a rock, and jotted a few words to secure this memory so he could write about it later. Two yellow butterflies pirouetted nearby and distracted him until they were out of sight. The rasp of a crow in the tree behind him brought his mind back to the forest and the trail. He stood, slung his backpack over a shoulder, and resumed his hike.

He tried to clear his mind of unwanted memories and simply enjoy the cool fall air, but the dam he had erected over the years to hold them back was breached. He saw his dad sitting in front of the television. He'd come home from work, turned it on, and settled into the recliner with a bottle of beer while he watched the news. He must have cooked when Hank was little, but Hank couldn't remember it.

As a teenager, Hank heated the usual four TV dinners, and they each ate two while they watched the news. They didn't talk. His father hated interruptions during the news. When the program ended, his father turned the television set off without a word and left for his basement shop to do small appliance repairs for extra income. Hank cleared the TV trays, also in silence, and did homework in his room. The only change in routine was Sunday, when his dad soaked in the bathtub—

Hank shifted his backpack and cast his gaze around him, looking for something, anything, to distract him from that last thought. A deerfly bit him, and he slapped it away, blaming it for the irritation he felt.

As Hank trekked through a small open meadow, he tried to recall any casual conversations with his father but couldn't. He had learned early on not to ask his father about his mom. "Don't ask questions!" He remembered the anger that rose quickly to his father's face. *Terrence Real says anger is a way to cover pain.* His Dad must have really been hurting.

Hank remembered Marjorie's journal assignment and reluctantly considered the memory. How did he feel when they didn't talk? That they never talked about Mom? *Lonely? Empty?* Some of each of those...and scared, too. Like he didn't know something important, something too big for him to know. *Okay, where did that come from? And why am I shaking?*

Hank sat on a fallen log to write in his notebook. Slowly, the shaking passed with the warmth of the sun through his plaid Pendleton shirt. He continued to walk deeper into the woods, eager to escape the memories.

Still, he wanted to know about his mother. What was she like? Why did she marry his father? Certainly not for exciting conversation. Had Dad loved her? What made him so mad after her death? How did she die? Maybe some illness he might be susceptible to?

An hour later, but with no more answers than before, Hank stood in front of Ramona Falls. Neither a particularly tall waterfall, nor wide, it attracted Hank with its lush greenness. The white water spilled over its top and then spread to veil moss-cushioned rocks. It fanned gently from top to bottom, a vision of gracefulness, rather than power or force.

The mist from the falls cooled him and a handful of other hikers. The surrounding old growth kept the whole area in refreshing shade. Hank decided a downed tree nearby would provide a good resting place to re-energize with his sandwiches.

After lunch, Hank pulled out his notebook and wrote, *I'm going to find out everything I can about my mother.* After adding three exclamation points and an underline, Hank hoisted his pack and set out at a brisk pace. Two trails led from Ramona Falls to the parking area. He had taken the longer, sunnier path to get to the falls but now chose the shorter, shadier route to return. As he walked, he began to plan.

He wished his dad were alive. He would insist his father talk to him. *And this time I wouldn't budge until he told me everything.* But Dad was gone, and so was his chance to learn what had happened to his mother.

Unbidden memories of his high school graduation day flooded him. His father had seemed like a stranger, a friendly stranger showing happy teeth all day. Hank remembered the heat of the day and how uncomfortable the black gown became. His dad insisted on taking pictures before Hank could take it off.

During high school, he had spent as little time at home as possible, preferring to be at friends' houses or just hanging out. Hank had expected to go out with the guys after the graduation, but they were all off to family parties. His dad surprised him by saying, "We're going out to the best restaurant in town. I've got something I want to show you after we eat."

Hank's mouth watered, remembering how good that first-ever T-bone steak had tasted. It sure beat the hamburgers or pizza with friends and the TV dinners at home. When Hank had emptied his plate and a second one of cherry pie and ice cream, his dad reached into his suit coat pocket and pulled out a savings register from a bank.

"Go ahead, look at it," he said with his eyes shining above that goofy grin. Inside the passbook listed a history of deposits, one made almost every month since Hank was four. Interest was reported and added faithfully every quarter. The last page showed a final deposit and the current balance.

Hank swallowed, as if struggling with that T-bone steak, and forced himself to recall the fateful conversation.

"More than a hundred thousand dollars!" Hank had whispered in disbelief.

"Every penny honest-made. All those nights taking in odd jobs, repairing vacuums and TVs, were leading up to this day, son." Here his dad's voice cracked. Still, he went on. "I'm so proud of you, boy. You've never gotten into trouble. You've worked hard in school, and now you can go to whatever college you set your mind to. You can be whatever you want to be! We've shown them all that a man can take care of his son alone and have him turn out fine."

Those were the most words he'd ever heard from his father in one day, let alone one breath. He relived the frustration and sadness of his answer. "Dad, I had no idea. I assumed money was tight. Money was always tight. I should have been applying to colleges months ago. It's too late now. I enlisted in the Army yesterday."

His father's eyes returned to their normal dullness, and his smile went flat. Hank tried to thank him, but his father's scowl cut off his words. They returned to their house without speaking, easily resuming the pattern so familiar between them.

It was too late for his father to start talking to him then. *I would rather you played with me all those nights I spent alone. Or talked to me about Mom. About things going on in my life and what was happening in yours. I wanted you, not a savings account.*

Hank stopped on the trail abruptly, too late to block the mental picture of the next morning, when he had found his father dead in the bathtub, electrocuted by a radio that had fallen into the bathwater. He took shallow breaths to fight the nausea that the scene always brought.

With an effort, he walked on as he pushed beyond that memory. The funeral had been small. Hank knew of no relatives to notify. His dad's coworkers expressed sorrow at the service: "Miserable luck just when he seemed to be the happiest he'd ever been."

Hank had received a deferment from reporting to boot camp while he put his father's affairs in order. Thinking that the sooner he could be away from the house the better, he boxed all their personal belongings, put them in storage, and turned the house over to a property management company to rent during his tour of duty. The deep sadness that had been his father's was all that he took with him. Like the backpack on his back, it weighed him down even now. He had to find out about his mother if he had any hope of lifting it. But how? There was no one left who could help him.

⌘ ⌘ ⌘

Tessa turned off the living room light and peeked around the corner of Joe's office doorway. His spicy scent filled her with anticipation. "I've sent the kids up to bed. What do you say to turning in a little early ourselves?" She watched him consider the paperwork still on his desk and held her breath.

He didn't even look up from the papers. "Honey, I have so much to do here. Maybe a little later?"

She exhaled and sagged. She knew she should understand, and she tried to be brave, but each rejection made the next one harder. Her silence made him glance up at her. She dropped her eyes, not wanting him to see the flood of emotions she was battling. She couldn't trust her voice, so she turned and walked to her room.

"Tessa, wait. What's wrong?" She heard him knock over the chair as he rose and then take time to stand it back up. He caught up to her in the bedroom and turned her gently toward him. "What is it?"

The warmth of his hands distracted her a moment. She looked up at him. "It's me, Joe. It's us. You can take time to set a chair right, but not our marriage."

He let go of her arms, and his confused look made her even more upset. Her control burst. "How can you not know what's wrong? Do I have to say it again?"

Still no answer.

"I want to make love with you, Joe." Suddenly, though, it was the last thing she wanted. She corrected herself. "I want *you* to want to make love with me."

"Of course I want you, honey. Who in his right mind wouldn't?" His grin didn't lighten her spirits this time. As he tried to guide her into a hug, she drew back and studied his face.

"Do you, Joe? Do you really?"

Joe met her gaze, then dropped his eyes. He released her and sat heavily on the bed, his shoulders hunched forward. Tessa waited.

"I don't want to hurt you," he whispered.

It was too late. His words cut into her heart, and she suddenly didn't want to hear more. She glanced at the door. She wanted to run.

"I didn't really notice it at first, but you're right. I don't feel any urge." Joe looked at her, and his eyes opened wide at the pain he must have seen. He jumped up and took her hands. "But Tessa, I love you. I swear. I really don't want to hurt you. I don't know what's wrong."

Tessa stopped a full-body quiver before it escaped. She straightened and lifted her chin. She was going to fight this unknown enemy. "Do you love me enough to talk to Doctor Zernick?"

Tessa watched the space between his eyebrows crease as he thought, then looked at her imploringly. "I can barely talk to you about this, Tessa, let alone someone else."

Nine

Secrets inevitably come to light.

For three days after his hike, Hank dug like an archaeologist through boxes in the storage building that held all the personal belongings from his childhood home. Each month since his father's funeral and his enlistment, the storage rent deducted from his account reminded him of unfinished business, but each month he had avoided examining the boxes and his past. Now the need to learn about his mother motivated him to keep at it.

He pushed between stacks of boxes in the poorly lit room. The dusty cardboard smell reminded him of his dad's workshop in the basement, a place he never felt welcome. His hopes rose when he found a box of his father's financial papers, but bills and statements relinquished no clues. Hank searched for personal correspondence, thinking maybe someone would mention his mother but didn't find a single letter. He impatiently set aside boxes of clothing and housewares to donate, then spent a few minutes distracted by his old report cards. With only three boxes remaining and his prospects dwindling, Hank lifted the lid from a carton that held paper clutter from around the countertops the day he had packed.

He remembered not being able to deal with the sympathy cards mixed in with bills and other mail. He had separated all the envelopes that looked like bills, turned them over to the property management company, and tossed the rest unopened into this box. Now as he opened each card and thought of the people who wrote—friends, teachers, his dad's coworkers—his stomach felt hollow. He came across a purple envelope, opened it, and found a note rather than a sympathy card.

Hank unfolded the purple stationary and saw *Dear Gordon,*

written in a feminine script. He checked the return address to see who was writing to his father, but he didn't know anyone from Spokane, Washington. Feeling slightly guilty but very curious, he read on.

If I figure right, this must be the June that Henry will graduate from high school. If you know where he is, could you send this on to him? I want him to know that his grandma hasn't forgotten him in all these years. I still love him, and I wish you happiness. I keep praying for the day when I'll see him again.

Love and prayers,

Esther

Hank released the breath he had been holding and quickly reread the note. He couldn't believe it. He read the note a third time, to be sure, and then inspected the envelope, hoping to learn more. Still folded inside was a check made out to Henry Glenn for $100. It was signed by Esther Wimsett. He knew from his birth certificate that Wimsett was his mother's maiden name.

He sat heavily on a stack of boxes and could feel the grin spread across his face. Eight years ago, he had a grandmother less than four hundred miles away who loved him and missed him. One who remembered him on his graduation day. If only he had opened the mail before he left for the Army. Or in the long years since. Eight years. Was she still alive? Still at the same address? Might he actually have family?

Questions pummeled him one after another. Why didn't she know where he was if she had their address? Why hadn't his father ever told him about her? Why hadn't they visited her? His eyes widened with realization. He could visit her.

Suddenly Hank couldn't sit still another minute. He folded the note quickly into the envelope and slid it into the pocket over his heart. He pushed boxes back enough to be able to close the storage building's door, locked it, and hurried to his car. He was almost to the interstate on-ramp when he realized he had to work that night and shouldn't miss class the next day. He slammed his hand against the steering wheel, hitting the horn by accident.

As other drivers looked at him, he shrugged and felt his face burn. Reluctantly he turned back toward his apartment, telling himself he could hang on a couple more days after waiting so long. He consoled himself with visions of a family reunion arranged by a smiling little lady with gray hair pulled back in a bun. He could almost feel her hug and smell her face powder.

⌘ ⌘ ⌘

Gwen tucked four-year-old Joe Pat back into bed and turned out the lights. After baths, stories, several attempts to delay, and this one last trip to the bathroom, it looked like the three boys finally surrendered for the night. Now she could read more about how to make her marriage healthier. She quietly slipped downstairs.

Brian looked up at her from in front of the DVD cabinet. "How about a movie, babe?"

"Not tonight, Bri, I have to get homework done for tomorrow." First the boys, and now Brian. Didn't he realize how much she had to do?

"C'mon, babe. Couldn't you do it during naps tomorrow?"

Gwen rolled her eyes and shook her head. "Yeah, right. When was the last time they all took naps at the same time?"

Brian slammed the cabinet door. "Fine."

Gwen's heart sank. Why couldn't he see how hard she had to work to keep up with her studies, as well as the boys, the empty refrigerator, and the overflowing laundry hamper?

Gwen studied until ten, but the reading made her feel guilty for the way she treated Brian. John Gottman's four marriage-damaging equestrians seemed to accuse her personally. Thinking over their last conversation, she admitted she had slipped into criticism, contempt, and defensiveness. She had even walked away, stonewalling—the fourth horseman.

Finally she closed the book and returned to the family room. Brian sat at the computer typing intently and didn't seem to notice her. "Coming to bed, Bri?"

He jumped and hit a key quickly before looking up. Pain shot under her ribs. Was it her imagination, or did he look like he was caught doing something wrong?

"Not yet, babe. I'll be up in a while."

She wanted to make up for being too busy for him. "You sure? Could be fun."

"I'm in the middle of something, Gwen. You go ahead."

Gwen felt like she had lost another battle, even without the normal shouting. She slowly made her way up the stairs to her room and finally to bed. She couldn't sleep and wondered how much longer Brian would be.

One of the boys called for his daddy. She waited until she heard Brian come up the stairs and go into Sean's room before she slipped down and sat in front of the computer. She had to know what was taking all his attention lately.

The computer screen had a private chat room conversation going. She recognized the other user name as Tad, Brian's pal from their hometown in Idaho. As she read the text that was still on the screen, she realized Tad wasn't writing. It was his wife, Shirley. Her pulse sped up, her jaw clenched, and every muscle tensed. Shirley and Brian had shared quite a long conversation, both commiserating about their spouses. Gwen fumed. *He's been griping to her about me!*

Brian came down the stairs.

"Brian, how could you?" she demanded in a strained whisper.

"What are you doing?" he hissed. "Can't I have any privacy in this house?"

Gwen forgot the sleeping boys and shrieked, "Privacy for you and Shirley? How dare you!"

"Well, *she* had time for me!" Brian answered at the same volume.

"Then go tell her to wash your toilets and iron your shirts. Get out! Get out right now!" Shaking with rage, she couldn't stand another minute looking at him.

"Fine." Brian stomped to the closet, grabbed a sleeping bag and his coat, and left, slamming the door behind him. Little Sean started to cry. She realized she didn't even have the luxury of feeling sorry for herself. Half wishing she had been the one who left, she forced herself back up the stairs to calm her boys and get them back to sleep.

⌘ ⌘ ⌘

The next evening, Hank could hardly wait to share his news with Tessa and Gwen. He hurried over to the two women, who had drawn three seats together in a corner of the classroom, pulled out the purple page from his breast pocket, and waved it. "I've got a grandma!" Seeing their confused looks, he realized he needed to backtrack. He dropped into a chair and quickly told them about the hike, his new determination to learn more about his mother, and his search through the storage boxes.

Tessa and Gwen exchanged glances. "You have a grandmother you never knew about?" Gwen frowned, as though she didn't quite understand.

He nodded. "Dad never mentioned her, but I found a note from her. Eight years ago, I had a grandma who loved me and missed me. I'm hoping I still do." He shook his head. "I can't believe I waited so long to do this. Four years in the service, college for three, and now work and volunteering and grad school. All that time this letter was waiting for me."

They read the note he handed them and passed it back, looking as happy as Hank felt. "What's next?" asked Tessa.

Hank wished he could leave immediately. "I'm going to drive there this weekend. It's only six or seven hours away, and I've arranged three days off. I'm hyped! There's so much I want to know." Hank dropped his voice. "Even if she's not alive anymore, maybe I'll find more family. Somebody, anybody, who knew my mom and can tell me what happened."

Hank's burst of words finally ran down and left him feeling spent. He rarely talked this much. Sure, he communicated fine with his patients, asking them questions, diagnosing problems, and instructing them on the solutions, but this expression of his emotions was a new experience for him.

Tessa put her hand on Hank's shoulder and looked into his eyes with a sincere smile. "Hank, I'm happy for you."

"I don't know; it sounds kind of scary to me," said Gwen, tapping her pencil thoughtfully on the table. "Maybe you should touch bases with Dr. Gloriam before you go, in case she has some advice."

Hank's heart sank. "Good point." He looked at each of them—Tessa with her kind dark eyes and Gwen with her restless energy. Despite the worry that Gwen had conveyed, he felt connected with the two women—the first time he'd felt connected in years, if ever. Still, to his mind, they were way ahead of him. They had real relationships they were working on. He was alone. *Perhaps not for long, though*, he realized with a lopsided grin.

"Enough about me. I've talked more than my share. Never thought I'd say that." He laughed. "Gwen, how are you coming with Gottman's four horsemen?"

Gwen's eyes filled, and Hank sputtered, "What's wrong? I'm sorry."

Hank felt horrible, but it was too late to take back his question. Why couldn't he keep his mouth shut? But he had kept it shut—too often, he realized, as he slumped down in his chair.

Gwen took a moment to compose herself and shook her head. "No, it's nothing you did. I've been reading so much and promising myself I'd fight those horsemen, and then last night I did everything wrong."

Hank, his earlier happiness fading, defied his father's voice that demanded he not ask questions. "What happened?"

Gwen haltingly told them of the fight the night before. When she finished, Tessa put an arm around Gwen, who by now was shaking, tears sliding down her cheeks. Hank surprised himself by reaching over and squeezing her hand.

"Gwen, I'm so sorry," Tessa whispered.

"I didn't even bother going back to bed." Gwen sighed. "I made a pot of coffee and spent all night and most of today trying to figure this all out."

Hank had been staring at the floor but looked up at Gwen. "Do you know where he spent the night?"

"He's working on fixing up an old house to resell. That's what he does for a living. He buys old houses, rewires them, and then updates them with paint and carpeting, sometimes even new cabinets and appliances in the kitchen." Gwen's voice softened. "It really is amazing to see how beautiful they are when he's done. He usually makes a good profit, enough to keep us going and buy his next fixer-upper. Anyway, I figure he's over at the old house."

Hank ventured, "I wonder if he might be willing to see your marriage as a fixer-upper worth remodeling?" The words sent a chill through him. Maybe that's what his own life was—a fixer-upper. He peered down at the letter still folded in his hands.

Time to start rebuilding.

Ten

Search for the answers needed.

F riday morning Hank slept for several hours after his Thursday night shift, then woke at noon, anxious to be on his way. *Maybe soon, maybe today even, I'll finally find out how my mom died and why my dad was so angry.*

He had arranged Friday, Saturday, and Sunday night off from the hospital. The Youth Club teens he usually spent Saturday with had teased him about a romantic weekend when he told them he'd be back on Tuesday. Finally, having packed the day before, he ate a quick lunch and set off.

As he merged east onto Highway 84, Hank thought over Marjorie's words to him after Thursday evening's class. She had seemed delighted for him to be on this adventure but had cautioned him, too. "Hank, you have a whole lifetime of emotions that you haven't gotten to share with anyone. There's bound to be a lot of feeling wrapped up in discovering you have relatives you didn't know about. Learning why you didn't know about them could open a floodgate. Be gentle with yourself these next few days. Get lots of rest, eat healthy, and don't take on anything else stressful, if possible." She had pulled a business card case out of her briefcase. "I want to give you my phone number so that you can talk to me if you start feeling overwhelmed. Call me anytime, day or night, all right?"

A shiver ran down Hank's back at the remembered warning. He had been so excited to find his grandmother's card with an address, he hadn't thought of what the emotional consequences might be. Sure, this would be quite a shock to her, if she was even alive, but a happy surprise, he hoped. Yet, how would he react?

The new questions circled in his mind as he drove. Why hadn't his grandma known where he was if she'd known where to write to Dad? Why hadn't Hank ever heard about her or from her before? Maybe his dad didn't think she'd be a good influence on him, but she sounded like a nice lady from the note. Could she have just found out where Dad lived when she wrote that card?

Since he had no answers, he finally pushed a tape into his cassette player and listened while a pleasant country voice narrated a Louis L'Amour story. At the next rest stop, he explored a short trail that passed a waterfall before it returned him to the parking lot. The fresh air and a bottled water renewed him, and he felt ready to drive the rest of the way.

As he arrived in Spokane, the sunset dyed the sky orange in his rearview mirror. At a gas station he bought a map of the city and drove directly to the address on Grandma Wimsett's card. He wanted nothing more than to run to the bright blue door, ring the doorbell, and hug the little gray-haired lady he pictured in his mind. He had stepped halfway out of the car when he realized he couldn't. He dropped back into the seat and rubbed the back of his neck, the heat rising in his face.

Shoot. Why didn't I think to call her? Now it was getting dark, and she'd be scared to have him knocking on her door unexpectedly. He'd have to check into a hotel, see if he could find her number, and call to introduce himself. Then, if it all worked out, he could see her in the morning. That would give her time to adjust to the idea. He shook his head, wishing he'd thought ahead.

He drove back to a Holiday Inn Express that had intrigued him. It stood on a giant protrusion of rock overlooking the Spokane River that flowed through the heart of the city. As soon as he dropped his suitcase on the bed in his room, he grabbed the phone book and turned to W. Only two Wimsetts were listed, one an E. Wimsett at the same address as on his card. He picked up the telephone receiver with a trembling hand, paused, and then set it back down. Looking out the window to the river, he tried to rehearse in his mind what to say. Finally, he shrugged and dialed.

A woman's strong voice answered on the third ring.

"Hello. This is Hank Glenn, and I'm trying to find an Esther

Wimsett." He realized he sounded almost desperate.

"Hank Glenn? Could you be Henry? My grandbaby! Where are you, boy? Oh, not a boy, you sound all grown up. Where are you?"

"I'm in Spokane, Grandma. Can I come see you tomorrow? I know it's kind of late now."

"Tomorrow! Absolutely not!"

Hank's heart skipped a beat.

He couldn't think what to say, but his grandma continued, "I've waited too long already. You get over here lickety-split. Are you hungry? I'll warm up something quick."

His head started bobbling like a dashboard toy. "I'll be right over. Are you still at the address in the phone book? And yes, I'm starved."

Hank said good-bye and, as he hurried to the door of his room, glanced in the mirror and caught his grinning but disheveled reflection. He forced himself to endure a few extra minutes of suspense while he washed, shaved, changed his shirt, and combed his hair.

When Hank rang the doorbell twenty minutes later, he heard footsteps hurry to the door. It flew open, and she beamed at him.

"Henry! Hank," she corrected herself. "Thank the good Lord. Oh, we have so much to catch up on, and first of all are hugs."

Hank stood speechless a moment and then was enveloped in warm softness, a vaguely familiar powdery scent, and complete love. He wrapped his long arms around her and felt every muscle in his body relax.

When they had both regained composure, he stepped back to look at his grandmother. She appeared younger than he had imagined, probably in her early sixties, and taller, too, maybe five-foot-seven or eight. Her hair wasn't white, but light brown with a stylish short cut. Her eyes struck Hank as riveting, perhaps because of how happy they looked through the last of the tears, but also because they were the same dark green that stared back at him each morning as he shaved.

"Welcome home, Hank." She placed a hand on her chest. "My heart's tap-dancing with joy. I've been praying for twenty-three years to see you again." At that moment, the microwave beeped. She guided him with her hand on his arm. "Come on in now, and let's talk all night if we have to, so we can catch up on lost years."

He followed her to the kitchen table, where she set a plate of roast beef, mashed potatoes, gravy, and beans in front of him. She poured them each a big cup of coffee, sat at the table with him, and waited for him to swallow a few bites. Then she asked, "Hank, where have you been all this time?"

Hank set down his fork and sat back. "Where do I start? For the last few years I've been living in Portland, going to school, and working as a physician assistant. I enlisted in the Army for four years. That's where I got the training for my work. As far back as I can remember before that, I was in Hillsboro, outside Portland, living with Dad before he died."

"He's dead?" She set her cup down, obviously stunned. She laid her hand over his. "I didn't know; I'm sorry. That's why my cards were returned. I figured he moved. But you say you lived with him all that time?"

"Yes, ma'am."

His grandma sat quiet a few minutes, her lips squeezed shut, and the hand that had been on his curled into a fist. "Just a day's drive away all those years, and he never told me. What could have made him so cruel?"

"I don't understand." He leaned toward her. "You didn't know I was with him? Grandma, there's so much I don't know." He sighed and decided to start at the beginning. "My earliest memory is Dad telling me Mom had died."

Esther inhaled sharply, and her lips disappeared so that the wrinkles above and below them touched.

Hank felt even more confused. Surely, she would have known his mother had died. At her silence he continued. "After that, he wouldn't ever talk about her. I didn't know about you until last week when I searched through his things and found the card you sent me for my high school graduation."

"Lord, have mercy on his soul!"

Hank had no doubt Esther Wimsett's words were the exact opposite of her feelings. Standing up quickly from the table, she turned away to slice large pieces of banana bread. He thought it lucky she had something productive to do with that knife. She seemed to struggle to compose herself as she brought the dessert to the table and set it before him.

"I can't imagine what he was thinking. It's going to take a lot of prayers to be able to forgive him for this."

"Grandma, tell me."

She briefly closed her eyes, and then opened them again, as though coming to a decision. "Hank, your daddy lied to you and to me, too. Your mama didn't die when you were tiny. She left him and abandoned you, it seems. He told me—"

"She didn't die?" Hank sunk back in his chair. His eyebrows tented in confusion and then tightened with anger.

Esther hurried to explain. "He told me she took you with her. I never dreamed he'd lie about that, or that she wouldn't have taken you with her, for that matter. She loved you so much, Henry—Hank; I don't think she ever would have left you by choice. He must have refused to let you go with her."

"She's still alive? She never came to see me in all these years?" His voice rose both in pitch and volume.

As Esther hesitated, the clock in the front room began to cuckoo, sweeping Hank back in time to a remembered sensation. He was being lifted in a man's strong hands and shown how to move a tiny wire that made the little bird pop out and cuckoo. He pushed the wire over and over, fascinated by the little bird, which added a cuckoo each time, as he and the man laughed.

Esther nodded toward the front room. "Your grandpa, Lord bless him, used to hike you up to torture that poor bird. The two of you would laugh together like it was the funniest thing in the world."

So many questions. Hank forced his thoughts back to the moment, surprised that he could have been distracted from his grandmother's revelation. "Where is my mom?"

Eleven

Our body affects
and is affected by our mind.

As Joe perched on Doctor Zernick's examining table, Tessa sat on the single chair in the room, remembering another time when she waited on that table, frightened about a lump she had felt that morning. The doctors had helped her through that trauma. Surely they could solve this problem, too. When the doctor came in, he shook hands with both of them. He had treated them separately before and looked pleasantly surprised to see them together this time.

Tessa closed her eyes a moment and prayed the Lord would give the doctor wisdom so he could help Joe. She felt like she was struggling to keep her head above water, and she wasn't sure how much longer she could swim. She tried to be grateful for any affection Joe showed, but she needed to be his lover, not simply his friend. There had to be something they could fix.

Please, Lord, help this doctor show us the answer.

"What can I do for you today?" the doctor asked Joe.

Joe glanced at the door, and Tessa understood that longing to escape. She smiled reassuringly at him, but he merely cleared his throat, making it obvious he wished he could be anywhere but here. "I don't seem to have much interest in making love lately. I wanted to see if there's a medical reason for it."

"Are you on any medications? Some can have this side effect. Even antihistamines can cause sexual dysfunction for some people."

"Nothing but an occasional aspirin for headaches."

The doctor made a note on his chart. "How long has your libido been low?"

Joe looked to Tessa, so she answered, "Several months." At Joe's surprised look, she added, "It took awhile for me to get up the nerve to talk to you about it."

The doctor pulled a stool over and sat on it. "How high is the stress in your life? Any changes lately that might be to blame?"

Joe shrugged. "Things are tough at work, but no worse than usual. I worry about finances and the kids, but that's nothing new."

Tessa cocked an eyebrow. She remembered the piles of papers on his desk.

"How about your sleep and your energy level?"

"Well—" Joe paused. "I'm tired all the time. Even if I fall asleep quickly, I wake up over and over. I seem to see the clock at some point of every hour."

"Do you feel rested in the mornings?"

Tessa watched Joe appear to deflate as he sighed. "No, I can't say I do. Even if we sleep in on the weekends, I feel like I drag myself out of bed."

"That doesn't sound good. Is your appetite normal?"

Joe nodded.

"What about fun? Are there things you enjoy?"

"I love my family—of course I enjoy them. But I can't say I ever have fun anymore."

Tessa's lips opened into a little circle. She thought back and realized it had been a long time since she heard him laugh.

"Anything you want to add, Tessa?" Doctor Zernick asked.

She chose her words carefully, still distracted by Joe's admission. "When we do try to make love, often it doesn't go well." She looked quickly at Joe to sense whether this admission might upset him. He looked down at the floor and his Adam's apple rose and fell.

The doctor nodded. "This is really more common than people realize and happens to nearly all couples at some point. Joe, let's do some bloodwork to check for physical problems. We want to rule out diabetes and other conditions that can have this effect. While we wait for those results, I'll prescribe something to help with your sleep trouble. Maybe better rest will do the trick. Hopefully we'll have more answers when you come back in about ten days."

Ten more days. It seemed so long to Tessa, but it would work. Things had to get better.

Joe and Tessa held hands out to the car. When they were seated, she turned to him. "You *never* feel joy?" She pictured the two of them with gray hair sitting in a silent, darkened room.

He paused, and she wondered if he already felt like he was in that room. "No, I don't think so. You do?"

"Of course. Just looking at you or the kids will do it. Or being together outside, like when we go to the beach or the mountains. Holding a baby. Lots of things bring me joy."

Tessa's heart ached at the thought of what Joe was missing, but then she noticed that Joe looked ashamed.

"Maybe the new medicine will help," she said quickly. "You were probably right that you're just tired."

She hoped, for both of them, that this was true. They leaned over and kissed. He hugged her and then started the car. Neither spoke during the ride home.

⌘ ⌘ ⌘

Joe took the new medication Friday night. Saturday morning he woke Tessa with a kiss and reported he only remembered looking twice during the night to check the clock.

He does look more rested. She dared to hope.

Tessa remembered when they used to spend a little extra time in bed on Saturday mornings, waking up more slowly and cuddling, rather than jumping to obey the alarm. However, this morning, like most Saturdays lately, Stephen had a soccer game, so they held each other only a minute longer while Tessa took a deep breath and reviewed the schedule.

"We'll have to take two cars to Stephen's game so that I can get Amy to her riding lesson before the game is over. After the game, you and Stephen can catch the second shift of recycling with the Scouts. We should all be back by one for lunch, I think. Then I'll go for groceries. Could you cut the grass?"

Joe groaned. Tessa forced herself out of bed. Another busy day had begun.

⌘ ⌘ ⌘

After her Saturday breakfast, Marjorie began the tidying her house so desperately needed. Collecting books and papers to put away, she stopped when she came across her journal. She set her armload down and sat in her prayer chair, looking tentatively at the journal. She glanced out the window to a cheery morning. For years she had journaled on the first of every month. This notebook covered the first painful year after Michael died. With a deep breath, she settled back into the chair and opened the pages that had served as self-therapy.

August 1

Sixty-six days since he died. I've endured two months in this solitary confinement. A show on TV last night portrayed a stereotype of widows (what an ugly word) as being sex-starved. What can I write about that? It's more comprehensive. I'm touch-starved. The first few weeks, friends called and took me to lunch. There were hugs of sympathy, pats on the shoulder, or an extra squeeze to their handshakes.

Now that phase seems to be over. I never realized how much it means to be touched. Michael and I loved to hug. Even when we were too tired for more, we always embraced each other for a few minutes before turning to sleep. We kissed when we awoke or when we came home to each other. I long for the backrubs, his finger caressing my cheek, his foot stroking my leg when we read together on the couch. I'm not lustful, I'm touch-deprived.

Marjorie held her breath and closed her eyes but couldn't quite recapture the sensation of Michael's touch. Disappointed, she turned a page.

Roger next door talked to me last night. He and Joan and the kids are going away on vacation for three weeks. He mentioned I'll need to get someone to take care of our yard. How can I have been so out of it that I didn't realize he was taking care of the mowing and weeding? I wasn't even aware that it needed doing and was getting done. I'll call a service today. Michael loved his yard. He would have been disappointed in me that I never even thought about its care.

We took the girls on some wonderful vacations. We didn't go far, but I treasure those weeks when we'd bump elbows in the trailer at the beach or a lakeside campground. I'm so glad we created memories. I need to take comfort in those.

Now what? Will I vacation alone? I don't drive farther than three hours without feeling sleepy. I'd have no idea how to dump a trailer sewage tank. What joy would there be in exploring new places, with no one to share them?

After a year of the trailer sitting unused she had sold it, surprised at how much it hurt to be admitting to one more end of an era. She took a moment to replace that sadness with a happy memory of the four of them sitting at the dinette table writing in their vacation journals. How different this journal of grief from those happy scribblings. She read on.

September 1

Staring at the clock in the dark, I waited until 12:01 so I could justify giving up on sleep and getting out of bed. First of the month. I need to write.

I was lying awake thinking that grief mimics all the different mental disorders. Or am I truly experiencing them? There's anxiety. Every nerve I own is—what did the surgeon say after Aunt Annie's back surgery?—insulted. Raw. On edge. High-strung. I'm so emotionally unstable. Understatement. I'm like Mt. St. Helen's a second before she blew. There's no way I could have returned to teaching or my clients yet.

Or how about hallucinations? Did I never before realize how many men look like Michael from behind? I keep thinking I've seen him at a distance, and my heart leaps. Then I remember, and my soul drops back into limbo.

Certainly there's depression. Though I hate going to bed, I dread getting up. I have no energy. Nothing is enjoyable. Life itself seems too overwhelmingly difficult, too disconnected. All my connectedness seems to have died with Michael. Shouldn't I be able to take comfort in my children? That sounds selfish. I should be trying to comfort them.

The girls came down for my birthday last weekend. I walked into the living room where Sophie was staring at the telescope in the corner. Just standing and looking at it. I know she was remembering how she and her dad would drive away from the city lights to watch a lunar eclipse or try to see Saturn's rings. She turned to me and tears were running down her face. I opened my arms, and we fell apart, together.

That memory had etched itself forever in Marjorie's mind. The sight of her daughter looking at the telescope epitomized the end of all the tender moments of quality time Michael gave each of them. She forced herself to continue reading.

I used to believe I'd rather have Michael die than be unfaithful to me. How incredibly self-centered. Yes, unfaithfulness would have devastated me, and I would have suffered such utter rejection, but he'd be alive. He'd still be available to Sophie and Colleen and all the other people who love him. Instead we all have to learn to live with a Michael-shaped hole in our hearts.

Michael's been gone almost 100 days. Seems like a century. Yet the ache is as unrelenting as if he died yesterday. Will this ever get easier?

October 1

I steeled myself to try again to go through Michael's clothes. I should give them to someone who needs them. I started to box them but, after a few shirts, I saw the suit he bought for our wedding. I slid his suit coat on and buried my face into the wooly smell. The sleeve got wet against my face. Of course, he never carried tissues in his pockets like I do; he was a handkerchief man. I left the closet to blow my nose, saw myself in the mirror wearing his coat, and sat on the bed doing that laughing/crying combination. Embarrassing and cathartic at the same time.

The extended family got together on Michael's birthday last

month. I can't say we celebrated it exactly, but I think we all needed to gather. I suggested they write me a list of Michael's things that they'd like to have as mementos of him. I told them I'd consider their requests when I was feeling brave and would try to see that they each got some of what they wanted.

In the middle of the night after everyone was gone again, the smoke detector started to beep. By the time I found new batteries, dragged out the stepstool, figured out how to open the contraption, and silenced the relentless nagging, I was furious. But there was no one to be mad at.

There always used to be someone to share experiences like that. Now every responsibility is mine alone. No one else to stop alarms or kill spiders or unplug drains. Worse, he's not here to confide in or bounce ideas against. Not a soul to take my hand and pray for our family, or be a witness to my days.

I didn't appreciate Michael enough. I should have thanked him often for the minor things and let him know how I cherished the major ones.

I was touched when I finally did sit down and read the girls' lists. They didn't ask for the more expensive things, but the meaningful little keepsakes: his wallet, his battered guitar, a few of his favorite jazz CDs, the cigar box of seashells he and Colleen gleaned from the beach ten years ago, the camera he taught Sophie to focus.

Sophie asked for one of his ties. She used to give Michael such a hard time about his outdated tie assortment. I cried. Again.

November 1

I was determined to be doing better. I'm not.

Thanksgiving is coming; time to be grateful. I'm not. Almighty, it's You I'm mad at. And me.

December 1

Christmas-card time. I used to put such care into creating our Christmas letter. I looked forward to composing a touching, meaningful way to share our family's love with others. This year I don't even want to begin. There are a few people who won't know about Michael until they read our card, the first without his signature.

I don't want a Christmas without Michael's joy, without his guitar carols. We always decorated the tree together, whether it was a real one he and the girls cut at the tree farm, or the pitiful pole with pre-drilled holes that we poked imposter branches into. I don't have the energy to do it myself, or the desire.

Still, this season isn't about me or my sorrow. I need to focus on something besides myself. I'll try to smile and wish people a Merry Christmas. I'll shop for gifts, but I'll miss him opening the car trunk when I get home, and lifting one eyebrow in that "how-much-did-this-all-cost" expression.

I'll give out the items of Michael's the family asked for. And maybe a few that they didn't. Not Christmas Day, but sometime during the season.

Marjorie remembered the barrenness of last Christmas. She kept reading, needing even now to confirm what she knew.

January 1

I survived.

The holidays were empty and awkward much of the time, but Sophie carved the turkey every bit as well as her dad. We put the centerpiece in front of Michael's chair at his end of the table. And though occasional tears escaped, they weren't all mine. Somehow, that lightened the burden.

My New Year's Resolution: I will find something to appreciate about every day. And I'll get back to my evening walk, even though alone. Today I'm grateful for every member of this wounded family. Each one has suffered this loss individually, but together we're going to pull through. Now I'm going to stop writing and take a walk.

February 1

There are crocuses squeezing color to the surface of a surprise late snow. I don't think I've noticed nature in a long time. The kettle will whistle soon, and I'll peruse the rose catalog that arrived today, as I breathe in the orange-spice aroma of my tea. I'm going to order a floribunda to plant on the one-year anniversary. It will commemorate his life and remind me to grow.

March 1

I'm dreading our wedding anniversary, not being able to add one to the number of years we'd been married. You start saying, "This would have been...," and that ranks right up there in the same gut-clenching category as, "You must not have heard...," or needing to check a new box in the marital status section of forms.

April 1

I reread my journal entries for the last few months. Wound-licking. I am bone-tired of feeling sorry for myself.

Resolved: By the first of May I will have something positive to write about.

May 1

I've leased half a horse! I can already hear Colleen asking, "Which half?" I need something to bring play back into my life. I couldn't bear reaching May 27—-one year since his death—alone.

Her name is Oasis, a sweet little Appaloosa. I can hardly wait to introduce her to the girls.

Marjorie closed the journal, feeling completely drained. She had hoped to find some release in those entries, but both her guilt and her grief seemed like reopened, weeping wounds. Still, hope glimmered in the last few entries. Could she gather enough of its light to even consider starting another relationship?

But how could she remain content and in love with anyone, if she couldn't with Michael?

Twelve

Discuss marriage problems with spouses,
not with untrained others.

Gwen awoke Saturday to an empty bed and a pit-of-her-stomach pain that had been growing over the last few months. She hadn't heard from Brian since Wednesday when she made him leave, though she did notice that his pillow and some of his clothes were gone. She knew they both needed a cooling-off period, but she hoped he wouldn't move past cool to cold. She loved him. She didn't want to lose him. If she hadn't already.

Still, he owes me an apology!

The phone rang, and when she heard her husband's voice, her heart surged with relief. Maybe she and Brian were more connected than she realized. She curved her body around the receiver and rested her head and shoulder against the wall, ready to listen.

"Gweny, I love you and the boys more than anything or anybody in this world. I'm a jerk, and you have a right to be mad, but can't we work this out? I miss you."

Gwen wiped a tear from her cheek. How could she deal with these simultaneous feelings of anger, loneliness, fear, and love? She remembered Hank's suggestion that they think of their relationship as a remodeling project.

"Brian, there's this rundown couple I know. They've got a few cracks in the plaster, but their foundation is solid. Maybe we could consider them our next fixer-upper." She paused to give herself time to calm the quiver out of her voice. "Come home, Bri. I miss you, too."

When Brian's car pulled up to the house a half hour later, Gwen followed Mickey, Joe Pat, and Sean, who poured out of the door singing, "Daddy's home. Daddy's home!" She hesitated at the porch, watching Brian lift the boys under their arms and swing each around in a circle. His muscular build and lithe movement stirred something inside her.

He looked at her, and his sandy hair, his trim beard, and the laugh lines that creased the edges of his blue eyes were as dear to her now as on their wedding day. She reached out her arms with a smile as he approached her. Through his hugs and her tears, they promised to work to make things better. They had too much to lose.

While the boys went to play in the tent in the backyard, Gwen and Brian sat down at the kitchen table with cups of coffee. Gwen took a sip, but the liquid unsettled her already uneasy stomach. She breathed shallowly to calm herself, feeling torn between some remaining indignation and her relief to have this frustrating man home.

Brian set his cup down. After a deep breath, he began to talk. His tone reminded Gwen of the speech project he had rehearsed and rehearsed in high school. "I was furious when I saw you looking at the computer screen. It took me awhile to figure out it was partly because I felt so guilty and partly because I knew how hurt you'd be. I wish I had apologized."

He looked directly at her. "Why did I go and write all that stuff in the first place? And to Shirley?"

Gwen nodded. Her questions exactly.

"I knew you and Shirley never liked each other. I must have seemed like a traitor. But I've been so frustrated lately. It felt good to have someone listen. At least, it started out that way."

Gwen saw the shame in his eyes but didn't offer any reassurance.

He sighed and plodded on. "I've been thinking this through the last few days while I worked, trying to understand how we got to this point. When Shirley first found me online, it was good to hear from one of the gang. She knew I didn't want to move here. She said she guessed how much I'd be missing everyone. Heck, I'd been friends with the guys since kindergarten. But then you wanted to go to graduate school and talked me into moving here."

Gwen felt her anger rise. She crossed her legs, sat back, and watched her foot jiggle. Was he trying to blame her? With great effort she kept from interrupting him.

"Babe, you've always been jealous of my time with my friends. Shirley said you probably were glad to get me away from them. That made it easy to pour out my complaints to her. Felt good to have her gripe about Tad, too. Nice to know we weren't the only couple having trouble."

Gwen's jaw eased out of its indignant lift, and she looked down. She had to admit he was right about her jealousy. She had hoped that by getting him away from the guys, and their hunting and fishing and basketball playing, he'd be forced to focus on her and their boys.

Brian lifted her chin with his finger and held her eyes with his own. "But I shouldn't have started writing like that." He dropped his hand back to his cup, and it was his turn to lower his gaze. "And then, once I did, I think I knew it wasn't right. But that made it kind of exciting. Going online, hoping Shirley would be online, too. Kind of sneaking off to meet her."

Gwen imagined Shirley sitting in sexy lingerie, typing at a computer in the dark. She wondered what mental pictures Brian had of his chat-room partner. Did he ever ask her what she was wearing? Gwen felt wickedly justified as she added curlers and green night cream to a suddenly very heavy, cigarette-drooping, flannel-clad Shirley. But the picture didn't relieve the ache in her heart. He had cheated. Not sexually, but he had cheated all the same.

Gwen pushed her hand against the sharp pain in her stomach. Here she was, living proof of a women's magazine article she had doubted last week. She had read that an emotional affair could be as damaging as a physical one. Now her Brian had talked to Shirley about their most private problems, and she felt like he had destroyed something precious. Her trust. Their privacy. He'd given away the intimacy that should have been hers alone.

Fear overtook her anger as she remembered more from the article. It claimed a man had a much harder time breaking off an emotional affair than a physical one. That he was more likely to leave a sexual partner than one he felt connected to. Could she lose him to Shirley, or someone like her? What if he left her and the boys? How could she support her family? She wouldn't finish school for another couple of years. What would life be like without Brian? Her hands began to tremble around her cup.

Brian took her hands in his, and their warmth drew her thoughts back to the present. He shifted his weight forward on the chair, as if trying to ground himself to this place, and met her eyes again. "When I think of that sneakiness, it doesn't sound much different than having an affair. But I swear I never would do that to us."

Could she believe him?

"Oh Gwen, I'm so sorry." Brian, whom she hadn't seen cry since he broke his arm in third grade, had tears in his eyes. "I was thinking of myself, of what I—"

The door burst open, and the three boys ran through the kitchen squealing that they had heard the ice cream truck. Gwen turned her attention to them, but the image of Brian holding his broken arm on the third-grade playground stayed with her. Even at nine she had wanted to hug him and make him feel better, but then, like now, she hadn't reached out.

Thirteen

Good intentions, bad decisions.

The same Saturday morning found Hank and Esther at IHOP eating blueberry pancakes at 5 a.m. They had talked through the night, and Hank had invited his grandmother out for breakfast. He was still reeling from her words, "I'm sorry to give her back to you, only to take her away again, Hank. She *has* died, but not when you were three."

Though Hank's neurons and synapses were screaming to know what had happened to his mother, it was clear Esther would need to work her way around to the full story from the beginning. For the last two hours they had simply been getting to know each other. Hank talked about his work at the hospital and about some of his favorites at the Youth Club. Esther spoke of losing her husband two years earlier, after forty years of shared love.

"I sure wish you had more time with him, Hank. You two would have gotten along fine. You know, we would have offered to have you live with us after your mom left your dad, if we had known she left you, too."

Her face registered realization. "Now that I think about it, that could explain why your dad kept your living with him a secret. Maybe he feared he'd lose you to us. It would be so much like what happened to him. Your dad's mom died when he was small, maybe six or seven. His father, your grandfather, fell apart when his wife passed on. He took to drinking and got mean. There was some talk that he got pretty rough with your dad, so his mama's folks fetched the boy to live with them."

She shook her head and her eyes seemed to focus in the past. "They

81

were a kind couple. They lived near us, and I know they gave Gordon lots of love and understanding. We used to see them walking back from buying ice cream cones on Sunday. Still, he never forgave them for taking him away from his dad. Even though his father had alternated between neglect and abuse, the boy loved him and wanted to protect him."

Esther patted Hank's arm. "Maybe when your mom left, Gordon couldn't risk the chance of losing you, too. He'd already lost too many people in his life."

Hank tried in vain to picture his dad as a little boy, dealing with his own problem father. Hank had never thought about what his dad's childhood was like. One more thing they didn't talk about. That little boy never learned how to be a loving father because he didn't have a role model of his own. Hank wondered if he would ever get a chance to break the family cycle. He yearned to be a good father, better than he or his dad had experienced.

Was his grandma right? Did his dad keep his mom from taking him with her because he loved him? A sudden realization hit Hank like pure adrenaline. Every nerve seemed to fire simultaneously.

Dad knew no other way of showing love than through hard work and money. He acted on his love every night when he went downstairs to earn extra money, but all I knew was his silence.

It must have deeply hurt his dad when he'd said he couldn't use the savings. Hank could feel his pulse quicken.

"Was he good to you, Hank? Did he do any of the mistreating his father had done to him?"

He hesitated, pondering what she'd asked. "He never hit me, and I never saw him get drunk. But I guess he didn't know how to be a dad. Didn't talk much, but he provided for me. He worked hard." For some reason that Hank didn't understand, he hesitated to tell his grandmother how quiet and lonely his life had been. He wanted to protect his dad.

Maybe like my dad wanted to protect and take care of his own dad.

"Why did Mom and Dad marry?"

Esther sighed. She said she would like to forget the hard times, but she told him a child had a right to know the stories that began his own story.

"Janie, your mom, came into this world angry." The wrinkles around his grandmother's mouth became more pronounced. "I know that sounds like an awful thing for a mother to say about her daughter, but it's the truth. Babies are born with strong personalities, and Janie started out ready for a fight. Some growing-up stages were better than others; some were worse. She settled down during her first few years of school, but by the time she hit junior high, she became a force to be reckoned with."

At that point, Esther stared down at her hands folded in her lap, then peered up at him through misty eyes. "She and your grandpa would lock horns, each more stubborn than the day before. They loved each other dearly but couldn't figure out how to show it."

She lifted her right hand, palm up. "Your grandpa wished for her safety, security, and happiness." She raised her left hand, level with the first. "Janie pushed for freedom, adventure and excitement." His Grandma clapped her palms together. "I was caught between them, loving them both, desperately wanting them to get along."

Hank apologized for putting her through the pain she was so obviously suffering, but she pressed on, her voice sounding determined he learn the truth, once and for all.

"When your mom reached her sophomore year in high school, she and your dad found each other. Gordon had dreams of leaving Spokane and making something of himself. I think that's what attracted her. She wanted to see the world. Janie already had a drinking problem by then, but we had no idea." She sighed, shaking her head.

"Gordon loved her; anyone could see that. He didn't run wild like some of the other boys she dated, so we hoped he'd help her settle down a bit. But, by the time she was sixteen, she was pregnant with you. Gordon was a senior. Right after he graduated, they eloped. Your dad took his responsibility for you seriously. He found work as a mechanic apprentice here in town. They still dreamed of moving away but couldn't afford it right off."

Hank could sense what was coming. Although his father had taken his duties in stride, his mother must have seen it as a prison sentence. He rolled the hot coffee mug between his palms, his heart still aching at the realization that his father had loved him.

"Of course, it thrilled me to still have her close, especially when I became a grandma. You were such a sweet little guy. Right from the start, as irritable as your mom had been as a baby, you were mellow. We called you Smiley. You always seemed easy to satisfy and gentle-natured."

Here, his grandmother's demeanor changed. The tempo of her words increased. "When you neared six months old, Janie got restless. She asked me to take care of you, so she could get a job. Those next two and a half years were some of the happiest of my life. While your mom burned off energy as a waitress, you and I played together."

"You loved going down to Riverfront Park and shooting down the slide in the giant Radio Flyer Wagon. I'd hold you on a horse going around and around on the carousel, too. You see, I hadn't been able to have more children after Janie, so time with you eased that hurt and gave me joy."

Hank strained, trying to remember.

A shadow took the light from Esther's eyes, and her smile wilted. She spoke more slowly, as though choosing her words carefully. "Then it all ended. Your dad called me one Sunday morning and told me Janie had left him and taken you with her. Put me into a state of shock. I loved your mama and hurt at her leaving, but oh, the pain of losing you, too. Your grandpa was fit to be tied. I think it broke his heart to lose Janie. He'd been afraid of losing her all those years, and then he really did.

"The next thing I knew, your dad called and said he couldn't stay in Spokane anymore. He'd decided to look for her and, if he couldn't find her, settle somewhere else. He wrote once from Oregon to tell us he hadn't found her, but he'd gotten a job there. Didn't say a word about you being with him. We lived from day to day, praying we'd hear from Janie and praying that you and she were safe."

Hank's heart felt like dead weight as he watched tears rise in his grandma's eyes. He wished he could have spared her such pain.

"About a year later, she called and asked us to wire her some money to come home. We did, but she never came. She did that a second time, too. The third time we said no but told her we'd come and get her. She hung up, and we never heard from her again."

Esther looked at Hank, and the sadness on her face filled his soul. Her voice lost all inflection, as if the pain had surpassed what emotions could express. "About three years ago, we got a call from a hospital in California. Janie had been brought there in an ambulance, dead on arrival. She'd died of a drug overdose. All she had with her was a Polaroid picture of you when you were three with our phone number written on the back of it."

Esther and Hank sat holding hands, her eyes dry, his burning. They looked down at their empty plates. What more could be said?

Hank and Esther agreed they both needed some sleep. He dropped her off at home and then drove back to his motel. Once there, he took off his shoes, pants, and shirt, and slid under the covers. Although he'd found some answers, he had new questions to think about. His body desperately wanted sleep, but his caffeinated mind replayed the night's conversation with his grandmother.

He curled up into a tight ball, determined not to fall apart. His father loved him. His mother left him. Eventually the long night without rest overcame his racing emotions.

He slept.

He dreamed of cuckoo clocks and giant wagon slides. He dreamed of a carousel that wouldn't stop to let him follow his mother, who had turned and walked away. He dreamed of being left all alone.

He awoke determined to end his loneliness.

⌘ ⌘ ⌘

Marjorie drove to the stable that Saturday afternoon, deep in thought about change. Most of the class had settled on books to apply to their relationships. It sounded like some of those relationships were getting worse instead of better, as the equilibrium was disrupted before it found a new balance. One person made a change, and then the other was pressured to change in response. But they resisted and pushed to return the relationship back to where it had been. It may not have been good, but it was familiar and comfortable.

Father, You know change frightens us.

A few fortunate couples had begun to discover the improvements that better communication brought. Marjorie prayed for the lucky, and she prayed for the struggling.

Please be with my students and the people who are so important to them. I know You want healing for each of them. Comfort and encourage them as they go through their growth spurts. Show me where I can help.

She bumped down the dirt road that led to the stable.

Direct my choice of discussion during class. Bring wisdom to my words as I write comments in their journals. Be present in the small groups so they can support one another in their growth. Lead them to the knowledge they need for their relationships, as well as what they need to learn for their future clients.

Marjorie's thoughts weren't only on her class. Teaching couples' counseling had become bittersweet. She missed Michael when she read about the students' relationships. Their journals reminded her of times when she and Michael had thrived; they had given in to so few of the problems that the students wrote about.

Sometimes teaching the class felt like a balm for her, therapeutic. Even though she didn't have her soul mate anymore, she had learned from their love and could find meaning for her life by teaching others how to enrich their relationships.

She had to admit that lately, though, she sensed an internal shift. She noticed qualities in some of her male students that charmed her. Just this week she'd found herself thinking, *I'd like to find that tenderness in the next man I love.*

The next man I love.

Until now, she'd assumed there could never be another person for her. She'd been holding on to God's promise of plans to give her hope and a future, but expected God to give her life meaning through her work as she counseled and taught. Could there be more for her life?

Father, might you have a new gift for me of a man's love? Could I be ready for that again? She sighed, afraid to even hope.

When she had parked the car, she reread the letter she had received at school the day before:

Dear Marjorie,

Thank you for your candor. I do understand. Even years can be too short a time to adjust to the passing of a great love. I lost a spouse, as well, and I know how difficult and pervasive the grief process can be.

I am grateful that your letter included your work address. I must admit that delivering my letter via "pony express" was an experience I am not eager to relive.

You work at a college, as do I.

May I suggest that we could continue our acquaintance by mail? I am much more comfortable expressing myself in written word than spoken. I don't know if that propensity led to my study of literature or was caused by it, but there it is. As they used to say of my profession, I am a man of letters.

Might you write to me? Tell me of your work, of your family, or what you do to relax. I, in turn, could tell you of my experience as a visitor to your country.

You are in my prayers,
Colm

Marjorie refolded the letter and pushed it back into her purse. *I don't know.* There couldn't be anyone as perfect for her as Michael. She couldn't feel right with anyone else. The truth was, she didn't want to be loved by someone who wasn't Michael. Especially someone who might be only visiting.

But wasn't Colm simply asking for friendship?

Fourteen

Stop criticism, contempt,
defensiveness, and stonewalling.

Gwen and Brian spent Saturday afternoon with their boys at the Oregon Museum of Science and Industry, a brick and glass complex on the bank of the Willamette River. They smiled at each other as they watched the boys run from playing with a wave machine to making flubber, and then to digging in a sand pit for "dinosaur fossils." The grownups held hands as they all watched a giant-screen OmniMax movie about dolphins. They toured a submarine docked beside the museum and then stopped at McDonald's and let the boys play in the ball crawl after they ate dinner. The younger two fell asleep in the minivan on the way home, and within a half hour, all three were sound asleep in their beds. Brian and Gwen decided the boys had a good idea. Brian took Gwen's hand and led her to their own room, where wounded feelings were salved and showed promise of healing.

Around midnight Gwen awoke and saw Brian propped up on an elbow smiling at her. He looked around and sighed. "It's good to be back in this room."

Gwen followed his gaze. In the moonlight, the furniture flanked their bed like guardians: the oak dresser that had been her grandmother's, the armoire that Brian's mother had cherished as a newlywed, and the entertainment center that their two fathers had secretly built together as a wedding present and then filled with a television, video recorder, and compact disk player. Their family still surrounded them, even in a new city.

Brian shifted to sit up. Gwen joined him, her back supported by the headboard Brian had carved with entwined wedding rings.

He smoothed her hair gently away from her eyes and told her he loved her. "I'm so sorry, babe. I've been frustrated. I felt us slipping apart."

Gwen nodded her understanding but had to speak her mind. "Griping to someone else was the wrong way to try to fix things. We need to talk to each other about what bothers us, so we can work on it together, not complain to someone else."

Brian defended himself. "It's hard for me to get up the nerve to tell you when I don't like what's happening. I don't want to upset you."

She frowned but wanted to keep him talking to her. "Like what, Brian?"

"This whole move, to start with. I didn't want to leave our home. I love that town and all our friends—"

"All *your* friends. They sure weren't mine!"

She felt him jerk like he'd been hit. "See, like that. As soon as I try to talk to you about what upsets me, you do that."

Gwen dropped her shoulders in concession. "Sorry. I've been reading about defensiveness being one of the destructive forces in a marriage, and still I slide right back into it."

Backing down was new to Gwen and must have caught Brian's attention, because he immediately softened. "Destructive forces?"

"Defensiveness, criticism, contempt, and stonewalling."

"What do they mean, stonewalling?"

She took a deep breath. "Mainly refusing to communicate or work things out. Like when I give you the cold shoulder when I'm mad at you. Or when you slam out the door and leave an argument. Although, that can be a good thing—well, without the slamming—if two people realize they need a cool-down period before they can communicate well. But let's go back to what you were telling me about your frustrations. I promise I'll just listen. Then maybe you can listen to me about mine."

Brian reached his arm around her so she could nestle against his chest. "Fair enough. I guess I've been feeling sorry for myself ever since we moved. I miss being able to call up a friend to help me with a house project, or going out with the guys for a beer at the end of a day. I miss playing basketball or going hunting. And I hate the city. Rush-hour traffic. Driving twenty minutes when I realize I need more supplies. I want to go back to walking to the store and knowing the people I pass. Or having family around to watch the boys so we can get away for a weekend. I miss how you used to always be home and didn't study every minute."

Gwen would normally have listed all the positives of the city to prove Brian wrong. This time, though, she realized he needed her to listen and she resolved not be defensive.

Marjorie says to rephrase what he said, so I get what he's saying right, and so he knows I'm tuned in.

Gwen sat up and turned so she could see Brian's face in the silver light from the window. She tugged the comforter around her shoulders, wondering briefly how Brian could be warm enough bare-chested. "You miss living in a small town, and you miss your friends and all the activities you used to do together."

"Exactly!" He drew her close. "You heard me this time."

"And maybe you feel mad at me because we left all that to come here for my graduate work."

He paused, as if to consider what she'd said. "Yeah, I guess. I know we talked about it, and I agreed to move here, but I wish we hadn't. I want to be back home. But then I feel guilty because it sounds selfish. I want you to be happy, too."

Although she felt vulnerable and tempted to raise her defenses, she was determined to keep trying what she learned in Marjorie's class. Her old reactions certainly weren't working.

"I like hearing the part about you missing when the family would baby-sit. Me too, Bri. I like getting to be alone with you. And I miss free time when I don't have to study." She caught herself. "But I'm supposed to be listening. What else?"

He bit his lip as though afraid to say more, but finally he leaned toward her, and kissed her hair. "Maybe I shouldn't get into this, but as long as we're being open, babe, you know I love the boys, right?" Brian shifted to face Gwen squarely. "But we went so fast from being a couple to having all these kids. Three boys in three years! Between the noise and the energy level and worrying about finances, a lot of times I feel

90

nuts! How did this all happen so fast?"

At first Gwen felt defensive, but then her eyes twinkled. "It happened so fast because we are both irresistible and sexy!" His grin rewarded her. "But I know what you mean. When we had all three in diapers I thought I spent all my time either in the laundry room or calf roping one to flip him over and change him. I still feel like I'm perpetually running after them."

She took a deep breath, as if she just finished the chase. "Let's take a good long break before we decide to try for a girl. Anything else?"

"No," he said, sounding relieved, "your turn."

Gwen paused to select her words, grateful the boys were fast asleep. She and Brian so rarely had uninterrupted discussions. "Okay. You already know I resented your friends. I have to admit part of my excitement to move here centered on getting you all to myself."

Brian nodded like he had suspected as much.

She needed him to understand how hard it had been. "I missed you when you were hunting or playing basketball or out for a beer with the guys. I struggled alone with our boys all day, and then when I thought I'd have your company or maybe even get away myself, you'd come home for dinner and then go out again. Or be gone a whole weekend hunting!"

Gwen noticed Brian's jaw clench, so she hurried to add, "But now you're the one coming home and staying with the boys while I leave after dinner for my classes. I get to see people, have actual adult conversations, and make new friends at school. You haven't had a chance to meet new friends here, have you?"

Brian shook his head but didn't talk. Gwen smiled at his determination to let her have her turn to vent. "But I don't want to go home yet. I want to finish this program. I love what I'm studying, and I want to learn how to be a good counselor. We could consider moving back when I'm done with the program."

"That's still two years away!"

"I could take more classes than I do now and finish in a little more than one year."

"But then you'd be gone from us even more." Brian sounded so much like the boys when they were frustrated that Gwen had to hold back a smile. He cleared his throat, inhaled, and let his breath out slowly. "It would be great to move back home. I'm glad you'll consider it, but don't go faster. I can wait. I sure don't want you gone more than you are now."

Gwen released the smile. "In the meantime, you better find some guys to play basketball with. Maybe once a week?"

"Sounds good, but did you finish what you wanted to say about your frustrations?"

"No, I guess not." Gwen met his eyes and silently begged him not to get upset. "When we moved here, I didn't get you all to myself like I wanted. Or even all to the boys and myself. You traded the time you used to spend with the guys for time in front of the TV or the computer."

Gwen's voice faltered, and she felt her eyes sting. "I'm lonely when you do that. I want us to talk when you're home. I want to hear about your day and have you ask about mine. And now I'm afraid that whenever I see you on the computer, I'll wonder if you're talking with some other woman instead."

Brian wrapped her in his arms and kissed her forehead. "I'm sorry, babe. I promise it won't happen again. You can count on me. No more chatting on the Internet." He paused and then, sounding as if he were forcing himself to be honest, he said, "I can't give up the TV completely, though. Some games I have to watch."

"But could you quit turning it on automatically when you come home?"

Brian lay back in the bed, lifting the comforter to invite her closer. "Speaking of turning on..."

Fifteen

Our soul, mind, and body
are interrelated.

Marjorie moved around the classroom from group to group the next Thursday night. It seemed to her like most were reporting happy progress with their relationships. She was glad for them, but sometimes it seemed they were all passing her by while she stood mired in loneliness. She stopped at Hank's group. She'd been wondering about his weekend in Spokane.

The lanky redhead leaned forward in his chair, grinning and talking fast. Marjorie quietly took a seat near their group while he acknowledged her with a smile and kept talking. "My grandma was amazing," he said, clearly excited by his weekend. "We talked for hours, and filled in lots of gaps about my past. I needed the whole ride back to Portland to process it all."

To Tessa's query about whether they planned to get together again, he said, "She's invited me to come back for Thanksgiving dinner. You know, I've never had a home-cooked Thanksgiving dinner before." Hank paused, then added, "It's like I've become more whole than I used to be. I fit somewhere."

Tessa and Gwen spoke at the same time, "That's wonderful," and, "I'm so glad."

Marjorie's thoughts echoed the same words. Hank deserved happiness. Yet she also recognized his vulnerability, and she sighed to herself. She too felt vulnerable these days. Every time she saw a happy couple or thought of something she and Michael used to do together, she ached. She felt like she should be sitting as a student and wished a wise teacher would come set her straight.

The thought brought the voice of old Professor Kohler to mind. She could hear his German accent intone, "Beware the client who shares your issues. Great harm can be done to him." She tucked the remembered advice away, promising herself to consider it in a quiet moment. For now she would focus on her students rather than herself.

"I'm doing more than my share of talking," Hank was saying to his small group. "How about you two?"

Gwen looked at Tessa, who nodded for her to go ahead. "Good progress to report. Brian's back home. We talked things out, but this time we both listened. I stopped trying to argue my side of everything."

Marjorie noted the strides Gwen seemed to be taking and imagined shaking her head in amazement at the progress some students made in a term. Why was it easier to guide others than to step out of her own stagnation? She'd been waffling for days on whether to write to Colm.

Gwen's words pulled her attention back. "Now I understand how hard moving here has been on him. He hates city life. He'd like to move back right now but knows it's important for me to finish this degree. But we talked about ways to make it easier for him, and my stomach hasn't hurt since he came home."

"Nice conflict resolution," Tessa replied. "I've been worried for both of you all week, but it sounds like things are going better."

Marjorie sighed. *Thank You, Almighty, for working in my students' lives and helping them to heal and grow. I could use a nudge toward growth, myself.* She slipped away to listen to another group and to discover where her Father had led them.

When the group discussion hour finished, and after a short break, Marjorie began her lesson. "Tonight I'd like to talk about the cutting edge of psychology, where it bumps up against spirituality. To study psychology and ignore spirituality is to disregard an integral part of each person we serve. Granted, not everyone believes in God, and even those who do believe in as many different ways as there are believers. Yet, all people with reasoning ability, at some point in their lives come up against questions that raise the issues of spirituality."

Marjorie looked at each student as she listed questions. "Why am I here? Does the world need me? How can I find peace...or love? Should I forgive? Are people intrinsically good? Intrinsically evil? Why is there suffering? Will I see my loved ones after I die?"

Marjorie paused to swallow past the lump in her throat. She could have added, what happens to the people left behind when loved ones die?

She gave her students time to ponder these questions as they fumbled for pens and notebooks. She had seen it in their faces and heard it in their voices. Like her, each of them had grappled with the queries. Some struggled to work out the details of sharing the commitment of love. Some grieved for a love rejected or a dear one who had died. From their drop-in visits to her office, she knew a few were desperate to know what direction their lives should take. Others suspected but were afraid of the path ahead. Again, her old professor interrupted her thoughts: "Beware the client who shares your issues..."

Marjorie drew a deep breath and continued. For the next hour, she discussed prayer in the medical field and studies that indicated prayer helped people heal faster. She shared her personal belief that the force within the person that psychology credited for growth and healing was actually love, or God. She recommended praying for their clients when they had established their practices.

Glancing at the clock, she concluded, "Let me suggest an experiment. You're each working on an important relationship in your lives and applying the recommendations of a psychologist author. Try adding prayer to your efforts. Don't pray for the other to change. Pray that you'll have the courage to do what's necessary to help the relationship. Pray for growth, healing, and happiness for both of you, especially when you're most frustrated. Write in your journals about what happens. Okay, time's up. Class dismissed. You're in my prayers."

You are in my prayers. The very words Colm used at the end of his letter. *Is that a nudge from You, Father?*

After she said good night to the last student, Marjorie sat down and opened her heart to her Father's direction. She wanted to contemplate Colm's request, but the pesky German professor was back with his warning. She took time to consider his words. Years ago, he had taught her to cautiously reconsider working with a client in an area where she hadn't resolved her own problems. It was usually best to refer them to another counselor.

Marjorie scanned the desks and imagined the students who had just left them. Who shared her issues? She looked to Gwen's desk and, as she thought of Gwen's arguments with Brian, she remembered her own parents' constant fighting. Newlywed Jessica had been writing about the death of her brother from AIDS, and Marjorie's heart clenched, still scarred from the loss of her older brother to war. Though he had only been a soldier a short time, she still pictured him the way she saw him last, in his dress uniform.

And Hank. Hank's pilgrimage to find his grandmother reminded her of the times in her past when she had returned to Montana to consult her wise Aunt Annie. The journal description of his silent childhood brought back her own experience of the tomblike atmosphere of her home after her mother shut down. Her mom had blamed her dad, the local Army recruiter, for their son's death. Marjorie relived the heart-yearning feeling of the day her meticulous father carried his two suitcases out the front door, an errant shirtsleeve reaching out to her. Her mood steadily darkening, she looked to the desk of Anna, who often rubbed her graying temples as she ruminated about her divorce. The eventual divorce of Marjorie's parents led her to study marriage counseling.

She glanced around the classroom and wondered instead who *didn't* have issues she shared. Her eyes settled on Tessa's chair and a bit of hope glimmered. Tessa was not yielding to the challenges that came her way but had struggled to victory against breast cancer and no doubt could overcome her husband's libido problem, too.

Marjorie's shoulders straightened as she considered other successes in this class and classes before. She had seen many through difficult times and learned from each of them. She would *not* beware. These were students, not clients, and she would continue to teach them the skills she knew, some from professors and theorists, some that she had learned from other students, and some from her own survival story.

She bowed her head to pray in both thanksgiving and determination.

Now, Father, what about Colm?

Marjorie couldn't help but admire Colm's willingness to face his fears. She thought of her own fears and how they had bound her in place for all these months. She remembered Colm's proud look when she had complimented him on facing his horse phobia to come to her rescue. She wanted to feel strong like that herself. To be courageous in the face of...what? Her fears were nebulous and undefined. Widowhood? The empty nest? Letting go of her girls? Or Michael? A shudder jerked her shoulders.

Remembering Colm's struggle for courage reminded her of the list he wrote of all his nemeses, ordered from smallest to greatest. Resolutely, she opened a drawer of her desk and removed a stack of index cards. She redistributed paper piles to make room to work. On the first card she wrote, *I'm afraid of loneliness.* That seemed both too general and too negative, so she moved the card to the bottom of the pile and began again.

On the new card she wrote, *I won't be afraid to let my girls be independent.* That sounded healthier. Since she intended to read these cards often as reminders, she'd rather engrain what she hoped to accomplish, rather than what she feared. She took a new card and tapped it with the pen a few times, then wrote, *I won't be afraid of my guilt over my irritation with Michael before he died.* Then, *I won't be afraid of my empty nest.*

On the next card she simply printed, *Colm.* This was followed in rapid succession with more abbreviated cards: *failure; letting my students down; living alone; losing my job; cancer; heart disease; loved ones leaving me; my girls dying; letting go of Michael; being lonely forever; God.*

That last card surprised her. She stared at it, feeling like a child who had just screamed, "I hate you!" at her mother. Afraid of retribution. More afraid it was true that she feared God. She quickly turned the notecard facedown and took another. *Being wild. Being too happy. Forgetting Michael.* His name brought the constriction back to her throat, but she wrote on with surprising relief at putting names to her worries, though the size of the pile became daunting.

When the flow of words ebbed, Marjorie patted the pile into order and paged through the fears, feeling like they were newly contained. She read the deck a second time, this time dividing them into two stacks—one for the fears that were holding her back, the other for those that were already serving their purpose to inspire her to action. Her concerns about cancer and heart disease contributed to her fairly healthy diet and her daily walks. She worked diligently to serve her students and clients well; she wasn't likely to lose her teaching position or jeopardize her private practice. She set those cards aside.

The remaining cards she categorized—fears about her daughters in one pile, Michael in another, Colm or any man in a third. That left the one bewildering card about God in its own pile.

Colm had faced his simplest fears first, but Marjorie had no idea what to do about any of the cards. How could she choose which was easiest to attack? Her determination stalled, Marjorie shrugged and secured the stacks with a rubberband, then slid them into her briefcase. She would call them her "growth cards" and carry them with her until she had overcome each fear.

Bowing her head once again, Marjorie asked for direction. After a few quiet minutes, she stood decisively. It was time for a visit to Aunt Annie.

Sixteen

Turn toward, not away.

G wen chatted for a while with Hank and Tessa after class, then noticed the time and hurried home in Brian's truck. She preferred her minivan, but Brian drove it when he had the boys so their car seats wouldn't have to be moved. Energized by Hank's story of finding his roots and looking forward to sharing time with her husband, Gwen hoped the boys would all be asleep. She imagined surprising Brian with a wink and a suggestion to head to bed early.

As she pulled into the driveway, all thoughts of romance were dispelled. Brian charged out the front door carrying Sean. "It's about time! Where have you been? I've been trying to get you on your cell phone!"

Her heart shifted into double time. Brian was obviously not at all happy, and neither was Sean, their two-year-old, who cried in his father's arms with flushed cheeks and glassy eyes.

Gwen clambered out of the car to meet them at the door. "I must have forgotten to turn the phone on after class. What's wrong?" Gwen's mood deflated under the weight of her worry.

"Sean started crying right after you left. He's running a fever. I've tried medicine for his fever and stuffy nose, but he hasn't stopped crying all night. I took his temperature again, and he's up to 103°!"

Gwen placed her palm on Sean's forehead but jerked away at the shock of the heat. "Here, give him to me." She kissed away his hot tears.

"I thought I'd have to wake the boys and take them all to the Emergency Room. You were supposed to be home half an hour ago." Brian's voice was shaking but loud, and his anger was contagious.

She resisted the urge to retaliate. "I'm sorry, Brian. I'll take him to the hospital. It's probably an ear infection. I'll call you when I know."

She jumped when Brian slammed the door behind him as he went back into the house. She could hear him stomp up the stairs and suspected the two older boys had been startled awake by the noise of the door. Gwen took Sean and headed to the minivan. As she buckled him into his car seat and backed down the driveway, both she and the toddler were crying.

⌘ ⌘ ⌘

As soon as Marjorie arrived home from class and let Nutmeg out, she sat at the computer to compose a letter to Colm. The nudge she had felt when she prayed after class had lifted her spirit and seemed to give her permission, even direction, to reach out.

> Dear Colm,
>
> Thank you so much for understanding and for your suggestion to write each other.
>
> I've always wanted to go to Ireland. What's it like? What do you miss?
>
> Yes, I do work at a college. I'm a therapist and a psychologist. I teach counseling at the graduate level, and I also spend much of my time helping couples with their relationships. I have two daughters, Sophie and Colleen....

When she finished her letter, she took a deep breath and printed it out. Reaching for the pages, she saw her husband's photo beside the printer and snatched her hand back. Could he see her from heaven? Did he know now that she had longed for a change before he died? Would he think she had been longing for someone like Colm? How could she even think of another man after Michael?

Feeling as if he had walked into the room and caught her with Colm, she backed away from the desk and sank into her prayer chair. Suddenly cold, she wrapped herself in the afghan she kept folded on its back. She desperately wished she were wrapping herself in someone's arms. Michael's? She'd never feel Michael's arms again.

Father, hold me!

Marjorie looked from the printer to the photo. The printer held an offer of friendship, a possibility of sharing herself again. The picture of Michael held her whole past, from delightful intimate moments to times of struggle. Michael was the person who was supposed to be the witness to her history, from the day they met to the day she died. But he was gone, and it felt like her story would never be read. Heat radiated from her face. Her eyes burned; her chest hurt from shoulder to shoulder. She imagined herself becoming smaller. No, not smaller, less solid. She rocked forward and back from the waist and gave in to the tingling in her sinuses. Marjorie sobbed.

When the stuttered gasps of breath subsided and her tears finally diminished, she realized Nutmeg was barking and scratching at the backdoor. She let the little beagle in, then sank down onto the floor to relish in the dog's squirming, nuzzling love.

"Nutmeg," she sighed, "my dear, sweet friend."

My Friend. That had been the way Michael addressed God when he prayed aloud. To Marjorie, God was Almighty Father. She returned to her prayer chair and folded her legs under her. She tugged the afghan around her, then took a ragged breath and bowed her head.

Help me to know what to do. Help me to deal with my loneliness as well as my guilt. Should I send this letter?

⌘ ⌘ ⌘

The grandfather clock in the living room struck 2 a.m. as Gwen returned with a sleeping Sean. She tucked him into his bed and then quietly slipped into her own. She cuddled close to Brian, who had his back to her. She rubbed his back gently and then rested her arm around his shoulders. His muscles tensed, but he didn't roll over. *Fine,* she thought, and turned away from him, her irritation postponing what little sleep she could catch before the older boys roused.

In the morning, she awoke when Brian came into the room. "I've fed Mickey and Joe Pat. Sean's still asleep. I'm going to work." He turned and left the room without a kiss good-bye.

Gwen sat up quickly and called, "Brian, can we talk before you go?"

Brian's only answer was the thud of the front door. Gwen's stomach echoed the slam with a sharp twinge. *Stonewalled.*

The day passed with the normal brother squabbles and housework. Sean already showed signs of response to the antibiotic the doctor started him on the night before. The fever subsided, but he rested on the couch, content to watch television and his brothers. Gwen sat with Sean's head in her lap during *Sesame Street* and replayed the night before in her mind.

She knew Sean's fever had worried Brian, and she knew she had messed up by not turning on her phone after class. But he was acting childish not talking to her. She pushed aside self-righteous feelings and tried to call him, but his phone must have been turned off.

Just to show me how it feels, I suppose. As if she didn't already know how it felt to be home alone with the boys when one of them was sick. Obviously he didn't like being in the position she'd been stuck in for the last five years.

She stroked Sean's hair.

She reminded herself it was good for Brian to be responsible for the boys while she was in class. About time he figured out how to take care of their needs. She didn't abandon him to hunt or play ball. She was at class—her work now—as important as his job. *I won't feel guilty for a half hour of conversation with friends.*

Her stomach spasmed again at the thought of his silent treatment. Like she wasn't worth the waste of words, or like she needed to make up for whatever he thought she did wrong. What about what he had done? He knew how much he hurt her when he treated her like that.

Two can play this game.

⌘ ⌘ ⌘

When Brian came home whistling, Gwen stayed at the stove finishing dinner preparations. She knew Brian hated macaroni and cheese, but she ignored her conscience. He peeked into the pot and then went to check the refrigerator. Gwen turned her back to him.

"Had a good day today." His voice was muffled by the refrigerator. "Covered old green walls with white paint. Always makes me feel like I've improved the world when I do that."

She could hear him close the refrigerator and approach her for his kiss. She didn't turn, so he tried to put his arms around her from behind. She walked over to the refrigerator without looking at him and brought out juice and the apples she had cut earlier.

Brian crossed his arms and stood between her and the table. "What are you upset about?"

"Oh, so you can talk to me now that you're hungry," Gwen replied.

Contempt! She pushed the little voice in her mind aside.

"What's the matter with you? Yeah, I was mad last night, but I was over that until you froze me out just now!"

"Like you froze me out in bed last night? Like you froze me out this morning, leaving before we could talk?"

Defensive, the voice accused.

"You're the one who didn't communicate last night. I didn't know what to do." His voice balanced on the edge between whining and anger.

"Why didn't you get on the computer and ask Shirley, then?"

Gwen pushed the juice and apples into Brian's hands and ran upstairs, her feet pounding *stupid, stupid, stupid.* She slammed the bedroom door but not loud enough to drown out her conscience's accusation: *Stonewalling!*

Brian called after her, "Oh no, you're not leaving me to feed and put the boys to bed again tonight. I'm going out to get a hamburger!"

Four-year-old Joe Pat sang, "McDonald's, McDonald's! I want hamburgers with Daddy at McDonald's."

"Tell your mom that!" Brian yelled and banged out the door.

Gwen wiped her eyes and pressed her hand against what was now a relentless ache above her waistline. What she needed was a good long run. But she knew her three active boys couldn't be left alone, so she forced herself back to them. With worried eyes and sober faces, they watched her come down the stairs.

"Sorry, boys, we didn't handle that well. C'mon, let's have some macaroni and cheese."

They didn't move.

Gwen forced a shaky smile and tried again. "How about if we put the tablecloth down on the floor in front of the TV, and we'll have a TV dinner picnic?"

Mickey broke the tension. "I get to pick the channel."

An hour later, the doorbell rang. Gwen found Brian on the porch with a bouquet of flowers and the newest Disney DVD in his hands. Relief and guilt battled within her.

"Hi, babe," he said, looking as hangdog as her dad's ancient basset hound. "I'm sorry. Want to try starting this evening over again?"

"Thank you. This time I'll leave my four horsemen out of it."

They started the movie, and Gwen noticed five-year-old Mickey's scowl soften as he became absorbed by the movie. They moved to the kitchen where they could have a little privacy but still keep an ear out for the boys.

By the time the Disney kiss ended the movie, Gwen had written the advice nurse number by the phone and placed a sticky note that said, "Phone on" in her backpack where she'd see it when she put her books away after class. Brian agreed not to give Gwen the silent treatment anymore. He'd tell her first when they could finish a discussion if he had to leave to cool off. Neither turned away when they slid into bed that night, but Mickey's scowl haunted Gwen long after Brian fell asleep.

⌘ ⌘ ⌘

Marjorie's trip to seek Aunt Annie's wisdom required a flight to Montana, followed by a snowy, thirty-mile drive from the airport in Butte to her hometown, Anaconda. As Marjorie drove the rental car through the little town and approached her aunt's home, she passed century-old brick storefronts where she had shopped as a child. She turned onto Main Street to see the Kennedy Commons, a square block where she had skated for hours when its inner circle was flooded to freeze into an ice skating rink, lighted by a giant Christmas tree in the center. In the summer it would boast a grassy park, but now the town's heart lay covered with the new snow.

She drove a few more blocks and then parked on Elm Street. She walked to the door of a little stucco house, wishing she'd thought to bring boots. Knowing it was too much to hope Aunt Annie could calm all her concerns, but wishing she would, she rang the doorbell. While she waited, she stomped her feet to warm them and recalled her childhood embarrassment upon learning of her misnomer for her aunt.

The neighbors next door to her little home on Fourth Street had a daughter a year younger than Marjorie named Ann Marie. She assumed her favorite aunt also had two names and was christened Ann Tanny. It wasn't until she heard her mother speaking directly to her one day that she realized why she called her Annie. She thought back to it with a smile as she rang the doorbell again.

No one answered the door, but Marjorie noticed a scraping sound from the backyard. She followed the narrow walkway to the back of the house. Aunt Annie, at age eighty-five, was hefting quick shovelfuls of the snow that covered the walkway from her backdoor to the garage.

"Aunt Annie!" Marjorie called in disbelief.

The bundled figure stopped midscoop, then plunged the shovel so it stood upright in the pile of snow she had pushed to the side. "Marjorie! How's my favorite niece?" she asked as she approached her with outstretched arms. "I'm so glad to see you."

"Isn't there someone else who can shovel for you?" Marjorie objected as she returned the hug.

"Whatever for?" asked the older woman. "Keeps me fit as a fiddle." She paused with a smile. "Though I'm more like a wheezy bagpipe nowadays." She grabbed Marjorie by the arm and pulled her toward the backdoor. "C'mon in, dear, and I'll put on a kettle. You can tell me all about your girls."

With one more glance back at the offending shovel, Marjorie allowed herself to be drawn indoors to the welcoming warmth of the kitchen. The room itself reassured Marjorie that some lives didn't change drastically. On the shelves above the stove, Franciscan Appleware still sat next to the apple-shaped cookie jar, which had always yielded a treat for each hand when she visited as a child. The tea kettle waited in place on the back burner. The kitchen table wore the familiar red-and-white-checked tablecloth, though the white wasn't as bright as it once had been. The painted cupboards also showed the yellowing of time.

Marjorie sat at the table, eased her coat off, and draped it behind her on the chair. Aunt Annie hung hers on the hook on the back of the swinging door that led to the living room, then bustled about getting tea and homemade cookies set out. Aunt Annie had always been like that. No matter what she was doing, when a visitor came, all work stopped and all attention focused on the guest. Even as a child, whenever she came to this house Marjorie had felt as important as a queen.

They chatted briefly, updating Aunt Annie on Sophie and Colleen. Marjorie asked about her health, but knew the reply would be predictable, "Can't complain when God's so good to me." Even so, the refrain didn't make Marjorie reluctant to confide in her aunt about her concerns. Rather, Aunt Annie always made her feel that, no matter what the problem, God was in control and all would be well.

Her aunt was looking at her closely and with a gentle voice observed, "Margie, dear, you're still grieving. Pain simmers right behind your eyes."

Tears welled briefly, but Marjorie blinked them back. Strange how quickly a little empathy always moved her.

"What's holding it there, Margie?"

Marjorie felt a jolt of anger at the obvious answer, then let it subside and sighed. "I guess it's still there because Michael's still gone."

Aunt Annie regarded Marjorie steadily, set down her cup, and laid her hand over Marjorie's, saying simply, "God is good."

When Marjorie didn't answer, the older woman cleared the path to the point of the visit. "What's on your heart today, Margie?"

Marjorie considered the question. Where to begin? She missed her girls and was afraid they'd drift away. Sophie's boyfriend, Niko, worried her. Marjorie's own confounded restlessness was back, tormenting her with memories of her irritability before Michael died. And Michael. Her ache to have him beside her persisted but did no good. She still was alone every night when she came home from work. What would Aunt

Annie think if she knew how angry Marjorie felt with the Almighty sometimes? Could she talk about Colm's letters and her stubborn attraction for this man she'd only seen once?

And the guilt that attraction rekindled?

The tumble of concerns jostled in her mind. How could she express them all? Finally she met Aunt Annie's eyes and asked, "How do I learn to let go?"

True to Aunt Annie's conviction that if spiritual troubles were set right, everything else would follow, she probed, "Where's God in your worries, Margie?"

A warm flush crawled up from chest to cheeks. Marjorie stalled for time to gather her thoughts, asking, "What do you mean?"

"Are you hanging on to Him with both hands? If so, your hands would be full and you couldn't hold too tight to anything else."

If my hands are doing anything with God, they're trying to shield me and my loved ones from Him. The thought startled Marjorie, and her childhood fear that her aunt could read her mind returned.

When Marjorie didn't answer, Aunt Annie changed tactics. "When you pray, Margie, what do you call God?"

"Almighty Father."

"And how do you picture God?"

Marjorie gazed out the window to the blue sky and high clouds. "On a throne, with a long beard." She wished she didn't have to admit this childish representation.

"How do His eyes look?" her aunt asked gently.

"I don't want to look at them."

"Look at God's face, Margie, and tell me what you see."

Marjorie closed her eyes and felt her heart beat faster. She looked up from below the throne. God the Judge was staring at her, His eyebrows lowered, and His lips pressed flat. Marjorie opened her eyes and gasped, relief sweeping over her to still be in the kitchen.

Aunt Annie took a deep breath and patted her hand. "Margie, dear, why are you frightened? Tell me about it."

Words and emotion poured out of Marjorie. She confessed her fears to her wise aunt, fears she hadn't admitted to anyone. She told of her dissatisfaction with life and her longing for change before Michael died. How she was sure the Almighty Father saw her lack of gratitude and took Michael away because of it. And how angry she was with God. Though she could pray to Him, she couldn't trust Him, or herself, anymore.

"What are you afraid He'll do?"

Marjorie could barely utter the words. "Take my girls. Leave me all alone." Even to her own ears, she sounded like a small, frightened child.

Aunt Annie stood and poured more water from the steaming kettle into the teapot. They sat in silence as the tea steeped, then she refilled their cups before she spoke.

"Margie, dear, God isn't a four-star general, sending His military police to keep you in line. You call him Father, and that might be fine for someone who had a gentle, affectionate daddy. Yours, unfortunately, was military through and through. Expected everybody to be disciplined and obedient at all costs. You and your brother, God rest his soul, jumped whenever he gave an order. You both toed the line."

She shook her head sadly. "But I remember you before his heavy-handedness weighed you down. He was gone for a year overseas when you were little, didn't return until after you turned four. Do you remember that time?"

Marjorie shook her head.

"Such a little package of pure joy. You'd dance like your mama used to when she was single." Aunt Annie was silent a minute, then added. "God rest her soul."

"I can still see you twirling around and around out on the grass, chasing butterflies, and singing. Couldn't carry a tune, then, but you didn't care. The happiness trilled out of you in little made-up songs. But you grew more and more serious as you got older. Then the last of your lightheartedness went dark when your daddy left." Her voice trailed off. She seemed to catch herself and added, "I wonder if his soul found rest?"

"So what do I do now?"

"Get to know the Papa God that Jesus came to teach us about. Imagine God in a new way, as a brother or friend or companion who wants to encourage you and help you anyway possible. The mama hen who shields her chick with her wings."

"Michael called God his friend when he prayed aloud." Marjorie's voice broke.

"There you go. Would the ultimate Best Friend hold it against you that you got tired of keeping that dancing little girl inside? That maybe she had to burst out? You weren't wishing for a different husband. You were wishing for a different you."

Marjorie looked at her aunt. Her heart felt strained, pulled between wanting to believe her and holding on to her guilt. Father... Friend? She tried out the appellation to test the sound. She imagined a father and thought of authority and judgment. Aunt Annie was right, her own had been a taskmaster. She imagined a friend. Someone to journey with her, alongside her. Someone to help her lift her burdens and share her joy.

"Margie, dear, God doesn't sit on a throne looking down watching for you to make a mistake. He's that prodigal son's father who is anxiously waiting for His child to come to Him so He can give her all the gifts and love He wants to pour out on her. Even if we were foolish enough to ask for a scorpion, He gives us bread instead."

"He didn't stop Michael from dying." Marjorie felt betrayed by all the songs and stories of God keeping His loved ones safe.

The older woman exhaled softly. Her face told of a great sadness that had been accepted, reminding Marjorie that Aunt Annie, too, had lost a husband. "He didn't keep his own Son from dying, but that doesn't mean He didn't love Him. Or Michael. Or you. Doesn't mean He didn't weep with you. But He knows death isn't the end of life."

The two women looked into each other's eyes for a long time. Marjorie felt love and understanding from her aunt. Slowly she began to realize Aunt Annie was sharing what God offered to them both. Marjorie bowed her head. "Dear Friend," she prayed, "teach me about Your gentle side. Forgive me for my mistakes. Show me whatever You want me to do." She paused and then added, "And give me the courage to do it."

Seventeen

Opposites attract
so that we learn balance.

W hen Marjorie hugged her aunt good-bye at the end of the weekend, she felt like a hero ready to set out on a quest. She would banish her guilt from the past and focus on doing her best with the present. Though it would go against her nature, she would try to stop worrying about the future and learn to trust her new Friend to be there with her. She didn't have new answers to where her road led, but she would be traveling with the best of companions.

The next Thursday evening, Marjorie wandered among the discussion groups happy that, at least in this area of her life, she was competent. She could offer her students theories and experience to help improve relationships and give them a few tools to help their clients. Like Tessa, for instance. After reading in her journal about Tessa's reluctance to divulge their libido problem, Marjorie had recommended she consider David Schnarch's *Passionate Marriage* for her small group discussion.

Tessa began to tell Hank and Gwen about the book. "Schnarch's point that I'm going to focus on is that somehow we enter into intimate relationships with the exact type of person we need to help us grow, often a polar opposite in some area. He says marriage's crucible can take our opposing personalities and refine us into healthier, better balanced people while strengthening and enriching our relationship."

"Crucible?" Gwen interrupted.

Tessa nodded and Marjorie did, too, as she listened. "Schnarch's word. A crucible is the container that metals are melted in. So he's saying marriage is the container that, through the heat of our day-today relating, refines us into something priceless."

Gwen pulled in her cheek between her teeth, but Tessa continued. "Unfortunately, much of the time, we avoid the growing pains that lead to our full potential. Instead of stretching to learn from each other's strengths, we minimize the part of us that is like the other, letting our spouses take responsibility in their areas of strength."

"You lost me," Gwen said. "How about an example?"

Tessa paused, and then brightened. "Rather than the stereotypical passionate woman nurturing her logical side, she delegates all logic to her husband. In turn, the logical man, rather than learn from her to appreciate his own emotions, encourages his wife to be the heart of their marriage. The agreement is subtle, and usually unconscious. But both spouses become more extreme and, ironically, more irritated with the other for not being more like them."

Marjorie was caught off guard by the example. Tessa had portrayed the very problem in Marjorie's parents' relationship. Shaken, she consciously relaxed the muscles that had tensed in her face and checked to see how the small group responded.

Hank was leaning forward, obviously intrigued, but Gwen sat back and crossed her arms. Marjorie considered the reaction. The concept Tessa was covering would provide a good topic for the whole group to discuss, and frankly, Marjorie had a feeling they could all benefit from its consideration. Her parents certainly could have.

She broke in, saying "Excuse me, Tessa. Would you consider summarizing Schnarch's theory for the whole class? I'd like to get deeper into this."

Tessa agreed, though with a worried look, so Marjorie dismissed the class for a short break before proceeding.

As Marjorie reorganized her stack of lecture materials during the break, she thought about opposites attracting. *How were Michael and I so different?* She laughed as her pile of notes slid off the desk. *He was certainly more organized than I am.*

An envelope that she had found in her office mail slot peeked out from under the notes. Feeling both anticipation and anxiety, she opened it.

Dear Marjorie,

I was delighted to hear from you. Thank you for writing.

Like you, I'm a professor, from University College Dublin. I've taught Irish literature there for twenty years now. About a year ago, a cousin who lives here and teaches American literature at Portland State University proposed we trade positions for a year. Both schools readily agreed and our respective departments initiated arrangements, assuming I shared my cousin's enthusiasm. I had become quite set in my ways and only reluctantly consented. Before I knew it, all was in motion for me to live for a year in his home here, and he and his wife in mine....

Marjorie felt a ripple of excitement reading the words. Touched by his old-fashioned formality, she held the letter against her heart for a moment. But then the old sharp stab of guilt struck. She felt she was abandoning Michael, the way she had been abandoned by her parents after their breakup. Angry at herself for being so foolish as to encourage Colm, she stuffed the letter into a pocket. She wasn't ready. She probably never would be. No matter how lonely she felt.

She pictured Aunt Annie with her hands on her hips and decided to rethink the matter after class.

After the break, Marjorie listened with only half her attention while Tessa reviewed what she had learned from Schnarch's book. When Tessa had finished briefing the class, Marjorie stood and refocused her thoughts. "Well done, Tessa. Schnarch writes about a very real phenomenon, but a hard one to grasp. We can learn so much from the ways our spouses differ from us."

If only I'd appreciated those differences instead of wanting change and excitement. Why couldn't I be satisfied with what I had? Michael had been her steady rock. Always before she had appreciated that—needed that—but then the restlessness.

"Unfortunately, we often spend more energy thinking they should be the same as us, rather than learning what their differences can teach us. I'll be looking forward to reading your journal, Tessa, to see how you apply what you're learning."

The class laughed at Tessa's expression, and Marjorie opened the subject for discussion. "So, what do you think?"

"Sounds interesting," gray-templed Anna said. "So he's saying that people choose each other and enter relationships, on one level, so that the other person can fill in their gaps and use their strengths to counteract each other's weaknesses. Yet, on another level, they're finding the perfect person to teach them to grow in the areas where they're weak."

"Exactly."

"It's hard to imagine my ex ever having been what I needed."

Marjorie waited for the class to respond.

Newlywed Jessica ventured, "I can't imagine my parents helping to balance each other, but maybe somewhere along the line they didn't grow. Dad was always the fun one, and Mom took life seriously. Maybe they ended up resenting one another because they'd both become too extreme. They didn't work to achieve their own inner balance but counted on the other for balance, instead."

Gwen quipped, "So I should learn to watch more TV and drink beer like my husband?"

The class laughed, but Gwen looked thoughtful. "What if a wife focuses totally on nurturing her kids so that her husband can focus on his job? She starts to resent him for not helping more with the kids, and he might resent her for not helping out financially."

"Right," Marjorie replied. "He won't grow in his ability to show affection, and she won't learn the self-confidence or independence that working outside the home can bring."

At the look some of the older women gave her, Marjorie hurried to add, "That's not to say that a mom has to have a paid career. She can grow through other means, like volunteering. But going to extremes causes problems. When she thinks that the only thing worthwhile is mothering, or believes she isn't capable of assuming other types of responsibility. Or if her husband thinks that he can't parent well, or that spending time with his children isn't important." ·

Hank cleared his throat. Marjorie looked at him and thought he seemed to pull his attention back from a dark place as he added, "Or when an independent mom gets so independent, she leaves, and a responsible dad gets so responsible, he can only work, not relate."

The class was silent, and Marjorie found herself at a loss for words.

She wished she could simply place her hand on Hank's shoulder but sensed the gesture would embarrass him. The pain in his comment was contagious, and Marjorie was suddenly a teenager again, watching her father carry his suitcases out the door. He had left without a good-bye.

As Marjorie felt tears rise, she walked to the dry-erase board to give herself time to blink them away. She lifted a marker. That was the day, she realized, that she decided to never be like her mother. She'd never let her free spirit drive a man away. But had she? Was the repressed energy of her maverick heritage what caused her restlessness and called on the heavens for change?

She couldn't think of a single thing to write on the board, so she set the marker back down. Her face flushed warm, which led her to walk to the window and open it. Aware of the uncomfortable silence in the room, she squared her shoulders and turned back to her students.

"But relationships don't have to end when the couple polarizes. At that point, tremendous growth is possible if both people realize their relationship is worth the work. What pushes the growth is when one of the two realizes he or she can't go on without the integrity of holding on to who that person really is deep down. Schnarch calls it 'differentiating'…"

Marjorie continued the lesson, finally concluding with Schnarch's self-validation, his term for refusing to adopt other's negative emotions, but relying on self-approval for personal happiness instead.

When everyone had gone, Marjorie shook her head as she turned out the lights. She certainly hadn't practiced what she preached. Not only had she caught Hank's emotion but nearly let it disrupt her class, the one area she had felt in control. In spite of the uplifting message of the tremendous growth a relationship can achieve, her heart lay heavy as she remembered premature partings. Her father's. Her brother's. Her husband's.

Could she really call God a friend, when He let such things happen? And could she endure any more loss? She pulled Colm's letter out of her pocket and considered it. He was here to teach for a year. Then what? She dropped it into the wastebasket on her way out.

Halfway to the car, she turned and argued with herself all the way back to the classroom.

Eighteen

Sometimes we need a little help from...
those trained to give it.

After Amy and Stephen had left for school Friday morning, Tessa and Joe drove together to Doctor Zernick's office. Tessa prayed silently on the way that this visit would bring them answers to help overcome Joe's loss of libido. She was ready to accept any explanation that would lead to improvement. Still, she had to admit that she hoped his lack of interest wasn't because of her, that it would turn out to be a physical problem.

She felt buoyed by Joe's report of progress to the doctor.

"Since I started the sleep meds, my energy level is great. I start my day feeling more rested than I have in a long time."

Doctor Zernick listened to Joe and then checked his paperwork. "Your tests came back looking good, Joe. No high blood pressure, no diabetes, and although your testosterone is a bit low, it's within normal range. Those would all be problems that could be responsible for low libido but don't explain your trouble. Let's go back to the sleep issue. You say it's improved?"

Tessa's reaction to the doctor's words vacillated between relief at the test results and disappointment not to have a physical reason to blame. She pulled her attention back to Joe as he answered the doctor's question.

"Definitely. I'm getting to sleep faster, and not waking as often in the night."

"So is our work done? Has your libido gotten back to acceptable levels?

Joe looked at Tessa before he answered, so she tried to smile away her disappointment and project encouragement.

He turned back to the doctor. "Maybe better, but nowhere near what it used to be. I'm interested enough if Tessa is persistent, but sleep always sounds better. And with the pills, I fall asleep too quickly. Once my head hits the pillow, I'm not much good for conversation or even a little cuddling."

Tessa thought of her lonely nights listening to him snore before she gave in to sleep herself.

"But there's improvement?"

He nodded. "In the morning I don't feel like I'm dragging myself out of bed. Used to be the hardest thing I did all day. Now I feel more rested."

"I mean with your sexual interest."

Tessa shifted uneasily in her chair. She hadn't noticed any improvement, so she wondered how Joe would answer the doctor.

"Well, it's at least alive again," Joe said. "When I come home and kiss Tessa, I feel aroused a bit, and I don't think that's been the case for a while now."

As hard as she knew this was for him to admit, it hurt to hear him say so. Still, she appreciated the look of reassurance Joe gave her before he continued.

"When we make love, I convince myself to do it for Tessa's sake. Since the medicine, though, once we do get started, I enjoy it for my own sake, too. When it goes well."

"And does it go well most of the time?"

Joe sighed. "Maybe half."

Doctor Zernick shifted his attention to Tessa. "This must be really hard for you." Tessa drew a deep breath and nodded, his sympathy bringing her closer to tears.

He sat on his stool, adjusting the knees of his slacks as he did so. He looked from one to the other. "I'm impressed with both of you. Tessa, it's wonderful that you're here supporting Joe. No doubt you've been feeling rejected, but obviously you two love each other. From what I've read, many couples grow apart rather than deal with a sexual problem. It's such a private, sensitive area that we don't talk openly about it even with the people it affects the most. You two deserve a solution, and I'm going to do everything I can to help you find it."

Tessa smiled her appreciation, and he stood to focus again on Joe. "How about enjoyment? Are you getting pleasure out of your work or your activities?"

"No."

Joe paused before he continued. Tessa felt like she was drawn into the depths of exhaustion as she looked into his eyes.

"Each day is a series of commitments—work, the kids' sports, Scouts, jobs around the house, car maintenance. I go through the motions because that's what the family needs, but I'd like to skip getting out of bed and let it all go. It's like I'm playing in a marching band but can't hear the music."

Tessa stopped a moan before it escaped. The tears that had threatened earlier rose again. One drop slipped out and ran down her cheek. She let it fall, rather than call attention to it by brushing it away.

When Joe added, in a low voice, "I want to hear life's music again," she didn't think she could bear it.

Doctor Zernick put his hand on Joe's shoulder and broke the silence. "I'd like to try you on an antidepressant, Joe. It sounds to me like your sleep problem has gone on long enough that it's worn you out and caused you to be a bit depressed. I don't think you'll need to be on the medication long, since we're working to improve your sleep, but I would like you to try it. Might take a few weeks to get up to full effect, but I think we need to get your music back."

Tessa held her breath. She knew Joe well enough to understand the struggle that played out on his face. He always resisted taking medication, saying that needing an aspirin made him feel like a weakling. But now, take on a label of depression? She was sure he'd think of that as a mental problem. A thousand times worse than admitting he had a headache. Her heart and her hope sank. If that's what getting his libido back would take, he'd never consider it.

Tessa looked at her hands and caressed the wedding ring there. She'd have to be strong and allow that some things were too much to ask. She gave Joe an accepting smile.

"We'll try it," he said.

Her lips parted, and her eyebrows shot up. Had she heard him right?

"Whatever it takes," he said to the doctor but held her eyes with his. Tessa had always trusted Joe's love, but now she was amazed at the depths of it. She had never felt more cherished. She could feel warmth spread up from her heart and imagined it pouring out from her eyes and her smile. The glow felt so alive she had no doubt Joe could feel it from across the room.

He took half a pill the first three nights, following Dr. Zernick's orders. On the fourth night he increased the dose to a full tablet. Tessa worried when he said he didn't notice any difference in his mood and kept quiet when he grumbled about doubting the medication would be worth the trouble. She hung on to her hope for their future.

⌘ ⌘ ⌘

Hank peered into Marjorie's office and saw the professor gazing out the window. She jumped when he tapped lightly on her door, then smiled at him like a guilty child.

"Hank! Come in and sit down. The beautiful colors keep claiming my attention away from my work." Marjorie swiveled her chair away from her desk to face him.

Hank glanced through the window as he approached the chair she indicated. Fall leaves had begun drifting down to cover the grass under a clear sky. Occasional breezes stirred them into small piles, but didn't lift his spirits. "Thanks, Dr. Gloriam." Hank settled himself in the chair.

"Students rarely come see me on such lovely days, so I'm delighted. What can I do for you?"

"I'm hoping you can help me work through something. Yesterday afternoon I was at the Youth Club like usual, hanging out with the kids. I'm there as a health resource, but a lot of time they just need someone to spend time with them."

Her nod encouraged him to continue.

"I was playing basketball with some of the high school guys when a kid came in and slouched on the bleachers. He looked pretty down so when we took a break, a couple of guys went over to talk to him. They asked him what was up, what's new, how things were going, but only got grunts out of him. Now that's pretty normal. Kids'll talk when they're ready. What's important is being there and being open."

Hank paused, feeling out of place. He looked around the office but was seeing yesterday's gym. "What wasn't normal was my reaction. His sitting there, blowing off their efforts to talk with him made me furious. I pictured myself shaking him until his mouth opened and words poured out. The thought made *me* shake. It really scared me that I could get so mad when he wasn't acting any different than most kids at the Club. I was so upset I had to leave."

Hank looked at Marjorie, but didn't see any judgment in her face, so continued. "What's going on? Lately I can get so riled up. I finally find family—my grandma's great. I should be happier. I'm usually pretty easygoing. This doesn't make sense."

Marjorie seemed to pause to consider what to say and then looked as if she had decided. "Hank, you're reading Terrence Real's *I Don't Want to Talk About It* for this class, aren't you? Tell me what the author says."

Hank hadn't expected a pop quiz like this, so it took him a moment to shift mental gears. He leaned back in his chair. His voice took on the professional tone he used as a physician assistant.

"Well, he talks about men being covertly depressed. They don't usually express depression the way women do. Sometimes they show the same sadness, lethargy, hopelessness, shame, eating and sleeping disturbances, but more often their depression is hidden, since men become so good at hiding their feelings or hiding from them."

He wondered what this had to do with his dilemma but continued dutifully. "Rather than experience the shame they've buried from whatever trauma or neglect brought them to this point, they often put up defenses. The defenses can become real addictions since they make the men feel better and keep the pain at bay, at least temporarily."

"What are some of the different defenses men use?" Marjorie prodded.

Hank's mind raced to understand where she was going with this. "The typical escapes, like alcohol or drug abuse, anything that keeps the pain at bay. Like becoming a sex addict or a gambling addict. Some men immerse themselves in a relationship or in their work. Anything that gives them a feeling of importance. They've grown up without a strong sense of self-esteem, so they borrow it or bolster it with other people's attention. They need someone else's approval since deep down they don't have any realization of their own value." He hoped he'd get to whatever point she wanted to make soon before he recited the whole book.

"The author says that often they overcompensate for feeling worse than everyone else and find a way to convince themselves that they are better than everyone else. Some boost their lack of self-esteem by controlling others. They need to feel bigger and better, so they need power over others. Since they convince themselves that other people aren't as good as they are, they have no issue with hurting people. Some even take this to extremes, like wife and child beaters."

Hank continued his summary in the same factual way he educated patients, all the while watching Marjorie nod or smile encouragingly. He had to admit, it was starting to irritate him. How did any of this pertain to him? He was about to say so, but the way Marjorie looked at him made him realize she had something up her sleeve and if he talked long enough, it would all make sense. He sighed, wondering what on earth he could possibly be missing.

"Some deny their sense of shame by tapping into 'a greater good.' Religion or love. Not that those are bad, but when something happens to their faith or their relationship, they're devastated. They convince themselves they've become better than others through their faith or their love. But the threat of losing that can turn them into fanatics or stalkers.

"Whatever way men try to feel better—unless they realize their equal worth with everyone—any threat to their illusion can make them lose control. If they get sober, or their drug supply dries up, if their lover leaves them, or they become disillusioned with their minister, in short, if their defense fails them, they're likely to explode. Rage might overtake them, and they're apt to hurt someone."

Was this what she was getting at? Something to do with rage overtaking him? He waited, but she still didn't speak, so he continued. "Or they might implode, and their deep shame might make them turn on themselves. If they do that, there is a real danger of suicide."

A picture flashed into Hank's mind of his father, dead in the bathtub with the radio. Sucker-punched by the image, he gripped the arms of the chair, his senses reeling. Hank barely heard Marjorie's next question.

"Hank, are you wondering where your recent anger is leading you?"

Hank's mind snagged, eight years back. It took awhile for Marjorie's words to reach him and, when they did, he sat confused. He couldn't quite pull himself to the present.

"I'm sorry, Dr. Gloriam. I drifted there." Hank stood up too suddenly, and his vision blackened. "Talking with you has given me lots to think about. Thank you."

Marjorie reached out to stop him. "Hank, you've been through so much, meeting your grandmother and learning about your childhood. I think it would be a good idea for you to talk to a professional counselor about this. Let me give you phone numbers for a couple of therapists I can recommend."

Hank took a deep breath to steady himself, and his vision cleared. "I'll consider that. Thank you again, Dr. Gloriam." Hank accepted the paper she handed him with the numbers and stuffed it into his pocket, his mind preoccupied with leaving her office. He needed time alone.

"Hank, are you all right?"

Hank nodded quickly, then paused, aware of Marjorie's concern, and smiled his reassurance. "I will be. I need to think through some things." He turned and hurried away.

Once out of Marjorie's office, Hank took long strides to cross campus. He needed to walk off his confusion and flood of emotions. A nature park bordered the campus so he headed toward it, hoping for the calm of the woods to envelope him.

Instead, his thoughts ensnared him. Did his dad use some defense to keep from feeling depressed? He had a clear story of him in his mind: a young widower doing his best to raise his son. But now he needed to edit the story. Dad wasn't a widower. He was an abandoned husband.

The woman he loved left him and never returned. Yeah, plenty of reason to be mad at the world.

Even when he was little, he knew it would make his dad mad if he tried to talk about his mom. Now he finally realized why.

He was traumatized. And rather than feel the pain, did he use a defense? An addiction?

His dad didn't drink too much. No drugs. Not even any sex that Hank knew of. All he ever did was work. Workaholic? Hank supposed he could call him that. If not at work, he was in the basement fixing things. Building up the savings account for his son. He was so proud of that. The happiest Hank had ever seen him was when he'd given him the passbook.

He kept the pain away by working for me and my future!

Then Hank had rejected the money. Told him he'd enlisted. Which was worse, that he was leaving or that he didn't appreciate the money? Both were blows, he supposed. So, from what Real's book said, he took away his father's defenses and left him with no way to ward off the pain. Then he died that night. An accident?

Did he kill himself? Because of me?

Hank felt suddenly dizzy and leaned against a tree. For a minute his mind went numb. Then he gasped for air, realizing he had held his breath since his last thought. His back against the tree, he slid down to sit on the ground. His heart began to jump hurdles. His breath came in short bursts. As sweat chilled his whole body, Hank became aware of a tremendous need to escape. He tried to stand, but his legs were shaking and wouldn't hold his weight.

He sank back down against the tree and worked on calming himself. Hank took deep breaths and forced himself to let them out slowly. He unclenched his jaw and tried to relax his muscles.

No one is dying. It's over. Not fair, but over.

His mom shouldn't have left them, but her drinking problem or her need for independence or something had gotten the best of her. His dad should have talked to him. He should have been a normal dad, but he was dealing with his own loss and could have been a lot worse.

At least he had offered stability, and Hank could look back now and see his father loved him in his own way. Not the way Hank would have chosen, but the only way he could, he supposed. He sighed, staring out at the stand of trees.

What now? He'd spent the last eight years of his life completely alone. Eight years? He'd been alone ever since his dad took him away from his grandma. He was sick of being alone. He wanted to share his life with someone.

Did he have a life worth sharing? He had a good job, and did some good at the Youth Club. He was learning new things in the counseling classes.

Counseling.

Dr. Gloriam had said he needed counseling. To talk this over with someone. What did he know of talking about himself? He was good at listening to the kids. The few dates he'd had said he was a great listener. But talk about himself? Could he do that? He shuddered at the thought.

He had talked in class with Tessa and Gwen. However, trying it with Dr. Gloriam had ended with him practically running out of her office. There was his grandma. They had talked for a whole weekend—mostly about him and his life. Grandma was good at asking questions.

Maybe I could go for therapy.

Kind of hypocritical of him to be studying to be a counselor, yet not want to be counseled. Where had he put those phone numbers Dr. Gloriam gave him?

Hank pushed his hand into his pocket and grasped the note where she had written the numbers. He leaned his head back against the tree and closed his eyes. Dappled sun filtered through the leaves to his face. The solid trunk warmed his back. He smelled the rich, moist earth. The peacefulness of the woods began to work its reliable soothing effect upon him.

He thought about his grandma and felt an urge to see her again. She had called him several times since his trip to Spokane. He hoped she'd call soon. Would he tell her about how lonely his childhood was? Or how his dad died? He hadn't talked about that with anyone. Maybe he should.

If not to a counselor, maybe to Grandma, he thought as he stood to walk back to his Jeep. But when the time came, could he?

Nineteen

Turn back to each other,
even when it's hardest.

Tessa brought a cup of hot cocoa to the garage and heard Joe whistling while he changed her car's oil. She smiled. "Sounds like someone has some music back in his life."

His grin reminded her of Stephen's when caught in the middle of mischief.

When Joe came in for dinner later, Tessa met him with a longer-than-usual hug. "Love you," he responded. "Gotta go wash up," he added, his mind obviously still focused on the car. He walked through the kitchen and disappeared down the hall, while Tessa watched him, her hands on her hips.

"Love you, gotta go wash up." He didn't even notice that she'd wanted to linger with that hug, wanted to kiss him—stir him up. *Men! Spend a little time with a car, and that's all they can think about.*

Tired of feeling rejected, and embarrassed at how easily her hopes had lifted when she heard him whistle, Tessa's frustration surfaced. Here she was thinking maybe things were going to start being better. He seemed happier, but not the least bit more interested in her. She had hoped it was the fault of the depression. Then they could fix that and go back to normal. A few years ago, they used to make love three or four times a week. Now maybe once a week, if she pushed for it. She was so tired of pushing.

Is this the way I'm going to be from now on? Never satisfied?

Tessa walked to the refrigerator but couldn't remember what she needed. She rested her head against the cool door. *What's with me?*

Here she was griping about sex, and she had a wonderful husband.

124

She knew he was good and considerate about everything else, that she was making too big a deal out of this. If they ended up never making love, she should still be grateful for what she had. He loved her. She loved him. He was a wonderful dad, a good provider. For that matter, a terrific person.

Then, there's me. Only able to think about wanting him to want me. Lord, help me get through this. It's so hard.

Tessa looked up at the ceiling and gave herself a few minutes to let her eyes clear. She called the family to dinner and forced a smile. As they held hands for the blessing, she knew she had been petty and decided to do better. *Lord, help me to be grateful, to not always want more. Thank You for my good husband and kids.*

When they finished praying, she squeezed Joe's hand on her right and Stephen's hand on her left. Tessa couldn't help but add to her silent prayer, *But if it's Your will, please fix whatever's wrong.*

She smiled across the table at Amy, whose look showed concern that Tessa wanted to allay. "Amy, how was school today?"

When dinner was over, Joe drove Amy and Stephen to church for the junior high youth group. When he had returned and come into the kitchen, he paused to give Tessa her honey-I'm-home kiss. She had just finished dishes and turned into his arms, responding with a kids-are-gone-and-we're-home-alone kiss. This time Joe got the message.

"Guess I'm not going to get the bills done tonight." She heard the laugh in his voice as she led him to the bedroom, but was there an undercurrent of regret?

As Tessa unbuttoned his shirt, she caught him glance toward his office and could imagine him thinking, *The electricity bill is due in a few days. I'd better at least get that one done tonight.* She willed his mind back to her and hoped maybe it worked, because he slid his hands under her blouse, up along her back, and unhooked her bra. He sighed and she relaxed. Tessa tilted her head up and closed her eyes as Joe's lips touched hers.

"I love you," he murmured.

She looked up, hoping to connect through their eyes, but he was again glancing toward the office. *Why can't he keep his mind on what's happening here?* She decided to increase her efforts. When she pressed against his chest, he pulled away.

"Tessa, stop, it's not working!"

Tessa jerked back and looked down. Her tear ducts always seemed ready to overflow lately.

Gentleness replaced the frustration in Joe's voice. "I'm sorry, honey."

"Never mind. I shouldn't have tried so hard." She turned away and fumbled with bra hooks and blouse buttons as she started to move toward the door.

"Tessa, please. Stop. Don't go!" The emotion in his voice could have been anger or fear. Tessa stopped before she got to the door and hesitated with her back to him. She remembered Marjorie saying anger often comes from fear. Well, she was angry and afraid, too. She wanted to run, to get out of the room and away from him.

Like weeks ago, a tune played in her mind. *"Come back to me, with all your heart. Don't let fear keep us apart."** When she did turn, the vulnerability and tenderness in Joe's face rewarded the tremendous effort it took.

Please, Lord, help me always turn back toward him, even when I hurt this much.

He reached out his arms to her, and she slid back into them. She felt a tear from Joe drop to mingle with her own. By the time they had both begun to relax into their embrace, nine o'clock approached, when Amy and Stephen would be waiting for a ride home. Tessa washed her face and headed for the car. She was relieved to have the cool night air and the drive to help regain her composure.

Lord, I love him so much. I don't want to feel like this anymore. You've got to help us! Marjorie had said prayer helped with recovery. Well, Tessa was praying. *We could both use a mighty dose of Your healing.*

---

*Lyrics from the song "Hosea" © 1972, from the recording *Listen,* The Benedictine Foundation of the State of Vermont, Inc., Weston Priory. Used with permission. Composer: Weston Priory, Gregory Norbet, OSB.

Twenty

Sometimes, we just need
a little help from our friends.

G wen glanced in her rearview mirror to check on the boys who, for the moment, were each absorbed in their various car toys. She turned onto the street of Brian's new venture and confirmed the address written on the note that she had stuck to her dashboard. Ducking her head to read house numbers, she parked in front of the corresponding house. Brian had left his lunch behind. Remembering his recent apology and flowers, Gwen offered to bring it to him.

Besides, it gave her an excuse to check out the new property. He had sold the previous house he had been working on and made more of a profit than expected. His new project, a large bungalow that he said had great potential, brought him to this time-worn neighborhood. He had talked excitedly about the spacious rooms and beamed ceilings and, as he pulled up the green shag carpet, he was discovering fine hardwood floors throughout the house.

Gwen rolled down the window and looked at the old home with pleasant surprise. Its deep columned porch and solid earthy appearance exuded stately character. With fresh paint and a new door, its street appeal would help it sell quickly.

The noise of neighborhood children playing outdoors cheered her. *Nice to hear the kids so happy.* She watched Brian drag a roll of carpet out to his truck. Before he noticed her, several children gathered around him.

"What're you doing?" she could hear one boy with short black hair ask.

"I'm going to fix up this old house," Brian answered in the same patient tone he used for Joe Pat's constant barrage of questions.

"You gonna move in?"

"No. This is what I do for a living. I buy old homes and fix them up. Once they're nicer looking and safer, I sell them."

"The Joneses used to live here. They had lots of kids. You gonna sell it to a family with lots of kids?" asked a little girl with more hair slipping out of her braids than bound.

"Maybe so. It's got four bedrooms, so probably a family will buy it."

"What kind of fixing up you planning?" asked the dark-haired boy.

"First I'm taking out this old rug. Smells kind of bad and there's beautiful wood underneath that will shine up real pretty. I'll probably put in new windows and rewire the kitchen. The old wiring wouldn't be safe with new appliances. The kitchen needs new counters, but the cabinets are in good shape. They'll be fine with some fresh, white paint."

Most of the children drifted back to their game, bored, she assumed, with the details of house repair. The inquisitive boy stayed and asked one more question.

"You need help?"

Brian really looked at the boy at this point. He was nine or ten, Gwen guessed, and even from the car she could see a face that held both determination and yearning. The boy looked down at his feet as soon as Brian had stopped his work to consider him, but then looked up with a smile that reminded Gwen of her own boys' innocent goodness.

By the way Brian rubbed the back of his neck, she could tell he was figuring out how to tell the boy no. He probably didn't want to be pestered by kids while he was trying to get work done. Brian occasionally could use some extra muscle, but this boy had none to spare. However, something in the boy's voice and her own motherly heart made Gwen hope Brian would agree.

"I wouldn't charge you nothing. I want to learn about fixing up places."

"You've got a place in mind you'd like to fix up?"

"Yeah. I want to make our house better for my mom. She deserves a nice house."

Brian visibly softened. Gwen thought of all the time Brian had spent with his dad on house projects to please his own mother.

"What's your name?"

"Mo."

"Nice to meet you, Mo. I'm Brian. I tell you what, you think about it overnight, and so will I. Ask your mom about it. If it still seems like a good idea to all of us, we'll plan a time so your mom can meet me. Sound good?"

"Yes, sir!" The boy grinned and looked up at Brian. Brian reached out his hand, and Mo met it with his own to seal the deal with a shake.

Later that evening, while sitting to take off his shoes, Brian and Gwen talked about the boy. "You know, in a few more years, maybe my own boys will be working with me, learning how to remodel. We could be 'O'Connell and Sons, Incorporated!'"

"Sounds great, Bri. It's good that you arranged to meet his mom. I'd be nervous about our boys spending time with someone I didn't know." She kissed the top of his head. "Very considerate."

But I hope she isn't pretty, Gwen left unsaid.

⌘ ⌘ ⌘

Thursday at their early dinner before class, Brian told Gwen and the boys about meeting Mo's mother. The boys loved it when their dad spoke in his storyteller voice.

"I found myself in the backyard of a little house whose better days were long gone. 'Mom, Mr. Brian's here,' Mo yelled before we'd gotten to the door."

The boys stopped with forks, spoons, or fingers partway to their mouths.

Brian winked at Gwen and continued, as if he'd been on a great adventure. "Mo's mother opened the backdoor. She seemed to fit the house perfectly. She was small like it, and tired looking, but with an air of dignity. Her skin reminded me of Oregon myrtle wood."

Brian pointed to the stemmed bowl that held a pretty display of fall leaves and nuts on a kitchen shelf. She and Brian both loved the fine-grained wood. Its dark honey color was so attractive that, according to Brian, woodworkers never stain it. The Made in Oregon shops carried the rare wood crafted into smooth, rounded bowls or animal shapes whose curves enticed Brian to stroke them. Gwen cringed, hoping Mo's mother's skin didn't inspire that urge in Brian.

"Mo's mom's face held both caution and courtesy. 'Nice to meet you, Mr. Brian.'" The boys laughed at Brian's falsetto imitation. "'I'm Siara. Come in. Would you like a glass of iced tea?'"

"'Call me Brian, Brian O'Connell,' I said as I wiped my feet on the mat outside the door and went in. 'Iced tea would be great. Thanks.' Well, I looked at her kitchen and that told me as much about the owner as other folks might learn by reading titles on someone's bookshelf. Mo's mother works hard. Every surface shone as clean as could be. The chrome that was left on the faucet was polished. Counters were covered in contact paper but free of crumbs and clutter. The empty counters told me money was tight—no microwave or mixer, no blender or coffee maker. Only an old toaster sat tucked into a corner, and a pretty bowl of fruit brightened the center of a little table-for-two."

Brian paused while the older boys looked around their own kitchen for comparison. "When Mo opened the old curved-top fridge to get the iced tea, I could see the shelves. Orderly and clean but not much on them."

Gwen imagined her own shelves and the clutter that kept leftovers lost in the back of the refrigerator.

"'Do you and your wife have children, Brian?' Siara—that's Miss Siara to you three—asked as she took out three glasses.

"*Guess she's observing me pretty closely, too,* I thought. *She must have noticed my wedding ring.* 'Yes, ma'am,' I said. 'We have three boys, ages 'tuna half,' four, and five.'"

Brian tugged out his wallet now, as he must have then to show her their picture. "That's Sean, there's Joe Pat, and the oldest is Mickey." The boys examined the picture and nodded. Gwen smiled at their seriousness.

"The photo of you boys seemed to help Siara relax a bit. 'Oh, they're sweet,' she said. 'Your wife must be so busy.'

"I told her that in the evenings I watch you boys while your mama goes to counseling school."

Gwen figured Brian had been trying to impress her, pointing out that he was busy with the boys, too.

"'You sound like a good dad,' Siara said, and with her words and her smile, I realized I had passed a test. Well, that and when she asked, 'So, what will you and Mo be doing?'"

Gwen listened while Mickey declared he'd help Daddy when he was as big as Mo, but a nagging fear played in her mind, and she wondered how young and how pretty Siara might be.

Twenty-one

If your friends are going through hell,
go with them.

Marjorie paused in her lecture and smiled as Gwen whispered an apology and slipped into the empty chair closest to the door. She hoped Gwen was all right. She certainly looked harried, like a runner close to the finish line. Marjorie continued what she had been saying, determined to do better this week at keeping her own issues out of the classroom. To keep from blushing, she had to push aside the memory of her emotions nearly taking over last week's lecture.

She addressed the class. "What kinds of things happen that turn the honeymoon to a moonscape?"

"Real life happens." The newlywed said this, which brought a sad smile to Marjorie.

"Tell me more."

"Suddenly there's dirty underwear, and you find out he won't eat what you cook and he doesn't think you should spend so much money on books."

"Yes, reality sets in, but that's when you can get to know the true person, not a romantic idealization of him. What other challenges hit relationships hard?"

"Children." This from Gwen, whose arms were above her head, recapturing her hair into a ponytail.

"Go on."

"As much as you love them, they're exhausting. They don't leave a lot of time or energy for being a couple, apart from being parents."

Marjorie remembered those days, and how grateful she felt when

Michael insisted they start a weekly date night. "And how might that make the couple feel?"

"Typically the woman feels overwhelmed and angry at the man for not helping out more."

"And the man?"

Gwen shrugged.

A student in his early thirties spoke up. "He feels confused and lonely. Maybe he'd like to help, but he doesn't ever do it well enough to please his wife, so he gives up."

"And the lonely part?"

"He used to have more of her time and attention, so he misses her. He can even feel a bit jealous of the new baby and then feels childish and guilty about that. Plus, he's exhausted, too. No one sleeps enough or well in a house with a newborn."

"Sounds like you speak from personal experience." He looked it, too, Marjorie thought as she noted his red, baggy eyes. But oh, how she'd love to have a baby in the house again. She noticed Hank looked as wistful as she felt.

"I haven't had a full night's sleep in weeks, but it isn't all bad. I love my little guy more than I ever thought possible."

"So, as challenges to a couple, we can list disillusionment when reality hits, and exhaustion when they become a family. What else?"

"Those babies grow, and life becomes even busier." Tessa continued, sending a look of commiseration toward the young dad. "Before you know it, your calendar is full of parent-teacher meetings, volunteering for the schools, Scouts, music lessons, sports, and church school. You name it, and you're driving to it. You pour your energy into giving the kids every opportunity. But if you aren't careful, you become so busy being parents that you forget to be spouses."

Had she forgotten to be a spouse to Michael? Marjorie forced her mind back to the class. "So, how do you protect your relationship?"

Was that what he was trying to do with the Europe trip?

"All the magazines say to go out on dates to focus on each other. It's a great idea but hard to actually do."

"Yes, it's difficult, but crucial to find some way to invest time and energy in your relationship." Marjorie paused to add emphasis.

"Parenting well is extremely important, but the best thing you can do for your children is to maintain a healthy, loving relationship for them to see as an example for their own futures." Marjorie scanned the class. "What else will bring couples in for counseling?"

"Affairs." Poor Anna sounded wounded still. Marjorie caught a soft inhalation from Gwen that stood out in the otherwise silent room. She sent a quick message to her new Friend, asking for healing for the first student and prevention for the second.

She responded carefully. "Sadly, yes. A successful couple works continuously to grow in their intimacy. If they aren't becoming closer, they are probably drifting apart, and then the danger increases that one or both will drift into another relationship. Most people truly want their marriage to work, to bring happiness to themselves and their spouses. Unfortunately, when times get hard, they may turn away from each other and look for consolation outside the marriage."

She noticed Gwen nodding with a clenched jaw. "But going to their mothers, their coworkers, or their friends isn't going to help the marriage. Only the couple can do that. They may benefit from professional help, but it's going to take work from both of them to avoid the danger."

"Sometimes trouble hits couples that they didn't bring on themselves," a young woman volunteered.

"Absolutely. Can you give an example?"

"Maybe they find out they can't have children. Or one of them gets cancer, or laid off work, or hurt in a car accident."

This time the breath intake was Marjorie's own.

Marjorie felt blindsided even worse than last week, as the mental picture of Michael's last moments crashed into her consciousness. She had to steady herself with a hand on the nearest desk and swallow to be able to speak. "And how would you help clients like these?"

"I was hoping you'd tell us."

The class laughed. Marjorie couldn't share their lightheartedness.

The young woman objected. "No, seriously, I have friends going through hard times, and I don't know what to say to them."

Marjorie could relate to that statement and her desire to help her students overcame her pain.

"I'm sorry. The class laughed because we all have felt that way. Even after twenty years of counseling, I still often sit with a couple and wish someone would walk in and give us some wisdom, because I have no idea what to say."

A young man with numerous piercings said, "I've only been in this program a few weeks now, but already my friends come to me and ask for advice. Sometime in our studies are we going to learn what to tell people who are hurting?"

"Yes and no." The class groaned at Marjorie's honest answer. "Some counseling theorists think you can do cookie-cutter counseling, and one style will fit all. In practice, it doesn't work out that way.

"A couple whose child died came to see me recently. Nothing I can say will fix their brokenness. However, I can be with them, listen to them, and cry with them. If they want, I can pray with them. I surely will pray *for* them." Marjorie's eyes felt moist as she thought of the couple. The class gave her their full, quiet attention.

"I can encourage them to find meaning in the child's short life. I can point out if their reactions are destructive and help them choose healthier ways to grieve. I'll let them know that different people grieve in different ways and help them be tolerant of each other's means of dealing with their sorrow."

A shiver rippled up her spine. *Am I tolerant of my own sorrow? Won't it ever get easier?*

"If their grief reaches dangerous levels, I'll warn them. I can recommend books or give information on support groups and therapists who specialize in grief counseling. But mostly, I'll listen."

Maybe I need to listen to my own grief.

She took a deep breath. "When we must face something that can't be changed, we still need some sense of control. All we can control is our attitude, but with that, we can survive."

Marjorie looked with empathy at the students who had asked for answers, and then at the whole class. "So, no, I can't tell you what to say to your friends. These counseling courses will flood you with information about human nature and how we tend to react to situations, but each client will be different, with different needs. However, all clients come with strengths. Listen to them. Help them tap their own power, and together you'll usually arrive at a better place than when they came to you."

Marjorie suddenly felt weighed down by responsibility. She suspected her students felt the same. "On that note, go home. Go make it a better place."

When she was alone, she sat at her desk and took the growth cards out of her briefcase. She had made definite progress on her fear of God's punishment. She considered the others: fear of letting her daughters be independent, of upsetting them if she became closer with Colm, of forgetting, or disappointing, or being disloyal to Michael. Forgetting him didn't seem likely, judging from how hard it was to get through her classes lately. She tore and threw away that card, wishing she could as easily tear up the rest of her fears.

For my students as well as myself.

Twenty-two

Jealousy is one mask
fear hides behind.

As the three walked from class to the parking lot, Gwen apologized to Tessa and Hank for missing their hour of small group discussion.

"I always leave the minivan for Brian since it has the car seats for the kids, but halfway here his truck refused to go when the light turned green. I coasted over to the curb and called Brian, but it took all that time for him and the boys to come get me and drive me to class."

Tessa and Hank assured her they missed her but had done fine. Hank offered to stay until Brian came to pick her up, and Tessa left them to head home to her family. After a few minutes of waiting, Gwen realized Brian hadn't really said that he'd be back for her. Embarrassed by keeping Hank waiting, she called Brian's cell phone. Her heart sank when she realized he was still at home.

"Babe, I'm sorry. What with the tow truck and the boys, it didn't dawn on me until a minute ago that you'd need me to pick you up. Now they're all in bed, and it would take me most of an hour to get to you. Could you get a ride or call a taxi?"

"Shoot, Brian. I expected you'd be here by now. We got out a few minutes early so nearly everyone left."

"Are you waiting all alone?" Gwen felt gratified to hear the concern in his voice.

"No, Hank is here. He always walks Tessa and me to our cars and makes sure we get off all right. He waited with me for you to come. Just a minute."

Gwen explained the delay to Hank, who offered to drive her home.

"Brian, Hank can drive me. Put on some coffee. I'll invite him in when we get there. I'd like you two to meet."

"Tell him I appreciate it. I'll take one of your zucchini breads out of the freezer. And yes, I know, I'll tidy up a bit, too." Brian's tone didn't sound as grateful as his words.

When Gwen arrived with Hank, she opened the door and was pleased by the fresh coffee aroma that filled the house. Gwen gave Brian a quick kiss and scanned the tidy room with relief. As she hung Hank's coat in the closet, she discovered a large box with a load of laundry, various puzzles, trucks, Legos, and several days' worth of newspapers hidden there.

Brian shook Hank's hand, saying, "Thanks for bringing Gwen home," with less than warmth in his voice.

"No problem. It gave us a chance to talk more about class," Hank replied.

"I've got coffee ready and some of Gwen's zucchini bread. Have a seat, and I'll bring it in. How do you take your coffee? It's regular, but we have decaffeinated instant if you'd rather, since it's late."

Gwen winced. *Hank'll think he's hinting it's too late for him to be here.* She noticed a small white sock and pushed it farther under the sofa with her toe.

"Black, thanks." Hank seemed unperturbed. "I'm headed off to work in a little while so regular is fine."

Gwen led Hank to the seating arrangement as Brian left for the kitchen. They waited in an awkward silence and listened to Brian rummage in the other room until he returned with a tray of mugs and a plate of sliced bread.

"What do you do?" Brian asked, as he set the tray down on the coffee table between Hank, who sat on the loveseat, and Gwen, who patted the sofa for Brian to join her. The conversation stumbled from Hank's work as a physician assistant, to the Youth Club, and settled for a while on the basketball games played there.

Brian talked about his work remodeling homes and then about his new helper, Mo. However, when they discovered they had both been in the Army, Gwen sat back and relaxed as she watched these two good men begin to appreciate each other.

138

When the grandfather clock struck the hour, Hank jumped up suddenly, saying he'd be late for work at the hospital. All three agreed they wished their time together could have lasted longer. Gwen realized Brian, especially, had missed talking with other men. As he walked Hank out, she heard him invite Hank over to watch Monday Night Football sometime and was pleased when Hank accepted.

As they cleared the coffee mugs and went upstairs to get ready for bed, Brian told her more about meeting Siara, Mo's mom. "You should have seen her kitchen, Gwen. It is spotless. She doesn't have much, but what she does have is neat and tidy. She and her house seem to fit together. Small, but with a proud simplicity."

Gwen felt her defenses rise. What was he saying? That their house was a mess? Well, Siara didn't have three preschoolers running around all day. It would be easy for Gwen to keep a clean house, too, if she only had one son who spent the day in school. Could Siara become the next Shirley? *Already I don't like the woman.*

"You all right, babe? You seem a million miles away."

"I'm fine. She said Mo could work with you?"

"Yeah, I think showing her the boys' picture in my wallet convinced her. She says she thinks you're the one who could use extra help, because you must be kept busy chasing our little guys. She saw your picture and thinks you're pretty." Brian leaned over and gave Gwen a kiss. "She's right, too."

Gwen felt like a shrew. The woman sounded nice. *And Brian loves me. I need to stop feeling so threatened.*

"How'd I do tonight meeting Hank? I was all set not to like him. I really hated the idea of him giving you a ride home. Hank, the knight in shining armor. But he's an all-right guy."

She smiled in guilty relief. *Brian gets insecure, too. Jealous of Hank driving me home.* "You did fine. Thanks for tidying up. I wish our house could always be neat like Siara's."

"Our house is fine, babe. I wouldn't trade it, our three messy boys, or my pretty, busy wife for the world." Brian wrapped Gwen in his arms and looked into her eyes with an expression that reassured her he meant every word. At least until the next fight.

Twenty-three

Reach deep within to find what is needed for change
but reach out to others, too.

After their last attempt, Tessa and Joe avoided any try at physical intimacy. She didn't think she could handle disappointment one more time. Judging from Joe's similar behavior, he was afraid, too. As if to make up for their concerns, they were both especially affectionate during the day. Each took a minute to give a hug, squeeze, or quick kiss between their comings and goings. At night they would lie with their arms around each other but not try for more. Tessa suspected they both fell asleep feeling loved but sad.

Meanwhile, life during the day significantly improved for Joe. He told her he felt more energy and realized work problems could offer interesting challenges, rather than drain his limited resources.

Tessa had taken Schnarch's words to heart, realizing she had let Joe polarize to be the financial manager of the family, and that she should grow in that area. Thinking fewer responsibilities might help him be less tired, she seized the opportunity when Amy and Stephen asked him to help them turn the garage into a haunted house for Halloween.

"Sorry, kids, I need to balance the checkbook tonight and get some bills paid," he had answered.

"I'll do that," Tessa offered.

"But you don't..." His voice trailed off, perhaps seeing the determination Tessa felt, perhaps thinking better of the insult his words might cause. The decision was made as the children pulled him toward the garage. The end result was that Tessa struggled with budgets and bills but thoroughly enjoyed watching the fun her husband and children were sharing.

One evening, while Joe was helping them paint wall paneling scraps black, Tessa overheard Amy announce, "Don't forget Mom's birthday is in a couple of weeks. I already know what I'm getting her."

She moved out of earshot quickly to avoid ruining any surprises, but her thoughts turned to the past. Over the fourteen years they had been married, Joe and Tessa had learned much about gift giving. She particularly remembered their first Christmas. Tessa had given Joe a ring, even though he had hinted about the Sears tool sale, and then he had struggled to keep her from realizing his disappointment. He hadn't told her how hard it was for him to get used to wearing a wedding ring and wasn't looking forward to trying to become accustomed to a ring for his other hand.

To make matters worse, she had cried when she'd unwrapped a hand-mixer from Joe. He hadn't known what was wrong but drew her into his arms. They sat together on the rug next to the Christmas tree and learned how to give the kind of gift the other wanted to receive.

Now, fourteen years later, Tessa was confident Joe was much better at choosing something that signified his love for her. She didn't think about the subject again until the next night, when she returned from class and found Joe sitting in front of the computer, looking dejected. She dragged a chair to sit close to him. He turned to her, and his expression spoke of failure.

"While you were at class, and Amy and Stephen were doing homework, I logged on to the Victoria Secret website to look for a birthday present for you. I thought maybe some new nighties would rekindle our love life." Tessa smiled sadly, knowing from her own lingerie efforts that the answer wouldn't be that easy.

"I clicked on the nightwear selection and rationalized my guilty feelings away, thinking, *It's not Playboy, and I'm shopping for my wife. No harm in the fact that I get a little tingle out of seeing the pictures.* This time, though, no reaction. No turn-on. Not even a little stir. Nothing."

When Joe looked into Tessa's eyes, she knew he was looking to her for answers. Answers she didn't have.

He took her hands in his. "Guess that proves it isn't about you. This is all about me, and my sexual interest is definitely nonexistent." He stared at the computer, which still showed scantily clad, pouting models. "I couldn't bring myself to order anything." His voice rasped with discouragement.

Tessa drew him to his feet and hugged him. "Oh, Joe, I'm sorry." His weight sagged against her momentarily; then he straightened and gave her a resigned, lopsided smile. After a pause she ventured, "I guess I'm relieved that your lack of interest really isn't because we've been married too long or because of my surgery. But I'm sad, too, because it takes away my hope that I could change something and fix this problem."

He nodded, embracing her tighter. "I have to admit, deep down I wanted to blame you, but it's about me. I need to be the one to solve it somehow." They went to bed and held each other but struggled alone with their thoughts.

⌘⌘⌘

Hank called the two counselors named on the card Marjorie had given him. Both were men; perhaps Marjorie thought it would be easier for him to talk to a man. He asked each about his counseling philosophy, length of time in practice, and the fees charged. One man seemed easier to talk to than the other. Hank scheduled a time to see him.

When Hank arrived for his appointment, he liked the counselor's office. The building looked like a family home someone had divided into small offices. The receptionist seemed friendly and efficient. The smell of leather somehow lent an air of competence.

Hank tried to imagine himself as a counselor and picture his office. He admitted this experience could point out things he didn't know about counseling and that hadn't been covered in his classes, such as what he might need in a waiting room or how to establish an atmosphere that put clients at ease. What magazines would he have available? Would he have a receptionist? Consideration of paychecks, benefits, hiring, and firing made him feel tense again.

The empty waiting room failed to calm him. Embarrassed at the possibility of being the only counseling student who needed counseling, he fought temptation to walk back out the door.

Too late. Hank stood to shake hands with the man who came into the waiting room to meet him. "Hank Glenn? John Stein. Come in, please."

Hank walked into the counselor's office and wondered what his choice of chair might say about him. It wasn't clear which chair John Stein would use. It didn't look as if he would sit at his desk, which filled a corner away from the seating arrangement. Hank avoided the black leather sofa and chose one tan suede chair that flanked it and faced another. *I wonder if people ever lie down on the couch anymore like in the cartoons.*

The counselor took the seat opposite Hank's and made small talk about Marjorie. Hank had mentioned her referral on the phone. John once attended a seminar Marjorie led, and he had been impressed. The conversation moved smoothly to the reason for Hank's coming, and Hank felt relief at how easily he could talk to this man. He retold the story of his surprising anger at the silent teen and expressed his confusion about his irritation lately.

John Stein leaned forward. "Has there ever been another time when you wanted to shake someone to get them to talk?"

"No, not really. I usually accept people not wanting to talk. That's the way I grew up."

"Tell me more about that."

Hank spoke about his quiet childhood home. He described the typical silent TV dinners while he and his dad watched the news and then how his dad went down to work in the basement for the evenings.

"But how did you and your mom do at communication?"

"My mom died when I was three." Hank took a deep breath. "Wait, no, that's not right. That's what I grew up believing, but recently I've learned different."

Stein waited while Hank sorted out what to say.

"My mother left us when I was three." Hank suddenly felt like a small child again, and he didn't like the feeling. All he'd wanted to know was why he'd gotten so mad at the kid at the Youth Club, not dredge through his childhood.

The counselor responded to Hank's agitation by saying, "Let's come back to that a bit later. I don't want to make you uncomfortable, scare you off on your first visit." He sat back in his chair. "What's going on recently in your life, Hank? Any changes lately?"

Hank pictured his grandma and relaxed a bit. Now that was something upbeat he could talk about. *I don't want him to think I'm some loser who's still bogged down with what happened when I was three.*

"Yeah, some really nice changes. I discovered I have a grandma I hadn't remembered, and I went to visit her in Spokane. She's great, and it feels good to have family again. It's been several years since my dad died."

Hank pushed his clammy palms against his jeans and eased his shoulders back. "Grandma hadn't known where I was and, like I said, I didn't remember her, so it was quite a surprise for both of us. I pretty much showed up on her doorstep, and we spent a weekend catching up on our lives. We talked all through the first night. Feels really good to have her to talk to."

"So, you call her and chat now?"

"She's called me a few times. Invited me to Thanksgiving dinner, too."

John made a note on a tablet. Unnerved, Hank wondered what it said.

"Hank, what are you hoping to gain from our time together? What changes would you like to see that will mean success?"

He thought carefully about how to answer. *I'm not going to say I'm here because my teacher thinks I need it. What do I want to gain from this?*

He rested his elbows on his thighs as he clasped his hands between his knees and looked at the therapist. "I guess I have a short-term goal and a long-term goal. I want to understand why I'm getting so riled lately and resolve that, so I'm easygoing like I used to be. That's the short-term goal.

"Long-term, I'm tired of being alone, and I'd like to have a special woman in my life. If there is some psychological reason I'm alone, I'd like to resolve that, too. Do what it takes to be part of a couple."

John made a few quick notes, then propped his ankle on the other knee. He adjusted his glasses. "Those sound like great goals to me. I think we can make real progress on both of them. If you feel good about how things go here today, we'll make a few more appointments and then evaluate how we're doing." He tapped his notepad with his pen. "First, though, I want to return to something you said earlier. When I assumed you called your grandma, you corrected me that she calls you. Do you ever call her?"

Hank's brow tensed, and he smoothed it with the back of his hand. "No, I guess apart from the first time when I called before visiting her, I haven't been the one to call."

"Now, a hunch. You've dated?"

Hank nodded.

"Did you call the women after the first date?"

Again Hank felt caught off guard. "No, I don't think so. Some called me."

The counselor shifted forward slightly. "Hank, have you ever asked a woman out on a date?"

"I guess not. I've gone along with buddies, or on dates arranged by friends, or when the woman asked me." He frowned, wondering where this was leading.

"Hank, have you heard in any of your classes of John Gottman and his idea of bids for emotional connection?"

⌘ ⌘ ⌘

The next Thursday night, during discussion time with Tessa and Gwen, Hank raised his voice above the noise of the other groups' conversations and recounted his experience with John Stein. "He started talking about Gottman. Remember a few weeks ago when Dr. Gloriam reviewed Gottman's idea of bids for connection? She told us that people constantly make small attempts to connect with others."

Gwen's foot stopped jiggling, and she sat up. "Oh, right, and people can ignore them, accept them, or reject them," she said as she tapped each of three fingers.

"Right. This counselor suggested that maybe I'm alone and haven't built a relationship with anyone because I never learned how to make or respond to bids for connection. There never was much connection in our family, so I didn't learn how to do it.

"I must connect some, since I manage fine in my job. Though, now that I think about it, I've never made many friends at work." He shook his head, puzzled. "Looking back, the friends I've made reached out to me or circumstances brought them my way. Like how I came to know you two; we were assigned together." He looked at his classmates, realizing how much he appreciated their friendship.

"It never would have occurred to me to suggest starting up a study group. Like it never occurred to me to call back any dates, or even my grandma. I'd been waiting and hoping she'd call again soon. Never dawned on me to call her."

Both women seemed amazed by his admission. Gwen was shaking her head with a wry smile. Tessa's expression was more sympathetic.

"Maybe women in the past have interpreted my not calling as actually ignoring their bids for connection. Remember, Dr. Gloriam said that having your bids ignored is even worse than having them rejected. People give up and quit trying to connect."

Hank thought of Kaya at the Youth Club and wondered how long it would take before he really learned this lesson. "Who knows how many dates gave up trying to connect with me. Even Grandma has been calling less often." Hank's face and neck felt flushed. "I'm a dolt. I probably gave up connecting with my dad as a kid and then didn't try much with anyone else."

"At some point we all give up," said Tessa.

Hank noticed her slight blush, but images of his childhood overshadowed it. He shook his head, clearing unwanted memories. "Now I have homework from the counselor. I'll try this week to be aware of other people's bids for connection with me. And, at least once, I'm supposed to make a bid for connection with someone on my own initiative." The thought made his diaphragm tighten, and he forced himself to exhale.

"That's my update for the week. How about you two? Hey, does asking that count as a bid?" He chuckled, and they laughed with him. Something about the glint in Gwen's eye made him uneasy, however.

146

Twenty-four

Take the first step to change.

Hank's talk about connection gave Gwen an idea that she hoped would benefit everyone concerned. Besides, she was supposed to be learning from Brian's strong points. Maybe she could use a little more fun in her own life. What better way than a party?

When she arrived home from class, she checked on the sleeping boys, kissed each one, and then returned to Brian in the family room. He lay in his recliner, arms crossed behind his head, watching a football game. She sat on the couch until a commercial and then ran her idea by him.

"Bri, what would you think of inviting a few people over Monday night to watch football? You've already extended an invitation to Hank. Let's ask Tessa and her husband, too, so you can get to know them. How about inviting Siara and Mo? Tessa has kids a little older than Mo. She could bring them. We'd all visit over dinner first, and then whoever didn't want to watch the game could keep talking in the kitchen. What do you think?"

Brian straightened the chair into the upright position and muted the television. "Sounds great to me, but why Siara and Mo?"

Gwen couldn't say she wanted to size up Siara and see if she was competition. Or that if Hank and Siara hit it off, Mo's mom wouldn't be a lonely single that might tempt Brian. Gwen had to admit those reasons were what first appealed to her, but since then, the invitation seemed like the right thing to do. Siara was alone. So was Hank. Maybe she could help them both.

"I wouldn't want Hank to feel awkward not being part of a couple, so I thought it would be nice to invite another single person. We're talking about how people make connections in class, and Hank has a little trouble with that. I thought it might be a way to help him out."

"Matchmaker, huh? Want me to ask her?"

"No, I think she'd be more comfortable if I did. I'll call Tessa and Siara tomorrow."

⌘ ⌘ ⌘

When Gwen phoned Tessa the next morning, she seemed reluctant to accept the invitation. "It's nice of you to ask, but Monday night's a school night, and the kids will have homework to do."

Gwen persisted. "I know it's short notice, but after hearing Hank talk at class last night, it made me think of inviting someone over for him to meet. You know, help him connect. She has a son about your boy's age so I thought it would be nice to include them, too."

"Oh, ulterior motives," Tessa responded conspiratorially.

You have no idea, thought Gwen guiltily.

"I get it. You're sweet to do this for him. Hank's such a nice man."

Gwen was relieved at the new tone of collaboration in Tessa's voice.

"Even if she isn't the perfect someone for him, it will give him a chance to practice making connections. Maybe the kids can get homework done ahead. I'll check with Joe, but we'll try to come."

With a little trepidation, Gwen called Siara that evening after dinner. Siara's voice sounded young and cultured. Gwen pushed aside her insecurities, introduced herself, and said, "Siara, I thought you and Mo might like to get to know our family better, since Mo is spending time helping Brian work now. I've invited a couple of my classmates from my counseling program to come over for dinner and to watch Monday Night Football. One of them is bringing her husband and their kids. They're just a little older than Mo."

"How nice of you. Mo would love it. But please let me bring something. I have a good rice dish, or homemade bread rolls are one of my specialties."

Gwen felt ashamed when she heard the sincerity in Siara's voice.

She forced a smile and inhaled deeply. "Mmm. I can almost smell the bread rolls. I plan to do spaghetti, so they'd go really well."

Gwen began to give Siara driving directions, but Siara asked for the nearest bus line. Gwen had no idea, so summoning her generous nature rather than her suspicious side, she suggested that Brian could bring Siara and Mo home with him after work.

When Gwen hung up the phone, she turned and critically scanned her kitchen and family room as if she were a new visitor. Toys and books lay scattered like shrapnel after a bomb. She sighed. "What have I gotten myself into?"

⌘ ⌘ ⌘

Marjorie mulled over her visit with Aunt Annie—amazed, as always, at the insight of the uncomplicated woman. She hoped thinking through their conversations would help her find answers for her worries. To her dismay, it wasn't Aunt Annie's bits of wisdom that kept claiming her attention, but rather her description of Marjorie dancing as a little girl. Finally, she gave in to the mental image. She closed her eyes and pictured herself as a child twirling and whirling, watching a little skirt spin out around her and making her feel like a ballerina. She couldn't help but smile. Her spirit felt lighter than she could ever remember feeling.

Marjorie pictured the growth card *Being wild* and opened her eyes, a decision made. "I'm going to dance!" She checked the college's course catalog online and then hesitated. She wouldn't be able to rediscover her lost free spirit in front of students or colleagues. Instead she turned to the phone book to look for dance studios.

The next night Marjorie climbed the stairs to a second-floor studio, ready to release her inhibitions. To her dismay, her classmates were all teenagers, wearing sports bras and skin-tight shorts. She looked at her reflection in the mirrored wall. The exercise pants and long-sleeved top she had just bought made her overdressed compared to them and underdressed by her usual standards.

She smiled to see the dance instructor looked nearly her age. The woman nodded at her in acknowledgment, clapped her hands, and commanded brusquely, "Let's begin." Marjorie was quickly overwhelmed as she discovered the Freestyle class seemed to be anything but free. She had imagined herself swaying to the music as the spirit moved her. Instead, she frantically tried to follow orders to point, ball change, stand up straight, and stay on beat. By the end of the forty-five minute lesson, she was thoroughly exhausted, embarrassed, and sticky with perspiration. Vowing to chalk this up to experience, a *one*-time experience, she gathered her belongings and headed to the stairs.

She stood back to let a nicely dressed man reach the top of the stairs. As he did so, he looked up and her heart lurched. Colm! His face broke into a beaming smile.

"Marjorie! Lovely to meet you here. But you're leaving?" His smile disappeared, and his hand reached as if to detain her.

Marjorie took quick inventory of her appearance and was humiliated. She didn't smell much better than the first time he met her, covered in horse muck. She felt the heat rise up her neck and into her cheeks. He looked so good. Crisp white shirt, black slacks, shiny dress shoes, the smile, the eyes. Ah, those hopeful green eyes stirred her soul.

She stuttered. "Colm. Hi." At loss for better words, she added, "What are you doing here?"

More dance students came in the door at the bottom of the stairs. A few began climbing the stairs, though most headed for the elevator. Colm moved alongside Marjorie to clear the stairs. He gently cupped her elbow to guide her back, saying, "Please don't go. Could you join our ballroom class, just for tonight?"

Marjorie vacillated. She imagined herself in his arms and, though her heart was beating like hummingbird wings, she imagined she would float like a swan.

Two gray-haired women, both in graceful dance dresses, passed her with cold stares. She looked down at her clothes. Ugly duckling. As two more women topped the stairs, Marjorie noted the blue-rinsed hair of one and an obvious wig on the other. She looked to Colm, her question unspoken.

He lifted his shoulders and grinned. "This was the class available in ballroom dance. I didn't realize it was for senior citizens, but they let me stay since they're a wee bit short on men. Actually, there are only three of us. I'm the worst by far."

Marjorie laughed in spite of herself. "Your class really doesn't need another woman then."

"Please, Marjorie. I'd love to dance with you."

For a moment Marjorie felt the little girl twirling inside her. Then she was a woman again, and the imagined feel of Colm's arm around her back became a hunger that caught her breath. She didn't realize he held her gaze until it was broken by the gaggle of giggling teens that burst through the studio door and flowed around and between them.

Colm watched them go and as he looked again at Marjorie, his lips pressed together with his effort to suppress laughter.

"I'm kind of out of place in my class, too. First night." She rolled her eyes. "Last, too."

At her words, Colm became agitated. "Marjorie, please come with me." But his request was vetoed by a diminutive octogenarian woman who had wheezed her way to the top of the stairs. She shook her head at Marjorie, saying, "Seniors only," and took Colm by the hand. "You promised me the first dance this week, Mr. McCloskey."

Marjorie watched him be drawn into the room, the plea still in his eyes. Then she hurried down the stairs, both relieved and devastated by her escape.

The next envelope she received from Colm held only three quotes:

When I pray, coincidences happen, and when I don't, they don't.
—WILLIAM TEMPLE

Coincidences are spiritual puns.
—G.K. CHESTERTON

There are no mistakes, no coincidences, all events are blessings given to us to learn from.
—ELISABETH KÜBLER-ROSS

Twenty-five

Reaching out, working together,
we overcome obstacles.

On Monday night, promptly at six, Gwen welcomed Hank into the house and thanked him for the bottles of sparkling apple cider he brought. Tessa and Joe arrived right behind Hank, and a nervous moment passed while Joe and the children were introduced, coats were taken, and the green salad Tessa carried was brought to the kitchen. Gwen felt flustered from the last-minute details and the challenge of keeping her eye on the boys. Brian hadn't arrived yet, and she told herself she felt so tense because she missed his help with the boys in the last few minutes before company came.

Her sons proved to be the icebreaker she needed, though. Sean hung back a bit, but Joe Pat and Mickey pulled Stephen and Amy into the family room to show them the fort they had built with all the couch and chair cushions. Not quite the tidy room Gwen had hoped to show company, but the fort had kept the boys busy while she prepared the spaghetti sauce. Stephen seemed happy to choose a video game to play with Mickey. Amy showed definite experience as a babysitter and had the two younger boys in giggles as she pretended not to be able to find them in their fort.

Hank watched the fun. "This is what a family home should be like. Siblings and friends and happy noise."

Gwen smiled her appreciation and then explained the host's absence. "Brian is bringing his little helper Mo and Mo's mother, Siara, to join us. Siara's a single parent and doesn't get home from work until almost six o'clock, so they'll head over here as soon as she's home. Actually, they should arrive any time now." The familiar pain lanced her stomach as she cast an accusing glare at the clock.

A full half-hour passed while suspicions tugged at her mind, distracting her in her efforts to be a gracious hostess. At last Brian, Siara, and Mo hurried into the kitchen where the guests chatted while Gwen stirred the spaghetti sauce.

"I'm so sorry to have made us late," Siara apologized. "The bus broke down, and they had to call another to finish the route. When I finally got home, I grabbed the bread rolls, and we came right over."

Gwen looked down at a face pinched with worry. Siara's black hair, unraveling from a twist at the back of her head, endeared her to Gwen. Tall blondes were the type of women who caught Brian's eye. Gwen hoped her face didn't hint at her earlier fears, or the relief that was making her legs weak.

She pulled herself together and gave Siara a full smile. "I never put the spaghetti noodles in until I see the whites of everyone's eyes. But the water is boiling, and the sauce is hot, so it will just take a few minutes. Come meet the rest of the guests."

Gwen introduced Siara to Tessa and Joe and tried not to be too obvious as she introduced her to Hank. Brian showed Mo into the family room. As soon as he was back in the kitchen, he made his way over to Gwen for a quick welcome-home kiss. Gwen introduced him to Tessa and Joe. Those who had arrived earlier all held a drink, so he asked Siara what she'd like and went to the refrigerator for her juice and his beer. Watching how Brian interacted with Siara, Gwen grew more relaxed.

The conversation had been centered on the counseling class, but with Siara and Brian's arrival, the nonclassmates balanced the number of students. Gwen shifted the talk so they all could get to know each other better. She hadn't figured a strategy to encourage Hank and Siara, so she turned toward Tessa's husband. "Tessa hasn't told us what you do for a living, Joe." He struck her as a good fit for Tessa, average in height and build but with kind eyes somewhere between green and brown. The eyes did strike her as weary, though.

"Makes me wonder what she *has* told you. You probably know more about me than I do myself." Joe's laughter lightened his words. He grinned at Brian, and Gwen suspected the husbands' shared situation could become a bond of friendship. "But to answer your question, I work as a loan officer at a bank."

"Do you enjoy it?" Besides the couples' class, Gwen studied career counseling. The different kinds of work that people chose intrigued her.

"I used to, more than I do now. A few years ago, I made decisions about which applications to accept or to reject. Now the home office decides."

"Brian has experience with buying and selling homes," Gwen said, trying to draw others into the conversation. Both Hank and Siara sipped their drinks but didn't make any attempt to talk. She arched an eyebrow at Tessa and tilted her head toward Hank. Tessa nodded, but it was Brian who succeeded at drawing out their quieter guests.

Brian explained about his business remodeling and selling older homes. "I'm working on one in Siara's neighborhood. Her son Mo took an interest in what I was doing and helps me now. He's a good little worker and catching on fast, too."

Siara brightened. "He's a big help at home. More responsible than most boys his age. We don't live in the best of neighborhoods, so I worry about him, but he's always busy." She glanced toward the family room where they could hear children laughing. "He even planted a vegetable garden in our backyard last summer. One of his friends' moms has quite a green thumb, so he goes to her with any questions. Today he brought in the last of the tomatoes since it's supposed to get frosty tonight."

"Oh, we forgot. He's got something in the back of the truck for the other kids." Brian called, "Mo! Let's bring everybody outside so you can show them your surprise."

"The noodles are almost done. Don't be too long," Gwen reminded them as her three boys ran out the door, followed by Mo, Stephen, and Amy.

Gwen decided the party was headed for success, even if her matchmaking attempt stalled. Mo had brought several pumpkins from his garden, and she watched him beam as the other children chose the ones they wanted and brought them indoors. Conversation flowed happily while they ate, and then the children clamored for an impromptu jack o' lantern carving session.

Tessa, Gwen, and Siara worked together to wash the dinner dishes, agreeing they were happy to let the men oversee the gooey scraping of the inside of the pumpkins and the careful planning of jack o' lantern faces at the kitchen table. Gwen knew, however, each mother would keep a subtle eye on the project.

As soon as her pumpkin was empty, Amy drew a horse profile and began to cut it out. The men and boys divided into groups. Stephen and Mickey decided to make their pumpkins match and worked together while Joe supervised. Brian helped the two younger boys. Gwen was proud of Hank when she saw him sit down next to Mo and hand the boy his pocketknife.

Mo looked up at Hank and gasped. "I've never done the cutting before."

Hank looked at him seriously. "Seems to me it's time to start. You go slow, and I'll watch and give any pointers you need." Hank returned the big smile Mo gave him, then the two focused on the pumpkin.

Siara had turned to put the spaghetti pot where Gwen indicated. She glanced to check on Mo just as Hank sat down next to him. Gwen watched her take in the whole scene, including their exchange of smiles, and saw Siara bite her lip. Siara looked at the other men, sitting around the table helping their children, and turned to the women.

"Tessa, do you think my Mo is old enough to be cutting the pumpkin himself?" she asked quietly. "How old was Stephen when you let him?"

Tessa turned to the intent group. "I know what you mean, Siara. I still don't like seeing either of my kids using a sharp knife, but the men will watch out for them."

"It's hard being Mo's only parent. I know I'm overprotective, and he doesn't have a man around to keep me from babying him."

"But you can't stand the thought of him being hurt?" asked Tessa.

Siara shook her head, eyes wide and forehead wrinkled.

"Me neither. That's why I'm doing dishes instead of watching."

"That goes for me, too," added Gwen. All three women looked over to the pumpkin work and then turned resolutely back to the dishes.

When the last pumpkin was finished and the table cleared of seeds, goop, tools, and newspapers, they lit the jack o' lantern candles and turned out the lights. "Ooooo," everyone said at the same time and then laughed.

"Great pumpkins! Mo, thank you very much," said Gwen. "Now, in case anyone is interested, the game has been going on for half an hour, and there are popcorn balls waiting in the family room." The surprise of the men, who had completely forgotten about the game, and the whoops of the little boys, who loved the sweet spheres, almost drowned out her words as she reminded her sons, "You can watch until halftime and then off to bed, no complaints."

The women took over the kitchen table and settled down with hot cups of spiced cider. They talked of motherhood and children, Halloween costumes, and what Thanksgiving plans they had. Siara told about the retirement home where she worked. Gwen's admiration for Siara grew when she learned Siara had started as an aide before Mo was born and had worked her way to being the recreation director. If only Hank were here listening instead of with the men.

At halftime, the aroma of the cider drew the game watchers into the kitchen. They ladled themselves cups of cider, and Brian cut slices of apple pie for everyone while Siara described the time she arranged for all the mobile residents of the center to make the seventy-mile trip to Seaside for an afternoon. She had even rented wheelchairs with extra large tires to make sure everyone could make it down to the water's edge.

Mo interrupted. "Mom says when we get a car she's gonna take me to see the ocean!"

"You've never seen the ocean?" Stephen voiced the general surprise. "It's totally cool. Seaside has an arcade and paddle boats, and you can rent bikes made for the beach."

"I like kite flying," Amy added. "Dad has a collection of different kites so we can fly something in almost any amount of wind."

"We made the awesomest sandcastle city there before Mom's school started," Mickey chimed in. Unfortunately, by speaking, he drew his mother's attention to the fact that he was still up, and that he and his brothers needed to get to bed. Sean shrieked and ran giggling away when Gwen stood up, but she swooped him up in her arms while Brian lifted Joe Pat onto his shoulders. Mickey ran for a book for storytime and followed his brothers and parents up the stairs.

"We'll be back in a minute," Gwen called over their boys' giggles. "Make yourselves at home." She telegraphed one more eyebrow signal to Tessa before shifting her attention to her boys.

⌘ ⌘ ⌘

Hank watched the family as they climbed the stairs to begin their bedtime ritual. He desperately wanted what Gwen and Brian shared, in spite of their troubles.

Hank thought Siara's face mirrored his own wistful feelings. She sighed and then turned to her son. "You know, Mo, I should get you to bed, too. You have school in the morning. I didn't think about the game going so late. Brian said he'd take us home, but I hate to take him away before the game is over."

Tessa caught Hank's eye and gave a slight nod in Siara's direction. Hank wondered what Tessa was trying to tell him, so he thought through Siara's remark until realization dawned.

Man, am I dense.

Hank took a deep breath. "Siara, can I drop you and Mo off on my way home? I'm more of a basketball fan than football, anyway."

"Oh." She glanced at Brian's second beer can, still at the table, and gave Hank a look of relief. "That would be nice. You're sure it's not out of your way?"

"Not at all. It would be my pleasure." Hank looked at her face now lit with an eye-brightening smile and realized he meant what he said. *It would be a pleasure to get to know you better.*

Hank waited with Siara and Mo until Brian and Gwen came back downstairs. They thanked their hosts for an evening they had all enjoyed. Gwen didn't seem disappointed that they were leaving before the others. In fact, she flashed Hank a wide smile. It was only then that it dawned on him what she had been intending. He shook his head at his own obliviousness.

As they walked to the car, Hank could hear one of the boys call from inside, "Mom! I can't sleep."

"Cool Jeep." Mo pushed the passenger seat forward with one hand as he hugged his carved pumpkin with the other. He climbed into the backseat, while Hank held the door until Siara was settled. On their drive home, Mo chattered about how much fun the evening had been.

Hank tried to figure out what to say to Siara but decided talking to her son presented less of a challenge. He glanced at the smiling boy in the rearview mirror. "Mo, that was great that you brought those pumpkins. And you grew them yourself. They were the hit of the party." Mo grinned at Hank in reply. Hank wished he could connect as easily with Siara as he seemed to with Mo.

Siara added, "Worth the hard work you put into growing them, I bet." She turned to Hank. "He did it all himself, from turning over the first shovel of dirt to harvesting them. When we get home, remind me, and we'll give you a few tomatoes from the last of the crop. There's no comparison between his home-grown tomatoes and the grocery store's."

"Speaking of no comparison—" Hank seized on the opening, but needed to clear his throat before continuing—"how about no comparison between your homemade rolls and any store-bought ones I've ever had."

Mo jumped in, "They're even better topped off with the raspberry jam she made this year."

Siara laughed. "Thank you, gentlemen. Guess I'll be making jam again next year, then." After a long pause, Siara said, "What a wonderful evening. They seem like good people."

Hank nodded thoughtfully.

Mo agreed. "I know Brian is cool from working with him, but I like Stephen and Amy, too. They didn't make me feel like I was one of the little kids."

After what seemed to Hank another uncomfortable pause in the conversation, Siara asked how well he knew the others.

"I've only known Tessa and Gwen from our discussion group in class. I met Brian one night when Gwen's car broke down, and I gave her a ride home. You see a whole different side of people at school than you do when you're in their homes." His thoughts drifted to the class. "We're all supposed to take what we learn in class about relationships and try it on our own families."

Mo yawned, then asked, "What family do you have to work on?"

Siara quickly corrected him. "Mo, that's a personal question. Sorry, Hank."

"That's all right. I don't mind." *At least it gives me something to say*. He gripped the steering wheel and nervously tapped it with his fingers. "I don't have any family and haven't had for quite a while. Not even a lady friend to get upset with me for analyzing her."

All three laughed.

"So I look back at growing up—try to make some sense out of those years. Figure out all the ways I'd like to do better for my own kids… if I ever have some."

"Me and Mom—"

"Mom and I," Siara interrupted automatically.

"Mom and I don't have any other family either. But we do all right."

Hank caught the pride in Siara's expression when she turned to wink at Mo. "We do even better than all right. We're happier than many people."

After more quiet moments, Mo set his jack o' lantern on the floor and lay down across the backseat. Hank's mind ground to a standstill around the words, *Say something, say something.*

With relief he finally parked the Jeep in front of the house Siara indicated. He hurried around to open the car door for her, but Siara had already stepped out and pulled the seat forward for Mo. Hank held the door and closed it for her instead, then walked them to the porch. After Siara unlocked the latch and Mo brushed between them into the house, she turned to Hank. "Can I give you a few rolls to take home as thanks for the ride?"

"Sure, that would be great."

Mo called out from the kitchen, "I'm getting you some of my tomatoes."

Hank forced himself to speak. "Siara, I didn't want to ask you in front of Mo, but I'd love to show him the ocean. Would you consider letting me take Mo to Seaside this Sunday?"

Siara's face lost all expression.

Her look and silence confused Hank until he realized she'd be uncomfortable about letting her son go off with someone she had just met. He thought he should have asked her to go to, but knew how much more uncomfortable he would be, not knowing what to say with her around.

Remembering his counselor's assignment, he plunged ahead. "Would you come, too?" *Now there's a bid for connection.*

Siara smiled and Hank really noticed her for the first time, from her white teeth to her smooth brown cheekbones and then to the gentlest eyes he had ever seen. Their color was so deep he couldn't tell where her iris ended and her pupils began. Those eyes pulled at him like magnets. He imagined bending closer to them for a kiss and then quickly looked down when he realized that he was staring. Suddenly he very much wanted Siara to come to the beach with him.

Please accept my bid. Don't reject or ignore it. Please don't say no.

Still Siara didn't answer, and Hank worried. *She's probably wondering if she can stand a whole day being with a man who doesn't know how to talk.*

Her decisive nod brought breath back to his lungs. "Thank you, Hank. How about if I pack a lunch?"

Relief flooded through him. "All right, but dinner's on me. Is nine too early?"

"Nine sounds great."

"Nine what?" Mo was back with a bag of tomatoes and bread rolls.

"Nine minutes until you jump in bed with teeth brushed. Then I'll tell you," his mom teased.

"Good night, Mr. Hank," Mo said.

"Good night, Mr. Mo. Good night, Siara. See you Sunday."

Hank whistled quietly on his way back to the Jeep. When he got home, he walked straight to the phone to call his grandmother and tell her about his day.

⌘ ⌘ ⌘

"Well, what did you think?" Tessa asked Joe after they sent Amy and

Stephen to bed and headed for their own room.

"Good game," Joe teased her.

"I meant, what did you think of the people?"

"I know, just giving you a hard time. They all seem nice."

He glanced at Tessa. She held his gaze and drummed her fingers against crossed arms. He wouldn't get away without saying more.

He raised his hands in surrender. "Brian's got a good little business going with his house remodeling. He's lucky he could move his business here when Gwen wanted to come to Portland for graduate school. Most jobs wouldn't have been that flexible."

Tessa folded down the bed covers. Joe sat in the bedroom chair and tugged at his shoelaces. "Hank's really quiet. At first he makes a person nervous, but then when he talks about his work at the hospital, or his volunteer time at the Youth Club, you realize he's got a lot of intelligence and depth."

Tessa sat across from him on the bed and tucked her feet under her. "Why nervous?"

"Oh, wondering what he's thinking, I suppose. I know you three are discussing each other's relationships."

She realized that Joe was afraid that other people knew about his problem. "That worries you, doesn't it?"

His jaw tensed, though he sat still staring at his shoes. "Our relationship is really private. I don't know what Brian thinks, but it bothers me that you're expected to talk to them about us. I got the feeling that Gwen could be pretty critical of Brian. I picture you and her having a gripe session about husbands, and Hank listening and feeling sorry for you both. Then tonight we're all thrown together—" he tossed his socks at the hamper and missed—"and I wonder what they know about you and me."

Tessa knew Joe's masculinity was vulnerable here, so she chose her words carefully. "Yes, Gwen does sometimes go beyond the privacy boundaries that I'd be comfortable with, but don't you trust me not to betray your confidences? Do you really think I'd sit and gripe about you? I'd never talk to people about things that I know would upset you."

Tessa walked to the hamper and picked up the socks to put them in. "Maybe tonight would have been easier for you if I'd told you what kind of things I talk about with them. For instance, I told them that you're always stressed about having too many things to do, so I offered to do the bills and checkbook so you could work on the haunted house with the kids."

He followed her. He pulled off his shirt and dropped it into the hamper before he wrapped his arms around her. "Thank you, by the way."

"For the socks or for paying the bills?"

"Both."

She looked at him seriously. "Sometimes it's hard to know what to talk about without getting too private. Right from the start, though, our professor made it clear that we're only asked to talk about things we're comfortable with. We don't need to divulge any deep, dark secrets. If we want, we can simply report what we're learning from the writer we're studying."

She could see that Joe wasn't convinced. His arms were tense around her and his jaw still clenched.

"Joe, I know that what we're struggling with right now is way too sensitive to be talked about casually. I don't, and won't talk to them about our sex life. Remember, I even asked you before journaling about it, knowing the professor would read what I wrote."

She reached up and cupped his face in her hands. His jaw relaxed and his hazel eyes softened. Those eyes were what had first attracted her to him. Joe took her hands in his, his hands so strong and warm. She missed that warmth.

"At first I wanted to say no," he said, "but I suppose you need someone to vent to sometimes. Since she's a professional, and I'm not likely to ever meet her, I figured that was all right. But this course makes me feel like a frog your class will dissect. Maybe I'm afraid you'll get disillusioned from studying the perfect marriage and comparing it to ours."

She slipped her hands from his and wrapped her arms around his waist. She leaned back to look up at him but was very conscious of their thighs and hips touching.

"Honey, we study seriously troubled relationships. In fact, the more I learn, the more I worry that I'm not quite strong enough to be a counselor. You and the kids are pretty easy; I don't have much experience working with difficult people." She realized she was focusing on her worries rather than his, made a mental note to talk to Marjorie, and shifted back to reassuring him.

"But my classes make me all the more grateful to be married to such a wonderful guy. We've got it good. Sure, some things we both wish were better, but we're working on them. Do you know how loved I feel, knowing all you're doing to tackle the libido problem? Especially knowing how hard it is for you to even talk about it?"

Joe visibly relaxed into the love behind Tessa's words. Even his thigh muscles softened.

"There's something else, too," she said. "We're focusing on changing ourselves, not our partners. I'm the only one I can change, so I need to realize what I contribute to a problem and fix that. I took on the finances when I realized I've let you do more than your share in that area. I'm trying to change myself to be a better partner for you and for our marriage."

"Don't change too much; I love you just the way you are." Joe kissed her to seal the deal. "You know what else I thought about Hank?"

"No idea."

"I have a lot to be thankful for. You and the kids, you make my life good. I don't want to ever be alone like him. I can't risk losing you."

Tessa leaned into Joe, needing to feel her chest against his and her cheek against his shoulder.

He rested his head on hers, and she took shelter within the sanctuary of their marriage. *Losing you. That's what scares me the most, too.*

Twenty-six

If at first we don't succeed...

The next morning Joe called the clinic and arranged for them to see Dr. Zernick over Joe's lunch hour. As they waited in the doctor's office, Tessa tried to draw confidence from the diplomas and certificates framed on the wall. She had hardly been able to sleep, praying that the emotional unity she had felt with Joe could overflow into their physical relationship. But prayers weren't always answered the way she wanted. She knew that only too well from sitting in this office two years ago, begging the Lord not to let the lump in her breast be cancerous.

When the doctor finally did hurry in to see Joe, he brought with him the same spirit of reassurance and determination that had helped her cope with the diagnosis of cancer. She wondered if someday she could bring that confidence to her own clients. He had fought right along with her to overcome the illness. She had to believe that he would do so again. He would figure out what had come between her and Joe, and he would know how to fix it. She hoped.

Tessa heard a new commitment in Joe's voice as he thanked Dr. Zernick for squeezing them in.

"I know you said to give this prescription a few weeks for it to hit full strength, but before we go any further, is there any chance it could make my libido even worse? I like how much better my mood seems. I'm having fun with my kids and work's not so bad, but what little sexual interest I gained when we started the pills to help my sleep seems to have disappeared since we started the antidepressant."

Tessa held her breath, once again grasping for hope, but her confidence wavered as the doctor looked chagrined.

"Yes, some antidepressants cause sexual side effects. I hoped that wouldn't prove the case for you but sounds like we've made at least that part of your life worse. I can look into an alternative."

I should hope so. Tessa couldn't believe he hadn't considered that possibility before prescribing. She found herself irritated with men in general, until Joe said, "Thanks, Doctor. I have to admit the antidepressant is an improvement, but it's not worth making things worse between Tessa and me."

She looked at her husband, as he relinquished his pride and privacy for her sake, and immediately regretted her irritation. She resolved to be more understanding and patient.

"I'll get back to you, Joe. I have a colleague I'd like to consult for a recommendation." He shook hands with Joe and Tessa and left with what seemed to her to be an air of retreat.

The two sat a minute before either moved. Then Tessa straightened her back and laid a hand on Joe's knee. "When we got married, we invited the Lord into our relationship, believing He'd be there to help us through the rough spots. I never thought we'd ask Him into our sex life." She gave Joe a lopsided grin. "But I know He'll be with us in this."

Joe put his hand over Tessa's and gave hers a squeeze.

By the time Tessa arrived home, the answering machine was blinking with a message from the doctor, asking Joe to call him. Since their children weren't home, as soon as Joe came home from work they made the call on the speaker phone.

"Joe, I have to apologize," Dr. Zernick said. "According to my colleague in urology, I never should have tried the antidepressant on you that I did. Another medication is preferred whenever a person already has libido issues. I'm putting a prescription for it into the computer. Take it a couple of weeks, and then let me know if we're on the right track."

Tessa's hope rose, and from the hug Joe gave her, she knew he felt the same.

⌘ ⌘ ⌘

Marjorie managed to unlock her front door while balancing a stack of papers, but then, as Nutmeg welcomed her by weaving between her steps, she nearly dropped them all. She slid her armload onto the last remaining area of the dining room table where the tablecloth still peeked through. Embarrassed at the piles of mail, papers, and books, she promised herself to spend the next Saturday morning clearing away the chaos.

The newly arrived offenders were the final papers from her Advanced Family Therapy class, a two-credit class that finished sooner than the regular three-credit semester classes.

The teacher side of Marjorie felt sad to see another group of students move on. She always wished for time to teach them more. However, she was sorry for another reason as well. She had come to look forward to the letters from Colm she found in her mailbox at work nearly every time she checked. Now without this Tuesday class, she would only be at the school twice a week, which would mean more days between receiving letters.

She hadn't given him her home address. Receiving the letters at school made Colm seem more like a colleague than...

She pushed that thought away as she took Colm's latest pages from the pocket before she hung up her coat. Marjorie knew they could have sent emails but preferred the satisfaction of holding the paper he had touched.

Dear Marjorie,

I brought a picture with me that I treasure from Killarney. It's a photograph I took one misty morning, of the River Nore. I wish I could show you, but I'll try to describe it for you. The colors are all muted grays and greens. You can see the river, but only dimly glimpse the trees beyond, through the fog. A lone woman is silhouetted, standing on the riverbank. You can't tell if she is facing the camera or the river. The picture, like the land itself, imparts a mystic feeling.

I took the photograph a few days before we knew of my wife Dympna's illness, so it reminds me of the last of our happier times. After she died, I imagined the shadowy woman to be my wife, looking away from me, looking beyond, perhaps to the heaven that now separates us.

Many emotions have become part of my love for that photo: the nostalgia for the happy days with Dympna; the melancholy of grieving for her; a gentle affection for the peacefulness of a soft, misty day; and my soul-deep love for my country. Now, however, I discover a new emotion when I look to that landscape. It is you I see there, facing me. I am time-bound, much like that photograph, hoping that you will take a step toward me.

> Your friend,
> Colm

Up to this point, Colm's and Marjorie's letters had remained light and newsy. He wrote of missing the obligatory teapot, symbolic of the spirit of hospitality in every Irish inn. She told of the Sunday night phone calls from her daughters. He praised the Portland public transportation system. She suggested he visit a local pumpkin patch.

Perhaps due to the new tone of Colm's letter, maybe because of the foggy photograph she could imagine so easily—for whatever reason—she sat, not at the computer, but at the table. She closed her eyes and mentally read through the growth cards. By now she knew the remaining ones by heart. In her mind she held the card with Colm's name, grasped it between her fingers to tear apart her fear, but couldn't.

She opened her eyes and let out a deep breath. Finally, she pushed a pile of papers aside and wrote to him in her own hand.

> Dear Colm,
> Your letter was beautiful, and I'm touched that you shared your heartache with me. You give me courage to try to tell you about mine.

Marjorie's hand trembled as she tried to figure what to write, how to put into words what had to be said. She was determined to take this first step, no matter how small. She continued, hoping he would understand the tangle of her feelings.

> Two years ago, when Michael died, it was the beginning of summer, the summer that he and I were finally to take a trip to Europe. With my clients transferred to colleagues, and no classes scheduled, we were ready for vacation. We were to leave as soon as

Michael returned from one last business trip to California. He never came home.

The finality of those words made her throat constrict and her lower lip quiver. She cupped her forehead in her hand. When would she ever get beyond this?

But he needed to know. She squeezed her eyes tight to clear them and then she wrote:

> On his way back to the hotel after a dinner meeting, a high school girl, who was celebrating her graduation in the brand-new sport utility vehicle her parents had given her, broadsided the taxi. Her airbag deployed, leaving her with only minor injuries. The taxi driver suffered a concussion. Michael died of a heart attack before the ambulance team could get him out of the car, but not before he whispered his last message of love for me and our girls.
>
> I told the friends who called or visited the next few weeks that I was managing all right and was spending my days going through Michael's things. One of the few lies I've told in my adult life.

She remembered those dreadful days so vividly. She'd bury her nose into his shirts in the closet, taking in the smell she dearly missed. She couldn't box them. She tried to gather his bathroom supplies to donate but couldn't bear the emptiness of his shelves. She only managed to move a few things out of the main rooms of the house and into their closet: his slacks from the laundry room, the last issue of *Motor Trend Magazine*, the suit bag that somehow made its way home from the California hotel.

She couldn't part with anything of Michael's except to give to family members. The girls took his car to Seattle. Colleen and Sophie both offered to change plans and spend the summer home with her, but she convinced them she'd be fine, as long as they came often to visit. The car would help them do that.

It took a full year before she surfaced above the worst of the shock and could return to work, determined to rebuild her life by focusing on her students and clients.

Marjorie realized she had been sitting with the pen poised above the paper. Michael's suitcase still remained packed in her closet; his aftershave loitered on the bathroom shelf. How could she weigh her undeniable attraction to a man she had only met briefly against the years of connection with Michael? Tears blurred her vision, but she quickly wrote:

> I'm still in my own fog, Colm, and to step out of it, I'd have to leave Michael behind.
> I'm sorry,
> Marjorie

⌘ ⌘ ⌘

Even by Wednesday afternoon the glow of satisfaction that Gwen felt from the success of the party hadn't dimmed. She could hardly wait to hear from Hank about how the ride home with Siara had gone. She could tell Brian had enjoyed the evening. Maybe this would be the beginning of sharing fun with friends they both liked. She could hear the boys giggling, and the world was looking like a brighter place as she moved clothes from the washer to the dryer.

At least until she heard a *thunk*, followed by silence, and then the mingled shrieks of all three boys.

Her heart lurched, and her mouth went dry. She dropped the laundry and ran to the family room. She was met partway by Mickey and Joe Pat, who both tried to tell her what happened while they grabbed her hands and pulled her faster. They all stopped at the sight of Sean, crying on the floor next to the coffee table, both hands on his forehead covered in blood.

Gwen felt faint but refused to give into it. She grabbed Sean up into her arms and ran to the kitchen sink on shaky legs. She grabbed paper towels and ran them under cold water, while holding Sean prone on the counter. She tried to dab away the blood to see how serious the wound was. Sean was still screaming and trying to keep her hands away.

Mickey's voice was strained as he explained, "Sean grabbed our movie and ran away. We chased him, and he tripped and hit his head on the coffee table."

The bleeding wasn't slowing, and the cut looked serious. Gwen tossed the paper towels into the garbage, grabbed a clean dishtowel, folded it with one hand, and pressed it onto Sean's head. "Mickey! Get my cell phone. Joe Pat, grab my purse. And your coats. We need to get Sean to the hospital.

"Sean! Be quiet and listen to me!" Her voice must have communicated the urgency she felt, because Sean settled into obedient stillness. "I need you to hold this towel and push on it until I can tie it onto your head. Can you do that for me?"

His wide eyes and shaky lower lip told Gwen she was frightening him worse. She forced herself to smile. "It's okay, Sean. We're going to make you a turban like Aladdin, and the doctor will help it stop hurting. All right?"

He nodded slightly and put his hands up to the bandage. Gwen rested his head on the counter and grabbed a roll of masking tape. She wrapped another dish towel around his head and then wound the tape around enough times to hold the bandage tight.

"We're getting you into your car seat. Then you're going to push on that turban until we get to the doctor, okay?" She lifted him and hurried to the car with the two older boys following meekly.

"I tried to call Daddy," Mickey told her, "but he's not answering."

"Keep trying. For now we're on our own."

She felt more alone than ever before.

⌘ ⌘ ⌘

Hours later, and with what surely must be the last of her energy, Gwen closed the door to the car gently, hoping not to wake little Sean, who was finally asleep in his car seat. She'd ask Brian to carry him into the house, seat and all. Surprisingly, both older boys were cooperating and closed their doors carefully, too. Gwen felt completely drained. Her stomach rumbled, and Mickey whispered, "Yeah, I'm hungry, too. I hope Daddy made dinner."

When she opened the door, the scene froze her mind. Brian was stretched out in his recliner with a beer can in his hand and a second on its side on the floor. The toys that had been left out upon their hurried departure were still strewn across furniture and floor. The television boomed at her, the base tones reverberating at the same frequency as the throbbing in her head. Dusk had made the room dark, lit only by the blue flickering of a scene from *Lord of the Rings: The Two Towers*.

To top it all off, Brian smiled at her, paused the movie, and said, "Hi, babe, I've been waiting to show you this great scene. Frodo and Samwise—"

The frozen moment thawed, and Gwen's temper hit white-hot. "Where have you been? We needed you! I tried over and over to call you!" She didn't care if neighbors three blocks away could hear her.

Brian matched her volume. "What's with you? Get off my back, Gwen!" He slammed down his beer and stood, leaning toward her like a mad dog straining at his chain.

"Off your back? Why don't you get off your backside? Look at this place. You were lying here boozing and watching TV, while your son was at the—"

"Quiet! You're hurting my heart!" Mickey stood between them, raising his hands like a traffic guard, as if to stop them both.

His words stunned both parents to silence.

Gwen watched Brian look from her to Mickey to Joe Pat, then scan for Sean. He patted the pocket where he kept his phone, and she watched the confusion in his face turn to question and then drain to fear. Before he could ask, she decided he didn't deserve to know.

She turned to Joe Pat and said, with a soft voice that quivered, "Go get Sean a clean shirt and then meet me and Mickey in the car." Joe Pat ran upstairs, and Mickey turned away from his dad and toward her. Without a sound he walked to the door, his shoulders seeming to struggle under a heavy weight. Gwen didn't meet Brian's eyes, or turn as he called after her, but followed Mickey out the door. When Joe Pat was buckled in his seat, she drove away without a glance back toward the house.

Twenty-seven

…Try, try again.

That same afternoon, Marjorie followed a strolling couple on the tree-lined path from her campus office to her car. The young man let go of his girlfriend's hand and put his arm gently around her back. She rested her head momentarily on his shoulder as she moved closer.

Marjorie longed for the feeling of Michael's arm around her shoulders. The pain of missing him struck instantly, as hard as it had the first few weeks after his death. She inhaled sharply, and tears rose in her eyes. As she had countless times before, she talked herself through the ache. It hurt so badly because she loved so deeply. Should she have loved less so that she would hurt less now? She knew the answer.

The fall smell of decaying leaves and wisps of wood smoke reminded her of incense and turned her mind to prayer.

Thank You, Friend, for my time with Michael, even though it ended sooner than I would have chosen. Thank You, too, for Sophie and Colleen.

You've given me so many blessings. I loved seeing the formation of geese fly over this morning. You know how much they thrill me, and You arranged it so I stepped out of the car in time to hear them and look up. Thank You for my work and my students. They give my life meaning.

Please, show me how to accept my life as it is. I miss Michael desperately. I want to feel his arm around my back again.

The sudden memory of Colm's strong arm against her back as he helped her after her fall sent a sensation through her as if God had

172

hugged her Himself.

The couple stopped beside the young woman's car and kissed each other good-bye. Marjorie managed a smile as she passed them, though a few unshed tears softened the scene.

The drive home didn't dispel Marjorie's loneliness. She walked through her house, touching the reminders of Michael in each room: his favorite chair in the living room, their wedding portrait on the stairway wall, the picture of their happy family at the top of the stairs, their bed, his pillow.

A draft from the master bath distracted her, and she went in to find she had left the window open when she aired out the room after her shower. As she leaned down on the handles, the motion recalled a forgotten moment from her last Ladies' Day Out with her girls.

After hugging Sophie and Colleen good-bye at the door, she had felt a draft from the same window and went up to close it. The girls were talking outside their car, which was parked below the window.

"Do you think Mom will ever remarry?" Sophie had asked.

"Doesn't sound like it."

"I didn't like her talking about that Colm guy, but I hate to think of her alone the rest of her life. Daddy wouldn't want her to be lonely."

"She's got tons to offer," Colleen had replied. "Somebody's out there who could use her love."

Sophie shook her head slowly, and they both climbed into the car.

The memory reverberated in Marjorie's heart like a door blown open to an abandoned room, fresh air dispelling stagnant haze. She went to her briefcase, pulled out the growth cards, and tore in half the one that said simply, *Disappointing my girls.*

⌘ ⌘ ⌘

Forty-five minutes after Gwen had left Brian, she sat in a booth at Chuck E. Cheese's restaurant with a slice of pizza untouched on her plate. The boys were eating their pieces. Sean seemed to have forgotten the bandage above his eye and though pale, he appeared to be feeling fine. Gwen, on the other hand, felt like she was the one who needed stitches to hold her together. Her mind felt heavy and slow to react when she heard Brian's voice.

"Hi, guys." He pulled a chair up to their table. The two younger boys hugged him and jabbered about the games they had already played before the pizza came. Mickey didn't say anything and didn't look up from his plate.

Brian looked haggard when he spoke to Gwen. "Babe, I'm really sorry. I'd left my phone in the truck, still set to silent after a meeting with the realtor, so I didn't know you needed me."

"We did all right without you," Mickey answered when Gwen didn't reply.

"I'm sure you were a big help to Mom, but you shouldn't have had to do without me. I'm sorry, Mickey. Sean, buddy, are you all right? What happened to your head?"

Sean reached up and touched the bandage gently. "I falled down. I bonked the table."

Gwen winced. Brian's face looked as wretched as she hoped he felt.

"Ouch! Did the doctor fix it?"

"Sean fell asleep while the doctor pushed the needle right through his skin," Joe Pat answered while Sean nodded. "It was cool."

The picture flashed back into Gwen's mind. Her baby on the examining table, his arms tucked into a pillowcase that they had then laid him on to restrain him. The doctor and two nurses working quickly to stop the bleeding.

"C'mon, guys, let's go spend the rest of our tokens." Mickey led his brothers back to the games.

"How did you figure it out?" Gwen finally asked.

Brian sat down across from her at the table. "I realized how much I should have been doing to help instead of watching TV, so I started clearing and washing off the counters and then saw the bloody towels in the garbage. It really scared me."

"Me, too. Sorry I yelled at you." She was, mostly.

"I deserved it. It must have felt like the last straw for you, coming home hungry and tired after an afternoon like that and seeing me lying there. I wish, at least, I'd made dinner for you. Or had the phone with me. I'm really sorry, babe."

174

"This parenting is harder than it looks."

"I could be more help, couldn't I?"

"And I could be more patient. I'm just so tired." Every part of her body felt like it was filled with sand.

"Gweny, we need to change things so we can both be happier. For the boys' sake and for us, too." Now she faced the mental image of Mickey standing between them, his hands outstretched and his little heart hurting.

Brian took her hand in his. "We can't keep up this fighting. The way Mickey looked at me before he left...it scares the boys." She watched him swallow before he admitted, "Scares me, too."

She hated to put her thought into words. "Should we break up so they don't have to listen to us? Share custody but live in different houses?"

To her relief, he shook his head adamantly. "Just the thought of you finding someone else...the boys with some stepdad instead of me...it drives me nuts." Brian's eyes lit excitedly. "That's what I was trying to tell you when you came in the house."

She felt her expression harden, and he ducked sheepishly. "Just listen, Gwen. I admit I was escaping into Tolkien's world, but this one scene...I wanted to show it to you because it made me feel..."

She couldn't resist. "All sentimental like you usually get after a couple of beers."

"Well, yeah, I suppose. But Samwise says to Frodo something like—" here Brian put on his best storyteller voice—"'It's like in the great stories, Mr. Frodo, the ones that really matter. Those were the stories that stayed with you, that meant something. Folk in those stories had lots of chances of turning back, only they didn't. They kept going. Because they were holding on to something.'"

Brian reddened but lowered his voice and kept on. "I was feeling like Frodo and wanting to know the answer when he asked, 'What are we holding on to, Sam?'"

He looked at Gwen with expectation, so she rolled her eyes and asked, "Okay, Frodo, what did Sam say?"

He moved to sit next to her. "That there's some good in this world, Mrs. Frodo, and it's worth fighting for. Let's start fighting together, babe."

They sat in silence.

Finally she said, "I wish we could go back to our dating days. I was more fun, then."

"That's it! We need to date again. Let's get a babysitter once a week and get away!"

How did he have the energy to sound excited? She shrugged. "I've thought of that, but kids over sixteen can drive and get better jobs. Kids under sixteen probably couldn't handle all our boys."

"What would you think of asking Siara? She could bring Mo over to help, and maybe I could do some work on her house in exchange." Gwen felt a stab of fear at the thought of Brian in another woman's home, but frankly, she didn't have any resistance left.

"We've got to do something. Mickey took our fight hard today, and I've been sitting here with no idea how to make things better." Maybe Brian had a point. She imagined going on dates with him again, her boys and Siara waving happily at the door. Siara did seem like a decent person. Certainly a good mom.

Gwen finally met Brian's eyes. "Then along you come, and you bring some hope with you. You're still exactly what I need, you know that?"

"I'm a jerk, but I love you, babe." He slid his arm around her shoulders.

She rested her head against his neck. "I'm a zombie, but I love you, too." She paused. "Brian?"

"Yeah?"

"Don't call me 'babe' anymore, okay? It makes me feel like a talking pig."

He laughed and gently drew her closer. "Ok, how about Bambi? Ariel? Nemo?"

Twenty-eight

Love will find a way.

Hank parked two blocks away from Siara's house on Sunday morning. In his nervousness about the day, he had arrived fifteen minutes early. He knew he'd be fine with Mo—he was comfortable with boys Mo's age at the Youth Club—but the thought of a day with Siara made him swallow hard.

To distract himself, Hank reviewed his careful plans for the perfect day. He'd rely on Mo's excitement to help with conversation on the way. Once in Seaside, he'd use the new digital camera he bought to capture Mo's expression when he would first see the ocean.

Hank could imagine the scene. He'd park the Jeep in a lot with a view of the ocean, miles of sand reaching out to meet white-edged cobalt waves, which, in turn, would stretch to meet the knife-sharp edge of a sapphire sky.

Mo would whisper, "Awesome." Then, like a child who realizes the presents beneath the tree wait for him, he would spring to life and leave Hank and Siara rushing to grab the camera and to catch up with him as he ran across the sand toward the water.

After kites, the arcade, strolling on the promenade, and a candle-lit dinner, it would be dark by the time he drove them home. He'd walk Siara to her door. The magic of the perfect day at the beach might even lead to a good-night kiss. Hank sighed at the thought, then jumped to realize nine o'clock had come and passed five minutes ago.

As he drove up to their house, Mo burst from the door, every bit as excited as Hank hoped. He helped Siara stow the picnic cooler and their gear in the back. When they took their seats in the Jeep, her perfume reminded Hank of the little purple flowers that grew near his apartment in the spring. He knew he should say something but could only smile. Her scent had made his mind go blank.

Mo didn't quite keep the conversation flowing as steadily as Hank had hoped, but he did ask occasional questions about what they would do and see. Siara seemed content to listen while Hank enumerated the small town's tourist attractions.

When Hank turned his head to glance back at Mo with his answers, he took in how fresh and feminine Siara looked, seated next to him. Her dark hair was gathered to one side of her head and fell thickly in front of her near shoulder. Sunlight made it shine. Imagining it mink-soft, Hank resisted his impulse to stroke it. Shaken, he shifted his attention back to Mo.

"Mom wouldn't let me bring a swimsuit. She said the water'd be too cold."

"She's right. With luck the beach can be beautiful in October, though not warm enough to wade or swim. We can build something in the sand, though, if it isn't raining, and I brought three kites for us to fly."

"I tried to fly a kite once, but I couldn't run fast enough to get it to go up."

"At the beach you won't need to run at all. I'll show you how to get it to catch the wind." Hank pictured himself on the beach, his arm around Mo's shoulder. He liked the fatherly feeling it gave him.

"I sure hope it doesn't rain," Mo said.

Hank had worried about the same scenario. "Me too, but if it does, we'll spend our time in the shops and at the arcade playing video games. You're not too old for a carousel ride, are you?"

"I don't know." Mo shrugged, obviously not thrilled with the idea. Hank's confidence about relating to children eroded slightly.

Hank glanced over at Siara and caught her eye. It glinted with nearly as much excitement as Mo's had before the carousel blunder. The childlike joy he saw there made Hank vow to do all he could to make this a happy day for all of them.

A ninety-minute ride through farms and forests brought them to Seaside. Hank had held out hope for a beautiful day even as clouds gathered in the Coast Range, but now, driving through the little town, he had to admit blue skies weren't likely. When he parked in the lot with a view of the ocean, low-lying clouds blurred the distinction between water and sky, both only incrementally different shades of bleak nickel gray.

He turned to Siara, dreading to see her disappointment. She seemed to be taking it bravely.

Mo peered out the window and asked, "That's it?"

Hank's heart sank. Not exactly a Kodak moment.

Sand and waves did call to the boy, and soon they all stood outside the Jeep, donning jackets and gathering their paraphernalia. Mo ran ahead with two drink thermoses, Siara carried the tube of kites and a blanket, and Hank followed them, his arms around the picnic cooler.

As Hank approached the spot Siara had selected to spread the blanket, Mo glanced up and shouted, "Mr. Hank, watch—"

But the warning came too late. Hank's foot caught on a large piece of driftwood he hadn't seen because of the load he was carrying. Cooler, food, plates, utensils, and Hank tumbled forward onto the sand. As Siara and Mo scrambled to help him, Hank wondered which was worse, the pain in his left wrist, or the shattered dream of his perfect day at the beach.

"You okay?" Siara asked, her worried eyes seeking his as she tried to help him up. Her eyes became a star-consuming black hole and he a willing captive.

He had to blink to clear his mind. "Bruised ego." He laughed and hoped she didn't notice the wince as he tested his wrist. Sprained, he figured. That would certainly add a challenge to kite flying.

Together they gathered their lunch, brushing off what sand they could. They shared turkey cushioned in Siara's homemade rolls and drained the thermos of hot chocolate. Hank chided himself for not preparing for weather the way Siara had when she packed both iced tea and hot cocoa.

They crunched carrots from Mo's garden, no one commenting on any extra grittiness. At Mo's urging, Hank dipped them in a container of peanut butter and was surprised by the tasty combination, but the pauses in chatter while Mo chewed made Hank uneasy. Siara sat quietly, and Hank suspected she was trying very hard not to show what she was really feeling.

When they were finished with lunch, Hank helped Siara return the leftovers to the basket. Then, with a few instructions, he gave her charge of the digital camera while he made good on his promise to show Mo how to fly a kite without running. Hank relaxed as he focused on Mo, rather than Siara.

"Stand with your back to the wind, Mo, and I'll walk the kite away from you while you unwind the string." About twenty feet from Mo, Hank faced him with the blue and red kite held out between them, stepped back to draw the line taut, and caught his breath at the stab of pain in his wrist. Determined not to let his sprain ruin the day, he bit his tongue, lifted the kite above his head, and released it. The wind caught the kite, and it rose immediately.

"This is so cool!" yelled Mo. The pure joy in the boy's voice encouraged Hank.

"You can decide how much string to let out. If it starts to come down, pull back a bit, and it'll rise again."

Siara was intent on photographing Mo's delight in his soaring kite, which left Hank free to watch her. The uncharacteristic carefree look on her face made him wish he had another camera to capture her happiness and hold it forever.

"Your turn!" He laughed, as he gingerly drew a second kite from a large cardboard tube. "This one has two strings so it can do stunts." Before long Siara learned how to make the stunt kite dip and spiral in the air by timing how she pulled on the control in one hand or the other.

Mo didn't want to be outdone, so they traded kites and Hank taught him the same moves. While Mo practiced, Hank tried to attach a parachute device to the single-string kite Siara now held. The little parachute, weighted with a Life Saver candy, was supposed to catch the wind and rise up the kite string until it hit a stopper on the line. Then it should release from the string and glide downwind. However, without full use of his left hand, Hank was having trouble attaching it to the kite string.

Siara watched his fumbling and then saw its cause. "Hank! Your left wrist is twice the size of the right. Oh, you hurt it when you fell.

Why didn't you tell us?"

Mo was distracted from his kite by his mother's words. Looking at her, he didn't pull out of the figure eight he had been trying to master. The stunt kite crashed into the couple, its full force striking Siara's head and knocking her into Hank before it hit the sand in pieces.

Mo's face fell as suddenly. "Oh, no, I broke the kite!" Then, seeing the effects, he sputtered, "Mom, are you all right?"

Hank steadied himself and Siara. He gently moved her hand away from her forehead and examined a scrape that was already swelling to walnut size.

Siara assured both Hank and Mo she was fine. "Just a little bump. No real harm done."

Hank guided her back to the blanket, gave Mo his handkerchief, and sent him to the water to get it wet. He couldn't believe how badly everything was going. He looked at Siara sitting wounded and Mo running to the water having first brushed away tears.

Hank's teeth ground against each other. This was his fault. He had imagined it all so much better. This morning he had let himself picture a good-night kiss. Now he'd be lucky if either of them even spoke to him on the ride home, let alone ever again.

Mo returned, soaked up to his waist. "A wave knocked me over. I was bending to get this wet, and I lost my balance." Hank shook his head, incredulous, and turned to give the handkerchief to Siara to hold against the swelling. At the sight of Mo's pants, Siara squeezed her lips tight and put her head down.

Hank's heart lurched. Siara had covered her face, and her shoulders were shaking. He'd never forgive himself for making this gentle lady cry.

"Siara, I'm so sorry." He wanted to hold her and comfort her but didn't dare.

She looked up at him with tears streaming down her face...but laughing! Hank was dumbfounded. He looked at Mo, whose worried expression quickly gave way to a grin and then giggles. He looked back at Siara. She pointed at Mo's pants, trying to say something but laughing too hard to talk.

She lifted her right hand for him to help her up, so he reached for her with his left and winced. She looked like she struggled for a moment to become serious but gave up, changed the handkerchief to the other hand and, gasping to catch her breath, stretched out her left hand to him. He shrugged, chuckled, and helped her up with his right hand. Their hilarity was contagious, and before long Hank was holding his sore arm against his stomach to ease his side ache as he struggled to breathe between laughs.

Eventually the kites were stowed in the tube, the blanket folded, and Mo loaded down. Hank and Siara carried the picnic cooler to the Jeep together, one on each side, both nursing their wounds with the other hand. Mo changed pants, shoes, and socks when he got to the car, and Hank again marveled that Siara came as prepared as an Eagle Scout.

They spent the afternoon exploring Seaside's Broadway Street shops, then started back toward Portland, the two-lane highway winding through dense coastal forest. At milepost eighteen, Hank turned off the road and parked, assuring his guests that dinner at a family-built log lodge, Camp 18, would end the day on a better note. They walked to the door and Siara chortled as she read the sign on the door, CLOSED FOR A PRIVATE PARTY.

"Of course," Hank groaned. "What did we expect?"

They drove farther, with Hank racking his memory to recall another impressive restaurant available before Portland. Finally, knowing they would rather not wait for a fancier choice, he gave up and turned off at a Dairy Queen with yet another look of apology to Siara. Mo was delighted.

They hadn't really had much opportunity for conversation, what with all the calamities at the beach. Now, facing Siara across the table, Hank once again worried about what to say. To his dismay, Mo filled the conversation gaps with a comedy review of the disasters of the day. Once back in the car, however, Mo fell almost instantly asleep in the backseat. The quiet of the ride home made Hank all the more nervous. In the dark he couldn't see whether Siara looked as uncomfortable as he felt.

He was still trying to come up with some intelligent comment when she broke the silence. "Did you go to the beach with your family as a boy?"

182

Hank cringed. *What do I tell Siara about my childhood?* Taking a deep breath, he ignored the emptiness that gnawed whenever he considered his childhood. "My family was my dad and me, from the time I was about three. He told me my mom had died..."

In the dark and with his eyes on the road while he drove, Hank found it easier to talk to Siara than he expected. When he had brought his story up to the point of his visit with his grandmother, Siara looked at him with moist eyes.

"What does your grandma look like?"

"Brown hair, green eyes, and taller than I expected. She kind of leans forward, but not from age. Gave me a feeling of her wanting to be close to me."

Siara glanced back at Mo, and Hank realized she was checking to make sure that he was asleep. "My grandmother is the one I miss the most in my family. She had warm eyes that held her smile long after her lips relaxed." Hank listened while, in a soft, wistful voice, she told of a close, religious family and a happy childhood. "It all changed when I had to tell them I was pregnant. My father couldn't accept it and wouldn't even listen to how it happened. He sent me away at seventeen and told me never to return. So I haven't."

Siara talked the rest of the way home about her younger sister and two brothers, both sets of grandparents, and numerous aunts, uncles, and cousins. She laughed about the pranks her brothers used to play on her, but her voice faltered when she talked about sharing a room with her sister.

"And you haven't had contact with them for all these years now?" he asked when Siara paused, lost in thought.

"Actually, I talk to my mother on her birthday each year. I call after Papa leaves for work at his jewelry shop. We both cry, and then she tells me what has happened in their lives over the year. She told me about my grandmother's death and about my sister going off to college. I tell her about Mo."

"You must be proud to talk about how well you've done by yourself. Mo's a great little guy."

"I am proud of him, and we have a good life together." Her voice had a pensive tone that made Hank look at her.

"But?"

She glanced at Mo, then faced forward again, squared her shoulders back, and smiled resolutely. "We're fine. I feel grateful for what I have."

Hank was surprised. *Grateful? She's lost her whole family and had to struggle to support herself and a child.* She probably hadn't even been able to finish high school. He looked in his rearview mirror. On the other hand, he'd give his schooling and his financial security to have what she had asleep in the backseat.

Hank looked at Siara. She understood family heartache. He suddenly felt completely at ease with her. "I see what you mean."

He wished he could reach over and put his hand on hers, but he decided he better keep his uninjured hand on the wheel. They'd had enough accidents to last a long time.

Mo awoke as the Jeep stopped at his house. "Awesome day. Thanks, Mr. Hank." He sleepily crawled from the backseat, over his mother, and out her door.

"Yes, thank you, Hank." She squeezed Hank's good hand, and then helped him carry the cooler to their door. She gave Mo the key and then took the cooler from Hank. He looked at the container in her hands. Even if the day had gone as perfectly as he planned, there'd be no hope for a kiss with that between them. But it had been far from perfect.

"I'm really sorry," he said one last time. There'd be no second date after a first one like this. "You were great about everything." He ducked his head. "Good night."

Hank turned to go, but Siara said quickly, "Hank?"

He looked at her, and her eyes twinkled. "It's my turn to provide a meal. Can you come over for a dinner soon?"

"You're kidding. After how today went, you'd be willing?"

Siara nodded and raised a lopsided grin. "I haven't laughed so hard in years."

Hank's heart soared. Even his head felt light. If it weren't for the sprained wrist, he might have cartwheeled down the sidewalk.

They compared schedules. Siara worked every weekday, arrived home around six, helped Mo with homework and spent time with him until he went to bed. Hank worked an irregular schedule of nights, with afternoons at the Youth Club and evenings either at class or studying. Saturdays he spent a full day at the club. Sundays he usually hiked. They settled on Friday, when Hank would leave the club earlier than usual, and neither Hank nor Mo would have to do homework.

"Well, good night, Siara."

"Good night. Thank you, again."

With the picnic cooler still between them, Hank just beamed and turned back to his Jeep. He had quaked at the thought of spending one day with Siara. Now he wondered how he'd wait until Friday.

⌘ ⌘ ⌘

The next day Hank had a return appointment with John Stein. Hank felt no reticence this time as he started his session. Today his therapist would see him as a success.

As soon as Hank was seated in the leather chair he announced, "I made a bid for connection, had a date, and even made a second one!"

"I'm impressed. Clients don't often take homework assignments that seriously." John Stein sat back and crossed his legs. "Tell me more."

Hank recounted the Monday Night Football party and admitted he had some helpful nudges from his classmates. Then he told about the day at the beach and how, though things couldn't have gone worse, it turned into a success.

"For a while there it looked like a second date wouldn't happen. Not just because of everything going wrong, but even when we agreed on a second try, we had trouble finding an available time."

"She keeps really busy?"

Hank shook his head and explained, "She's home evenings and weekends, but I work nights, and then there's the time at the Youth Club and my classes and studying—"

"Ah, you're the busy one. When do you make downtime?" John Stein began jotting on his notepad, and Hank's confidence faltered.

"I keep Sundays to myself. Even if I work the night before, I go hiking. You know, to stay in shape and be outdoors."

"Every Sunday?"

"Except when I went to Spokane to see my grandma and yesterday when I took Siara and her son Mo to the beach." A moment earlier he had felt proud to report his progress. Now he felt defensive.

John Stein consulted his notes. "Let's see. You work nights, sleep awhile, spend several hours at the Youth Club volunteering, study or have class in the evening, and on your one day to yourself, you hike all day?"

"Yeah. I guess that's right." Hank sat back and crossed his arms.

"Does that schedule remind you of anyone?"

"What do you mean?" Hank's forehead rippled, then his eyebrows jumped. He raised his chin and thrust out his chest. "I'm not at all like my dad!"

"You certainly have some of his good traits." The counselor's voice was conciliatory.

"What good traits?" Hank demanded.

"You're responsible, a hard worker, and loyal to a commitment."

Hank barely heard the answer; he was still so stunned by the implication. "I don't spend all my spare time alone in a basement. I'm out helping kids."

John Stein set his tablet aside, uncrossed his legs, and leaned forward. "Hank, I didn't mean to sound critical. I'm sorry. You live an 'other-oriented' life. Your career, your volunteer time, and even the classes you take all focus on helping others. But do you feel balanced?"

Hank deflated. "No, like we talked about before, I'm lonely. I want a relationship."

"And with your life the way it is, do you have time for a relationship?"

Their eyes met and held contact.

"I see what you mean. I'm busy, but I'm not building relationships at work, or even at the Youth Club. And now I'm at risk of not having time for a relationship with Siara and Mo."

The counselor sat quietly and gave Hank time to think.

"So you think I'm a workaholic like my dad?"

John smiled. "Unlike your dad, you've begun to connect. Now you have to make sure to nurture those connections, and that takes time.

What homework for this week would help you with that?"

"Guess I need to find a way to quit being so busy. I want time to get to know people."

"Great! So you'll make some changes this week to allow time for deepening connections with people. But I'd also like to see you add time to relate to yourself, too. Find out if you've made yourself busy in order to escape feelings or memories."

Hank stood, his mind reeling. He'd spent his whole life running from feelings, from memory. He didn't want to run anymore. Not if it meant losing Siara and Mo.

⌘ ⌘ ⌘

Gwen and Brian sat at a table and watched their boys play in the McDonald's ball crawl. She looked across at the man whose presence could still take her breath away. "Brian, I'm worried about Mickey."

Brian's eyes followed Mickey as the boy climbed to the top of a slide. "He's been really quiet since Sean got hurt."

She nodded. "I don't think Sean's accident started it, though. Our fight did."

Brian sighed. "Probably right. He's still mad at me."

"I've been thinking about that. About us, I guess." She knew things had to change. Staying together was hurting her children and her first responsibility was to them.

Brian turned away from watching the boys and looked directly at Gwen. "I don't want to lose you or my sons."

Gwen reached across and took Brian's hand. It felt solid. "It's easy to say we're not going to fight from now on, but you and I, we're both such emotional people. We have more explosions than the Fourth of July."

Brian paled a shade. "I keep swearing to myself that I'm going to do better, be more patient. Then, before I know it, we're at it again."

"And here I study marriage counseling. I know I'm not supposed to be critical or defensive or stonewall or...whatever the last horseman is."

"Contempt."

"Right, not supposed to show contempt. How'd you remember that?" She frowned at the irony. Her husband wasn't even taking the class and he remembered the destructive behaviors better than she did.

"I've been trying to be better at those, too," Brian admitted.

"But when we're mad, we go right back at it. I'm supposed to remember to lighten the tension with humor or reach out and touch you or do something to stay connected, even though I'm angry."

Brian moved his leg slightly so their knees touched under the table. "Way harder than it sounds, though, isn't it? I've been trying to be more helpful around the house when I remember, but I don't notice what has to be done the way you do."

"And I try to give you more space, to not always demand your full attention, but then I find myself feeling all hurt and neglected again," said Gwen, looking down at her tray.

Brian lifted her fingers to his lips and, holding them gently in his work-worn hand, kissed them. "I love you and the kids, but I want more than that. I want to have time with friends. I want to have fun. I want to go back home."

Without thinking about it, Gwen moved her knee away and let go of Brian's hand. "And I want more than housekeeping and spending all day herding the boys. I want to be a counselor, and that means staying in Portland." She felt like she lay on a torture rack and could hear the ratchet tightening.

Brian's voice faltered. "What are we going to do?"

"If we stay together, we'll keep fighting, if not about these things, then about something else. I don't want to hurt the boys, but I don't want to lose you."

Brian sighed and their eyes met. "Me neither."

She grasped for an answer, for one more chance. "I think if we're going to stay together without ruining our kids, we need a change we can stick with. Something simple."

"How about, 'No more yelling'?"

Gwen was surprised by Brian's suggestion. She knew they usually argued at full volume. She couldn't even imagine saying in a normal tone the things she had yelled. Maybe that simple rule would be easy to remember and might buy time to get herself under control.

"No yelling. Sounds straightforward. We'd still have to talk and work things out, but it would sure be better for the boys. And maybe it would make it easier to avoid the four horsemen."

Brian grinned. "No way can I picture you calmly saying, 'Brian, please get your rather large behind off the couch and do something around here, My Love.'"

Gwen giggled. "Gweny Dahling, get off my back, Deah. I know I swoah I'd play with the boys while you study, but I simply must watch one moah game fuhst."

They laughed and held hands again. Partners. With one last chance to make it work.

Twenty-nine

The best-laid plans…
often need touch-ups.

Gwen held little Sean on her lap in the family room and snuggled her nose into his hair to inhale the shampooed freshness. Brian called Joe Pat and Mickey to him. "Boys, I want to talk to you." They came close, and he took one on each knee. "I haven't been the kind of dad lately that I want you to grow up to be. I want to say I'm sorry."

"You're a good daddy!" Joe Pat protested. Mickey looked down at his untied shoelace.

"I want to do better," Brian continued. "The day that Sean-o got hurt, you must have been pretty scared, plus tired and hungry by the time you got home. Then you heard Mom and me shouting at each other, and I'm sure that didn't feel good. I didn't know Sean got hurt, but even so, I should have figured you'd be hungry and have made dinner and tidied up the place."

Mickey sat, still quiet, still no eye contact. Gwen gave Sean a gentle squeeze, wishing Mickey were in her arms, too.

"Your mom and I know we shouldn't yell at each other, and we've decided we're going to stop. We might mess up now and then but we're going to try really hard. We don't want you guys thinking fighting is a way to fix things."

Gwen nodded. She needed more for her boys than an unhappy home.

"How're you going to stop?" Mickey asked.

"When we forget and yell, we're going to put five dollars in a container. Then, when we know we've broken the habit, we'll give the

190

money to someone who really needs it."

"That sounds good," Mickey admitted.

"I need money. I want to buy this cool train at the toy store," Joe Pat offered.

Gwen smiled and shook her head. "Sorry, J.P., that's what your allowance is for. This money is going to someone who doesn't have a home or who doesn't get gifts at Christmas time."

Joe Pat's eyes rounded large at the idea of either tragedy befalling anyone. "Yeah, that would be better."

"Here's how you can help. If you guys hear us yell, or even better, before you think we might, hold up five fingers like this to remind us, Okay?" Brian raised his open hand high.

"Cool!" said Mickey as he high-fived his dad.

"Cool," said Joe Pat as he imitated his big brother.

Sean grinned up at his mother and they tapped palms together, too.

"One more thing." Brian's voice became more serious.

"Uh-oh." Mickey must have guessed what Gwen knew was coming.

"There's going to be a five-cent fine for you boys yelling, too."

"Oh, man," they both whined.

"Do you have to pay if you yell at us?" Mickey wanted to know.

They hadn't thought about that. Brian looked at Gwen. She shrugged and then smirked at his cornered expression.

"C'mon, Dad, it's only fair."

Gwen wondered if Mickey had a future as a lawyer.

"All right. I do want you boys to obey your mom and me because that's what's right, not because you're scared from us yelling at you. But let's call that a one-dollar fine and see if that works to stop it."

"Okay."

"I love you boys."

"Love you, too, Dad," said Mickey.

"You, too, Dad," parroted Jo Pat.

Sean looked up at his mom, humor sparkling in his eyes. "*I* two. Tuna half."

⌘⌘⌘

The next morning Brian called up the stairs, "I'm off to work, Gwen."

She came down to kiss him good-bye in time to see Joe Pat tap him. "Five dollars, Dad. You yelled." Mickey, who sat at the table eating his cereal, stopped chewing.

Brian lifted Joe Pat onto the counter so that their eyes were level. "I raised my voice to be heard, J.P., not in anger."

"So that's all right to yell?"

"I guess there is good yelling and bad yelling."

Joe Pat frowned, his little eyebrows coming together in a single line. "When else is it all right?"

"Well, if you need help. If someone is hurt or you're afraid, it's good to yell for help. Like you did when Sean fell."

Mickey joined the conversation. "Or if someone tries to steal us?"

Gwen ached to think her little boy had such big worries.

Brian ruffled Mickey's hair. "Exactly. Then you'd yell as loud as a siren so people would know you need help."

"And not have to pay a nickel?" Joe Pat seemed to want to be very sure about the rules. Gwen made mental note to keep an eye on him.

"And definitely not have to pay a nickel."

"Okay. Bye, Dad. Love you."

"Bye, boys. Love you, too."

Gwen watched Brian leave and hoped her boys would always have this kind of relationship with their dad.

She had to make this work.

⌘ ⌘ ⌘

Gwen and the boys decorated a shoebox that they dubbed the "I'm Sorry Box." When peace reigned for several days at the O'Connell household, and the box remained empty, she felt they might be on to something.

On Monday, Gwen had managed a normal voice to remind Brian to take off his construction boots after he had left a mud trail from the backdoor to the refrigerator.

Brian visibly choked back an angry retort and explained, "I called at the door for someone to bring me a beer. I get hot and dry raking leaves."

Gwen apologized and said it must have been when she took the boys for a walk around the block. Then she handed him the mop.

They even managed to have a civil discussion on Tuesday, when Gwen felt sure she had asked Brian to be home by five to take out the roast while she was having Sean's stitches removed. Brian insisted she had said six.

However, they both paid five dollars on Wednesday, when Brian found his hammer out in the rain.

"Gwen, how many times have I told you—"

"Not as many times as I asked you to pound down the nails that stick up on the deck stairs!"

"Tools get ruined in the rain!" Brian's voice rose.

"And boys trip over raised nails!" she defended herself as loudly. "The phone rang and I forgot to put it away, but I shouldn't have had to do it myself."

Mickey ended that fight when he held up his five fingers until they both stopped to look at him. "Daddy, Mama's worth more than a hammer."

The older boys lasted three days before they had to pay. It took that long for Mickey to fall for Joe Pat's scheme. On the first day, Mickey's treasured action figures were dumped out of their bin on Joe Pat's bed. Gwen heard the restraint in his voice as he reminded Joe Pat that he couldn't play with them without permission.

The second day, the action figure bin sat on the floor on Joe Pat's side of their room. Mickey was angry, but Joe Pat held up five fingers, so Mickey calmed himself enough to say, "Joe Pat, I told you yesterday you can't play with these unless you ask first."

Joe Pat grinned. "I didn't play with them. I only moved the bin."

"But you left them down where Sean-o might get into them."

"Oh, sorry."

Mickey put the bin back on his own shelves and scowled at his brother.

On the third day, right after Mickey had gone to the bathroom in the morning, he came back into the room and saw his action figure bin on Joe Pat's shelves and his brother grinning at him, again.

Mickey roared. "Joe Pat, you scumbag, you know I've told you not to move my action figures. This is the third time. Cut it out. Don't touch them ever again!"

"Five cents, Mickey! You yelled! Five cents for the I'm-Sorry Box!"

Unfortunately for Joe Pat, Gwen had been listening to their exchanges over the baby monitor and came into the room. "Sorry, Mickey, he's right. You need to pay the box."

"But Mom…"

"*And* so do you, Joe Pat, but I think you better pay ten cents for trying to make someone mad on purpose. That's a mean thing to do. Now put the bin back, don't touch it again without permission, and no cartoons for you this afternoon."

"No fair!" Joe Pat stomped, and his debt rose to fifteen cents before he calmed down.

Mickey struggled, but Gwen caught the small smile that escaped him.

Thirty

We might need tough love to challenge others,
or ourselves, to grow.

Tessa saw Marjorie studying a stack of index cards at her desk. She knocked quietly on the open door of her campus office, not completely sure she wanted to be heard.

Marjorie swiveled her desk chair toward the door and welcomed Tessa, who came in and sat opposite her. Tessa admired the way Marjorie's face lit with sincere affection, not just for her, but for every student. Probably every client, too, she guessed.

Tessa looked around, stalling to collect her courage. "I love your office. It's peaceful." The sky blue window wall set off the clean, white window frame. The three white walls made a nice contrast with the blue hydrangea that flowered in the corner. Books filled tidy shelves and family photos hung above the desk. A bowl of cloves added an exotic aroma. She realized the room's calm atmosphere was probably carefully planned to relax its guests. Tessa wished it were working better for her.

Marjorie looked around the room, and gave a little laugh. "Keeping it peaceful here wreaks havoc on my house. That's where I store my chaos."

Tessa sorted her thoughts. "Dr. Gloriam, if you have time, I'd like to talk to you about some concerns I have." She dreaded going on. Yet, if she wouldn't make a good counselor, better she admit it now and not risk doing someone harm.

Marjorie sat, not interrupting.

"I'm a quiet person, and I tend to avoid conflict. My husband does, too. We either figure something's not worth getting upset over, or we talk through the things that are. Our easy relationship means I don't have much practice with confronting people."

"A mother of two adolescents?" Marjorie voice held humor.

"Actually, even there I'm blessed with pretty even-tempered kids. I don't usually have to do much discipline. There's the normal sibling upsets, but they blow over fast." Tessa paused before she continued. "Last week you said confrontation is a necessary part of counseling. I'm not sure I can be that kind of a counselor."

"How so?"

"I won't have any problem being supportive and listening with empathy..."

Marjorie nodded. "You'll be good at that. It won't come so easily to all my students."

"But I'm going to have to deal with angry people." There, she'd said it. Her greatest fear about counseling.

"Wounded people who need help confronting their problems?" Marjorie smiled at her as if peering over the top of glasses.

Tessa recognized the technique. Marjorie had reframed her words to be more positive. "Right. I can't picture myself confronting, uh, wounded people."

Marjorie leaned toward her, kindness softening her voice. "What frightens you?"

"I don't want to hurt their feelings. I don't want them to be mad at me." She sounded small and vulnerable, even to herself.

Marjorie sat back and nodded. "And dislike you?"

"Right." This was harder than she'd imagined. Maybe she shouldn't have admitted all this.

Again Marjorie leaned forward, this time her serious expression added weight to her words. "Would you rather have them like you, or see them grow in healthy ways?"

Tessa smiled crookedly and lifted her open hands from her lap, as if in supplication. "Can't I have both?"

"Not always."

Tessa dropped her hands and looked down. "You see? Maybe I can't do this." Joe had been so encouraging about her studies. What would he think if she couldn't finish?

"Counseling goes beyond being supportive, Tessa. To help people, sometimes we need to confront them. Like when you made your kids brush their teeth when they were little. Or when you convinced your husband to go to the doctor. In cases like that, you've been able to be both supportive and challenging, for their own good."

Tessa looked up and whispered, feeling as if confessing, "I get so nervous when I disagree with someone. To avoid it, I usually stay quiet."

"Maybe you think they're too weak to take what you have to say. Or that your relationship isn't secure enough to survive some bumps."

The thought was new to Tessa and she considered it carefully. "Doesn't sound good, does it?"

"It comes from good intentions, but wrong motivation. You need to believe your clients are strong and have within them what they need to grow. Then you never have to apologize for helping them discover that force inside themselves. They'll believe it's there if you do."

Marjorie's words brought others to mind. Tessa paused and then ventured, "Our minister spoke about us all being called to be prophets. He says we need to be brave to bring the Good News, since people usually don't like hearing it. It requires them to change, and we all resist change."

"Exactly."

"And he said that to be true to the prophet call, we need to encourage change through a profound sense of love for the person." She could do that. Her mood lifted slightly.

Marjorie agreed. "Completely convinced that the Spirit to change for the better is inside of them."

Tessa straightened in her chair. "Not to put them down and come across as self-righteous."

Marjorie nodded. "The counseling relationship, like any relationship, doesn't go far if one person talks down to the other."

They sat together in silence a moment, as Tessa tested an idea in her mind. She met Marjorie's eyes. "I watched a sheep dog once. He pestered the poor sheep constantly. Nipping at their legs to keep them together. Counseling might need to be like that."

Marjorie laughed. "How so?"

She hurried to explain. "They don't like the dog. He nudges them and makes them move, but he keeps them safe by doing it. He doesn't worry about being liked; he simply does his job to help the sheep."

"Sounds like a Good Shepherd."

Marjorie's eyes shone, and Tessa knew her teacher was enjoying watching a student reach a pivotal discovery. Tessa glowed with her own realization. "I guess so."

"How about another example from your own journal? You wrote about how you ached after your first dragon boat practice."

Tessa groaned and rubbed at the imagined stiffness. "My arms felt like old-growth logs the next day."

"But you kept going and grew stronger. In time, your team was able to make it across the river and will ultimately win races."

Tessa closed her eyes and relived the exhilaration of their paddling success.

"Tessa, you know from experience that healing requires some pain and even suffering sometimes. You'll be encouraging your clients to heal. You don't ever need to feel bad about that. You can commiserate with them about how hard it is, but if you truly care about their welfare, they'll know. That's not to say they won't get mad at you, but deep down they'll know you want what's best for them."

"And they'll eventually like me again!"

Marjorie sighed. "Not always. But that isn't the goal. It's not about us, or our feelings. It's about them. Sometimes it doesn't go well. Sometimes they'll leave, and you'll never know if you helped them. That's when you put them in God's hands and let go, so you can be present to the next wounded person who comes to you."

For a moment Marjorie looked stricken and then softly repeated her own words, "You put them in God's hands and let go, so you can be present to the next person...."

Tessa watched Marjorie with concern until she gave a little shake and smiled at Tessa. "Think of yourself as that good sheepdog. Hold them together. Be strong for your clients when they've lost touch with their own strength."

"Thanks, Dr. Gloriam." She rose to leave. "You've given me food for thought."

Marjorie stood. "And you, me. Tessa, you have the makings of a fine counselor. The world needs prophets like you."

Tessa smiled appreciation and left, feeling much better than when she had arrived, though she wondered what food for thought she had given Marjorie.

⌘ ⌘ ⌘

By early November, Hank, Siara, and Mo settled into a routine of companionship. Hank finally began to experience the simple pleasures of family life. On Monday afternoons, he met Mo and Brian at the fixer-upper and helped on projects that required extra muscle. They finished in time for Hank and Mo to pick up Siara from work and stop for fast food.

Wednesdays were much the same, but the three worked together on Siara's house. When Brian went home for dinner, the others ate a slow-cooked meal that Siara had started in the morning. Hank and Mo both studied until Mo's bedtime, then the two adults would turn on soft music, nestle contentedly on the couch, and tell each other the stories that Hank knew had gone unspoken for too many years.

On Fridays, Hank still spent the afternoon with his friends at the Youth Club, but he left in time to drive Siara and Mo to Brian and Gwen's house, where they joined that young family for the dinner Gwen had made. Hank and Siara did dishes and looked after the boys, while Brian and Gwen escaped for their evening away.

Hank spent a few hours on Saturdays at the Youth Club, and then he, Mo, and Siara had their own evening out, taking turns to plan the excursion. Together they bowled, skated, did early Christmas shopping, or went to movies. Sometimes they played board games and made cookies. Hank grew more and more reluctant to leave for his nightshifts at the hospital.

Tuesdays and Thursdays dragged on as classes kept Hank from visiting. After work, when most people were starting their day, Hank would drive back to his apartment, which seemed emptier than it had before. When he climbed into his bed, he no longer ached with loneliness, but rather lonesomeness. He knew whom he wanted by his side.

Sundays he still hiked but used the time to turn his thoughts inward and to deal with facing the pain he had so long worked to ignore. Though the experience was healing, he found the hikes becoming shorter or his return pace faster. He was anxious to shower and join Siara and Mo for the evening, his need for solitude satisfied.

Though Hank loved his time with Mo, he particularly enjoyed the time he and Siara had to themselves. On one such night, Siara seemed quiet during dinner and didn't joke as usual with Mo as she oversaw his homework. Hank felt irritated by her silence and tried to remind himself, as his counselor had recommended, that he was reacting to his father's silence, not hers.

No reason to take it personally. I need to accept companionable silence. He hoped hers truly was companionable.

However, when Mo went to bed and Siara settled next to Hank on the couch, she seemed ready to talk. "Hank, you've never asked me about how Mo came to be."

He flushed warm and wished he had been satisfied with the silence. Now what could he say?

"I guess I figured you'd tell me about it if you wanted me to know." He paused and rubbed the back of his neck, unsure whether to continue. "But there's more to my not asking than that."

"Oh?" Siara straightened and drew back.

He felt he had to speak. "I grew up isolated by secrets. I spent my childhood thinking my mom had died and wondering why my dad was so angry. Now, as an adult, I'm trying to adjust to learning the truth." He took her hand in his and was distracted momentarily by how delicate it seemed. "I think family secrets are never good for families."

"Oh." Siara was looking down at her worn carpet, but Hank heard her sniff and his self-righteousness collapsed.

"Siara." Hank drew her closer to him. "I don't want to hurt you. You're a treasure to me." He smoothed her hair and marveled at its silkiness. He softened his voice. "But I don't want to see Mo hurt, either. I'd rather not know something than keep secrets from him. I can't stand the thought that he has a family somewhere that he doesn't know about. It's too much like me."

Siara pushed back from Hank and whispered harshly, "What do you want me to tell him? That his grandfather feels so ashamed of us that he doesn't want to meet him? That I used to be loved, but because of him, they consider me dead? You think that would be good for him to know?"

"No, of course not." Hank's pulse started to pound in his neck. His thoughts became confused.

"You want me to let him know how much easier my life might have been if I'd secretly had him aborted?"

"No!" The idea of a world without Mo seemed inconceivable. Part of his love for Siara was because of her devotion to her son. As much as silence made him nervous, he had never wanted to get into this conversation.

Tears were streaming down Siara's face. Her shoulders and her voice shook. "Shall I wake him up and tell him his father was a rapist?" She lifted her chin but wrapped her arms around herself.

"Oh, Siara, I'm sorry." Hank drew her back to him and held her while she cried out her anger. As hers subsided, his rose. He would have done anything to have protected her.

When her sobs had calmed, he scooted off the couch and knelt on the floor to face her. He took both her cold hands into his and blew on them to warm them. She seemed embarrassed by her outburst and was slow to look into his eyes. When she did, he spoke earnestly.

"I'm sorry for everything you've gone through. Especially that you had to go through it by yourself. I don't want you to be alone ever again." He squeezed her hands gently, and lowered his voice. "I love you."

Hank met Siara's gaze, aware she was searching his soul. Hank relived from his Army years the agonizing seconds spent waiting for his parachute to open.

"I think I love you, too, Hank." She smiled through her tears.

I think? He mentally activated the auxiliary chute. "But?"

"But this has happened too fast. Let's wait a few months to be sure before telling Mo."

Hank wanted to marry her tonight, immediately. But he didn't want to scare her off, or do anything to upset Mo. He simply nodded; he knew she was right. He also suspected that Siara needed healing that only her family could provide.

A thought occurred to Hank, and he offered it. "I have a present I want to give you."

"You what?"

"When you feel ready, I'd like to pay to help you go back and visit whoever in your family will see you." Siara looked frightened, so he hurried to add, "And I'll go with you if you want."

She shook her head slowly. "I'll have to think about that. And about what you said about secrets, too. I have to figure out what Mo can handle at his age."

"Of course."

"I don't ever want him to feel ashamed. He hasn't done anything wrong."

"Neither have you."

Siara's chin had been raised but slid down as she heard Hank's words. "It doesn't feel that way."

Hank lifted her chin with a gentle finger and kissed her tenderly, then said, "You are a precious gift, and I am proud of you."

⌘ ⌘ ⌘

Two days after the question of visiting her family had surfaced, Hank and Siara sat close to each other on her couch.

Siara asked, "Hank, were you serious about going with me to see my family?"

"Absolutely." Though his stomach did tense at the idea.

"I've been thinking about it."

"We could go whenever you'd like. I have vacation time available."

"Do you think we should bring Mo? Where would he stay if we didn't?" The idea of leaving him behind was obviously bothering her. She probably had never left him overnight before.

"He could stay with Gwen and Brian." Hank paused. "What would you tell him, though?"

202

"We could say we want to take a few days alone, but that sounds immoral. I wouldn't want him to wonder if we were sleeping together."

"We could wait and include the trip on our hon—later." The unspoken word gave Hank a tingling sensation.

"I should go soon or I'll lose my nerve, and I don't want any shadow on our... later." She smiled weakly.

"We'll take Mo. He'll be our chaperone." With the thoughts that *honeymoon* brought to mind, he might need a chaperone.

Hank's arm curved around Siara's shoulder, and her warmth and softness made him wish their honeymoon was soon. He looked down at her just as she looked up at him. They smiled and shared a kiss. Hank sank into the surge of love he felt, and he kissed her more intently. Siara jerked away.

"Sorry," he whispered, berating himself.

"No, don't be. This is overwhelming me. I've never dated."

"I don't want you to feel pressured or rushed. I just want to show you how much I've come to love you." He ached to show her. To feel her close. To heal her.

"Part of me can hardly wait for...later. I do love you, Hank." She smiled.

The second parachute billowed open, and Hank's heart soared with it. As he floated back to earth, he noticed her pinched brow and asked, "And the other part?"

"Is the mom who wants to do what's best for Mo."

"I would never consciously do anything to hurt him. Or you."

"I know. And then there's another part of me that is a frightened little girl."

"Siara, all your parts—the child, the mom, and the loving woman—are all treasures to me. I want to help you, and if that means putting you in charge of our, uh, intimacy, that's fine with me."

"If we travel together?"

"Separate rooms. Whether Mo is with us or not."

"Thank you, Hank."

"My pleasure, pretty lady." Hank tried to sound like John Wayne but then returned to his normal voice. "I want you, but when you are completely ready and not a moment before."

Siara moved close to Hank again, put her hand behind his head, and guided his lips back to hers. He kissed her but allowed her to direct the length. Her kiss remained gentle, so his did, too. She leaned back to look into his eyes. Hank thought of a Ukrainian egg he had seen once, beautifully painted but very fragile.

"Hank, I have a three-day weekend for Veteran's Day. Could we go then?"

"I'll make reservations in the morning. Where are we headed?"

"Seattle."

Thirty-one

Focus on the good times.
We were, and are, loved.

ank's foot tapping betrayed his nervous anticipation, and he knew his feelings must be nothing compared to Siara's. She had told him she would talk to Mo about her family at dinner that night. Now even dessert was finished. He was afraid she'd lost her nerve, but when Mo picked up his plate to carry it to the sink, Siara touched Mo's hand. "Wait. I want to talk to you about something."

Hank and Siara exchanged glances, and Hank nodded to encourage her.

Mo grinned at Hank. "Is it about you and Hank? It's okay; I really like him."

Hank gave Mo an appreciative look and then waited for Siara to find the words that seemed to elude her.

Siara closed her eyes a moment. "I'm glad you do, but no, it's not about him. Mo, I haven't been honest with you, and I'm sorry." She looked so troubled that Hank reached over and gave her hand a squeeze.

When Mo looked at his mother and then Hank, his lower lip sucked in. Hank had seen that face whenever the boy worried over difficult homework.

Siara trudged on. "A long time ago, my family and I had a disagreement and became angry, especially my father and me. I left them before you were born, but now I think it's time to try to make peace." She looked to Hank and he nodded again, wishing he could make this easier, but knowing she needed to be the one to tell the story.

"Hank offered to take us to see them next weekend. Going back will be hard for me." She shook her head sadly. "And I'm not even sure they'll see me." She straightened in her chair and smiled at Mo with reassurance that Hank suspected she probably didn't feel. But her voice was stronger as she said, "But I think we should try. They ought to have a chance to know what a wonderful person you are, and you should know them."

Mo sat back in his chair, visibly stunned. "We have a family?"

"You have a grandma and a grandpa and two uncles and an aunt. I'm not sure we'll meet them all, but will you go with me and give it a try?"

Mo's lip pulled in again. "Why didn't you tell me?"

"I should have," Siara answered. "But I was angry with them. I didn't want to say anything that would hurt your opinion of them, so I didn't talk about them. I guess I worried, too, that because they're upset with me, they might hurt you. Not physically, but your heart."

Mo sat up straighter. "I'm tough. I think we should try it."

Hank marveled at the maturity Mo showed, for someone only nine. As the boy stood and hugged his mother, Hank wondered whether he would have reacted as well if he'd learned the truth about his family at that age.

Suddenly, the thought of visiting Siara's family took Hank's breath away. What did he know about working out family conflict? In his limited experience, his father had always had the last few words. The idea of facing Siara's father with his secret desire to ask permission to marry Siara set his heart racing.

Why had he thought this would be a good idea?

⌘ ⌘ ⌘

The next weekend in a Seattle motel, Hank and Mo watched Siara as she picked up and replaced the telephone receiver several times from her nightstand.

"It's okay, Mom. You can do it."

Siara shook her head and wrapped her arms around herself. "I can't. He told me to leave and never come back. I thought I could try for your sake...." She rubbed her hand up and down her arm as if trying to warm herself. Mo snuggled close. Siara put her arm around his shoulder and rested her head on his, whispering, "I'm sorry."

Hank decided Siara needed distraction, and he needed to provide it. "Grab coats, people, we're going to explore!" They drove into the heart of Seattle and then rode the monorail to Seattle Center. Mo enjoyed a few rides at the Center's amusement park. They wandered through its science center and took in a performance at the children's theater.

Siara remained quiet and withdrawn. Hank's tension mounted. He wanted to share a life with this woman and boy, but the thought of joining an extended family marked with their own vows of silence was more than he could handle. He had to initiate communication.

The three ate at a window seat in the restaurant at the top of the Space Needle, and Hank shared Mo's fascination as the whole restaurant made a 360-degree circle each hour. Even more exciting to him, though, was seeing Siara's first smile of the day as she watched the fireboats on the Sound sprout butterfly wings of water. She pointed out the ferries that ambled back and forth to connect Seattle with Bremerton across the Puget Sound. As they revolved away from the water, she told them the names of some of the skyscrapers that stood sentinel for the green hills rising behind them.

By the time the three finished dinner they had come full circle. The sun had set, bringing new panoramas of city lights. Though Siara seemed calmer, she was quiet again, so Hank and Mo carried the conversation, both eyeing her with concern.

⌘ ⌘ ⌘

After a tired Mo finally fell asleep in the motel, Siara and Hank sat in silence in Hank's room with the adjoining door open. He hoped the time away from her worries had given Siara a chance to build her courage. Hank needed this to work, for all of them. He longed to be part of her little family, and the possibility of reuniting Siara's extended family and the joy this could bring to her and Mo made any effort worthwhile. Still, he didn't know how to express such hope to her.

Fortunately, she broke the barrier. "Hank, the Space Needle was the perfect place to take me today."

He tilted his head to one side. She had been unreadable all day. "You liked it?"

"My father and I had a date once, just the two of us, and he took me to eat at the top of the Space Needle."

As Hank tried to imagine the scene, the graduation dinner with his father came back to him in a rush of unresolved emotions that made his voice husky. "A date with your father."

"A tradition in our family. When a girl becomes a young woman, the mama tells the papa it's time for her first date. He takes his daughter out and talks with her about men and dating and the responsibilities a woman must take on."

"Responsibilities?"

"My papa did so wonderfully. First he told me how much he loved me and how happy I made him." Siara's voice quivered, but she continued. "Then he talked about protecting myself from men who might say what I want to hear, simply to get what they want."

"Oh." Hank reddened.

She looked at him shyly. "But he also talked about physical love being a precious, wonderful gift when shared by two people in a lifelong commitment."

Hank sighed. A life commitment with Siara was what he wanted most. But he also wanted this dear woman to be happy, and he knew that she might not be until this rift with her family healed.

"I felt so uncomfortable at thirteen to talk about these things with Papa, but excited, too. He made me feel proud to be a young woman." She looked down at the floor, then back up at him with shining eyes. "He even bought me flowers. I knew he treasured me."

Hank waited, hoping for the words that came next.

"Maybe if I keep thinking of that night, I can try to talk to Papa."

However, when Hank brought breakfast to Siara and Mo's room the next morning, she had lost her resolve. She wanted to go home. But finally, at Hank's and Mo's urging, Siara agreed to at least visit her mother after her father left for work.

Thirty-two

"The truth will set you free."
JOHN 8:32

Hank watched from the Jeep as Siara and Mo waited at the door of her parents' home. The door opened, and Siara blocked his view of her mother, but he knew that for a long moment the two just looked at each other. Then he saw arms reach out to embrace his beloved, and he released the breath he had been holding.

As Siara turned to introduce Mo, Hank had an unobstructed look at her mother, who swept her grandson into her arms. She was even more petite than Siara and quite wrinkled. He thought of a gnarled, windswept olive tree he had seen while in the service, and he figured Siara's mother must have stood firm through many storms. He decided he was leaving the two people he had come to love in very good hands.

After Hank watched the door close behind Siara and Mo, he drove around the area, trying to imagine her childhood. Did she play at this park? Attend that grade school? He turned a corner and found the commercial center of the neighborhood.

The businesses that once served the community's needs had undoubtedly changed as the area was overtaken by the growing city of Seattle. A small grocery store and a gas station seemed like old-timers, but what might have been clothing or hardware stores now housed a Starbucks coffee shop and an antique center. Tucked between them was a small jewelry store that looked like it had always been there. From her stories of her childhood when she'd walk to visit her father, Hank realized it could be the jewelry store that he owned. He pulled into the parking lot and stopped the engine.

Her father might work beyond that door. The thought made his heart race. Maybe he could talk to him, make it easier for Siara. But could he face him, knowing the stakes at risk? Her father should at least know how she became pregnant, though Hank shook his head at the idea. Siara should tell that tragedy.

Still, if Hank could get her father to see how much Siara wanted to be part of his life again, he might relent and welcome her. And eventually be willing to hear Hank's request. He took a few minutes more to build his courage, then climbed out of the Jeep. He smoothed his jeans, as much to dry his palms as to adjust the fabric. He cleared his throat and entered the store.

"Good morning, sir. May I help you?"

Hank looked at the impeccably suited proprietor, found his eyes to be familiar though his skin was darker, and knew he must be Siara's father. His courage nearly failed him, and he considered asking directions to the highway.

He remembered Siara's tears and forced a smile. He opened his mouth to say, "I'd like to talk to you about your daughter," but instead blurted, "I'd like to see some wedding rings."

Her father's eyes lit. "Of course. Please come to sit here, and I will help you find the perfect set. You will want also an engagement ring?" The man's accent was mild, but perhaps explained Siara's careful enunciation.

"Yes, thank you." Hank realized they were each discreetly sizing up the other, one to determine which rings to show first, the other to understand what type of man could so deeply hurt a beloved daughter.

"Your young lady has a preference for white or yellow gold?"

Hank suddenly wondered what had possessed him to come into this shop. Siara should be introducing him to her father. But what could he say now? Should he pretend not to have known her father owned the local jewelry store? He didn't want to pretend to this man; he wanted their dealings to be forthright. Her father made a slight move, and Hank realized he was still waiting for an answer from him.

He stood and offered his hand. "Sir, I'm Hank Glenn. I've fallen in love with your daughter, Siara, and I'd like your permission to court her."

Siara's father scowled, and he stared at Hank in silence. At the look on her father's face, Hank retreated behind his ruse for entering the store. "I was hoping you could tell me what kind of ring she would like." Mentally smacking himself on the forehead, he added, "More than that, I was hoping you could give us your blessing."

Hank watched her father scan his clothes and then look at Hank's hands, as if searching for clues. There were no rings to disclose his financial situation. His watch was covered by his shirtsleeve. Hank accepted the inspection without flinching, but his heart beat rapidly, and he could feel himself sweat.

"How long have you known her?" The tone was brusque. Dismissive.

"Siara and her son have become very important to me in a short time. I haven't asked her to marry me yet. I hoped for your permission first. I don't want to rush, for both her sake and Mo's."

At the boy's name, the jeweler's eyes widened and one shoulder twitched. A rumble came from his throat, yet he didn't speak.

Hank gave up on the blessing and fell back on the ring. "I know she likes blue. I thought maybe a sapphire and diamond combination."

Siara's father walked to a cabinet and stood in front of it, as if deep in thought. Finally, he unlocked the drawer, lifted out a small box, and opening it, brought it to the counter. "I've saved this for her since first I saw it. The day she was born." Hank, who had been watching him, broke his gaze and looked down.

Hank whispered, "It's perfect."

Both men exhaled.

The gold engagement ring held two stones, a heart-shaped sapphire and a simple round diamond. Neither stone was large. Hank knew Siara would be self-conscious if the ring were too showy. The sapphire flashed sparks of red in its depth of blue. The diamond lived up to the name of its brilliant cut and sparkled under the overhead lighting. The wedding band curved into the engagement ring gracefully, and added a twin sapphire to the other side of the diamond.

"The one heart and diamond, like Mo and Siara, and another heart to join them, like I will, on our wedding day." Hank hadn't quite realized he voiced the last thought aloud. When he did, he looked quickly up at Siara's father, who looked away.

He cleared his throat. "I'll take it. May I take your blessing, too?"

"My daughter has been…"

Please don't let him say "dead to me."

"Has been a long time gone. The blessing is not my right to give anymore."

"But we both would still treasure it," Hank persisted.

The tenderness he had demonstrated with the ring disappeared. His face closed. "I don't know you. You are not one of us."

Hank felt like he had crashed into a wall. He took a step back. "I'm a good man, and I do and will love your daughter and grandson. I can support them well. I work as a physician assistant, and I'm studying to get a master degree in counseling. I own a house and have enough money in the bank to live on for several years."

"Again, you are not one of us."

Not quite sure what the man meant, Hank didn't answer but stood firm.

Her father broke the silence. "You are a man of faith?"

"I worship God in my own way, out in nature."

The jeweler shook his head slowly and then looked down. "Siara still worships?"

"Yes, every weekend. I know she prays for the family she still misses desperately."

The older man's shoulder twitched. "When you share her faith, then maybe we will talk of blessings."

Hank had been dismissed. He paid for the rings, and as he reached the door, he turned with what felt like the last of his energy. "Thank you, sir, for the help with the rings. You chose perfectly, and I know what they'll mean to her, coming from you."

⌘ ⌘ ⌘

Back in the Jeep, Hank looked again at the rings and wished he could see them on Siara's finger right away. He closed the box and locked it inside the glove compartment.

Unsure what to do, Hank drove back to Siara's family home and

212

waited in the Jeep, hoping that all was going well inside the house. As he thought of her being sent from her home, a frightened pregnant teenager, Hank discovered within himself a Protector force that vitalized him. He inhaled slowly and yearned for a dragon to slay. He wished he knew how to pray, but he had to do something, so he went to the door and rang the doorbell.

Siara opened the door, her face looking young and exuberant. He was whisked into the kitchen and introduced. He didn't know what Siara had told her mother about him, but the older woman was beaming at him as she placed a cup of tea in front of him. Her complexion was lighter than Siara's, but she smiled the same smile. He could see and hear Mo in the backyard playing basketball with a young man who had to be her brother, judging from their identical laugh.

Siara put down the cup of tea her mother had refreshed for her. "Mama, I need to tell you what happened before I left. Maybe Papa will listen if you choose to tell him, but it's important to me that someone in my family knows the truth."

"Ai, my Sisi. Yes, time we talk of it."

Hank was still shaken from his experience with her father. He didn't know if he could bear to listen to what was to come. Then he imagined how much worse it must be for Siara and knew if she could tell it, he could listen.

Siara took a deep breath, as if to gather courage. "You remember Cousin Leah's wedding?"

"Of course, you were a bridesmaid." Siara's mother smoothed back strands of gray hair that had escaped her braid.

"And remember I stayed at her house the night before, to help with the party?"

"Ai, it happened there?" She covered her mouth with the tips of her fingers.

"Yes, Mama. So many people. Music. Dancing. I began to feel dizzy, so I went upstairs to lie down for a while." Hank could see Siara was struggling and took her hand to give her courage.

"And then?" The older woman looked as if she was torn between needing to know and not wanting to hear.

"I didn't wake up until the next morning. My underwear was gone, and I…hurt. Blood stained my dress, but I had no memory of anything that happened."

Hank had heard this before, but the telling still made his chest tense and his fists clench. How he wished he could have been there to protect Siara that night.

Siara's mother sat stoically, lips tight, but a tiny testament of pain escaped from each eye.

Siara took another deep breath and continued. "Mama, I think someone drugged me…maybe put something in my punch. I tried to remember who was around me the night before, but I couldn't figure out who would—" she seemed to force herself to continue—"hurt me that way. I'd slept late, and the whole house was in a hurry to be ready for the wedding. I showered and dressed in my bridesmaid gown and went on with the day. I was in a daze and didn't know what to do or even what to think." Hank watched her look to her mother, desperate for understanding.

"You didn't come to me, Sisi." It was a lament, not an accusation.

Siara's head dropped. "I felt so ashamed."

More tears traced the lines of her mother's cheeks. She reached both arms toward her daughter, and the two women held each other in an embrace that Hank hoped salved the years of their denied companionship.

Siara and her mother parted abruptly when they heard the front door open and footsteps approach. Hank stood quickly, as did the women, when Siara's father walked into the room. The older man paused when he saw Siara; he looked at her for a long time. His expression was inscrutable to Hank. What would her father say about their encounter at the store? How could Hank explain it to Siara?

A cheer from the backyard drew the older man's attention to his grandson.

"Papa?" Siara ventured.

His shoulder flinched. "A fine-looking boy."

"He's named after you."

Her father cleared his throat. "I must talk to your mother." He looked at Hank but didn't acknowledge him. "Leave a phone number where we can reach you. Give us time."

Siara quickly wrote the name of the hotel and Hank's cell phone number. She gazed one more time at her father, a look of longing mixed with stubborn pride. Her father considered her with the same expression.

"Sir," Hank began but stopped when he saw Siara shake her head quickly.

Siara rose, kissed her mother, and went wordlessly to the backdoor. She looked out at Mo and paused, turning back to her father, her back straight and her chin lifted.

"Papa, we went last night to the top of the Space Needle. It reminded me of the time you took me there. That night I knew how much you loved me." She lowered her chin slightly. "I'm sorry that what happened to me hurt you. And I'm sorry I was so stubborn that I let us be apart this long. I still love you, and I pray you still love me."

Her courage spent, she fled to the backyard, and Hank, after saying good-bye to her mother and nodding to her father, followed. His chest expanded with pride for Siara. She hugged her brother and introduced Hank to him.

Mo exuded joy. "Hank, I found a grandma, just like you did!" The boy walked backwards to talk to them on the way to the Jeep. "And I've got an uncle who played basketball with me. Did you see the hoop in their backyard? I think that's what I'll start saving money for. If we had a hoop at our house, would you play with me?"

Siara attempted a brave smile over Mo's head. She shrugged and shook her head sadly.

Hank turned to Mo. "I sure will, Mo. Great idea."

When they were back in the Jeep, he put his hand over Siara's ice-cold one. "I love you," he mouthed to her, and while Mo chattered about his newfound uncle, they drove to the motel.

⌘ ⌘ ⌘

That evening Hank and Siara talked quietly in Hank's room, keeping an eye on sleeping Mo through the door that connected the rooms. She perched in a chair, holding his cell phone like a lifeline. Hank sat across from her on the bed.

"It gave me hope when Papa asked me to leave a phone number. Now, though, so many hours have passed without word."

She told Hank about how wonderful she felt to sit and talk to her mother after all these years. "I'd like to have that chance with Papa, too. I wonder what made him come home. I don't remember him ever leaving his shop in the middle of the day."

Hank felt his cheeks burn with guilt. He made his confession. "Siara, I met your father at his jewelry store today."

"You what?" She looked at him, and her face drained of color. "You knew he owned it!"

"Yes, and I didn't plan to go looking for the jewelry store, but driving around I saw it, and I guess curiosity got the better of me. So I went in."

"Did you tell him who you are?" Her face reflected how bad a decision it was. Hank's heart sank. He might have jeopardized the whole purpose of their trip and his hope for being part of a healthy family. But worse, what if he had ruined her chance for reconciliation?

"At first I didn't plan to. Thought I'd pretend to shop. But then I realized that wasn't honest, and he'd remember me if we ever did get a chance to talk, so I told him."

"And?" One hand gripped the phone; the other grasped the arm of the chair.

"Hard to read. He was quiet." Should he tell her about the rings? It would help him explain, but this wasn't how he wanted to propose. He planned to only propose once in his life, and he meant to do it right.

Siara didn't respond, but her fingers clenched white.

"Then I asked for his permission to court you. He said you've been gone so long that it was no longer his right to give. I told him I'd like to have it anyway."

Siara nodded and some of the color returned to her face. "And then?"

"He said when I worship with you, I could come back and ask for his blessing."

"Really?" She leaned forward, and the light that had left her eyes when she fled her house returned.

Hank nodded.

"That's wonderful! There's hope that he might accept you, which would mean he might accept me again. Oh Hank, would you consider that?"

She sat back quickly and motioned to stop. "Wait, no. I don't want you to be pressured into such a thing."

Hank paused. Would he consider worshipping with her? He didn't know anything about praying with a group of people. Or praying at all for that matter. Still, the kind of thinking he did when he hiked might be a kind of prayer.

He realized she waited expectantly, so he verbalized his thoughts. "I do believe in a Creator who I can call God. And I think I worship when I feel awestruck and grateful for nature's beauty."

Hank looked at Siara's hopeful face, and the Protector arose in him again. He wanted to make this and all her wishes come true. "Yes, I'm willing to learn about your faith and try to share it."

"Oh, Hank, you're wonderful!" In her enthusiasm she flew to him and, caught off guard, he fell backward on the bed with her on top of him. They both laughed and then grew quiet as they looked into each other's eyes. From the color in her cheeks and the way she caught her breath, Hank suspected that Siara had discovered her own vitalizing inner force.

His cell phone rang, and she jumped back with a guilty jerk. She cleared her throat before answering.

Hank sat up and tried to figure what was being said, but Siara stood with her back to him, so he couldn't read her facial expression. She repeated "All right" several times, then "Thank you," as she turned toward Hank and beamed. "I love you, Papa." Her father's response brought wet sparkles of happiness to her eyes as the call ended.

Hank reached out, and she nestled into his arms. "Oh, Hank, thank you so much for bringing me here. It's going to work out. They want us all to come worship with them tomorrow and then to eat at the house."

The image brought a whole new range of concerns to Hank's mind, but Siara's smile made them seem inconsequential.

In the doorway, after a long good-night embrace that held its own promise for the future, Siara stepped back and looked up at Hank's face.

"Hank?"

"Yes, my love?"

She grinned like a little girl. "Permission to court me?"

His resolve crumbled. He left Siara looking startled and confused as he patted his pocket for his car keys and whispered, "Don't move. I'll be right back."

To his mixed relief and apprehension, she still stood in the doorway between their two rooms when he returned. He stopped, spellbound. His heart pounded as if it wanted to leap out and join hers. Her long sleek hair spilled over one shoulder. How could one woman be so completely exotic and demure at the same time? She looked up at him from under thick dark lashes, and the Protector filled his chest. He knew he would die for her, if need be.

He led her into his room by the hand, unsure whether the shaking was hers or his. He gestured for her to sit. He knelt before her, still holding her hand, and raised it to his lips to kiss. She quivered, and Hank noticed tears in her eyes. Unsure what he had done wrong, he loosened his hold and pulled back, but she laughed and tightened her grip.

Heartened, he looked into her eyes again, and only glistening remained.

"Siara, will you marry me? Will you let me treat you as well as you deserve? Let me be Mo's father?" He knew he was flushing, but the look on Siara's face made him disregard his self-consciousness. She was ready to answer him, and her eyes told him her words would be what he wanted to hear, but he hurried to say one thing more. "I swear I will never knowingly hurt you in any way, and I'll do all in my power to keep anyone else from hurting you or Mo." He would break the cycle of abandonment and heal it with steadfast love.

Siara opened her mouth, but no sound came out. Instead she nodded vigorously, and then threw her arms around Hank's neck. They kissed and held each other close. Hank didn't ever want to move, but Siara drew back, looking determined.

"Yes, Hank, I will marry you. I will hold your heart in mine, our souls side by side, all the days of my life."

He drew out the ring box from his pocket and handed it to her.

"Your father says he chose this ring for you the day you were born."

She ran a finger across the imprint of her father's store name on the box, then slowly opened it. She inhaled through parted lips and beamed her approval.

Hank lifted out the engagement ring and explained as he slid it onto her finger. "You are the diamond and Mo is the sapphire heart." Then he lifted the wedding band from the box. "I'll be the second heart, and I'll join you on our wedding day." In truth, he knew she already owned his heart. He wouldn't be at all surprised if it kept up its present pounding for the rest of his life.

He wished everyone he knew could be as happy.

⌘ ⌘ ⌘

When it rains, it pours. By the end of the day, Marjorie wondered if she should take lessons in ark building. The series of cloudbursts had begun the night before. Sophie phoned as Marjorie prepared for bed.

"Mom! I'm engaged! Niko asked me to marry him!"

"Engaged? Oh!" *No!* Could this be real? She had no idea Sophie had become so serious about that man. She hurried to cover up the pause. "Congratulations. Tell me more." She hoped her voice didn't hint at her thoughts.

Sophie described the pink linen, taper-lit tables, and the white-jacketed waiter who brought a champagne bucket to their table, complete with a ring-box on ice. Niko had taken the ring from the box and knelt beside Sophie's chair.

"Mom, he asked me to 'be his princess for life.' Isn't that cool?"

Princess for life? Sophie would have groaned if that were a line in a movie. And she hated pink. This was her engineer daughter who scoffed at romanticism. *Hold on, be supportive.*

"You sound happy, Sophie."

"I'm so psyched, Mom. I sure wasn't expecting this yet, but he's wonderful. We're going to drive down soon so you can meet him."

Marjorie's stomach clenched at the thought. "Sounds like a good idea." *I should hope so!*

"This is all happening so fast. Niko's company is transferring him, so we don't have much time."

"Whoa, Sophie, slow down. How fast exactly?" Marjorie could almost feel her blood pressure rise.

"He's heading down to Silicon Valley in January to take a new position with the company. He wants me to apply for a transfer and go with him."

"So a wedding in less than two months?"

⌘ ⌘ ⌘

Still reeling from Sophie's call the previous night, Marjorie decided to skip her Saturday chores and ride Oasis in the morning to unwind. When she approached the stall, she was surprised to find Melle Walker, the stable owner, and Suzanne, whose hyphenated last name she could never remember, having a serious conversation while looking at the horse.

Frightened, Marjorie glanced at Oasis. The horse's ears stood perked; her neck arched with spirit.

"Is something wrong?" Marjorie asked.

"Oh, Mrs. Gloriam." Both women smiled, but Melle had a worried look around her eyes. "Glad to see you. Suzanne has something to talk to you about. I'll leave you two alone." Melle seemed to be only too happy to go.

Suzanne was obviously not one to mince words. "Marjorie, I'd like to buy your half of Oasis."

Marjorie's mind went blank, and she couldn't form a reply.

Suzanne continued. "My offer on a piece of property has been accepted. The land includes a small barn, and I'd like to move Oasis there, if you'll agree to sell me your half ownership."

"Oh." Marjorie felt completely inarticulate.

"She'll have her own field to graze, and the barn is heated. The property adjoins a state forest with hundreds of acres to explore. She'll be happy."

But I won't! Marjorie closed her eyes and tried to slow the pulsing that seemed to be building up pressure in her chest.

Perhaps Suzanne read Marjorie's reaction, because she lowered her shoulders with a sigh, touched Marjorie's arm, and dropped her business-like manner. "Please, Marjorie, I love this horse, and I'll be able to spend time with her every day. Not a one-hour ride, three times a week, but time to really work with her and form a true relationship. I need this," she added softly.

Relationship! Can't she form a relationship with a person, instead of my horse? Marjorie forced herself to remain calm, pushing away an accusing voice in her head that said the same could be asked of her. "Suzanne, I want time to think about this. Right now, I need to ride. Give me a few days, and I'll get back to you, okay?"

The outing proved less than satisfactory. It could have been her imagination, but Oasis seemed bored with traveling the same trails, and Marjorie certainly didn't unwind.

⌘ ⌘ ⌘

The third blow came when Colleen phoned that afternoon. "Oh, Mom, I thought you'd be out. I planned to leave a message. Now I'm flustered."

"Hi, dear." Marjorie focused on using a normal voice. "You heard your sister's news?"

"That's part of why I'm calling. You know, if Sophie leaves in January, I can't afford this apartment by myself."

"You could probably find another student to share it."

"People are settled by the middle of the school year. I had a different idea."

Marjorie braced herself. She wondered if she should sit down.

"Mom, what would you think of me doing a semester abroad?"

"Of course." Marjorie was thinking, *Of course, that's the way things go. Everybody leaves at once.* However, to her dismay, she realized Colleen heard the "of course" as agreement.

"Oh, Mom, thank you so much! I figured you wouldn't want me to be that far away, since Sophie will be leaving, too. You're the coolest. I have a chance to study in London...."

Marjorie listened to Colleen's enthusiastic plans, all the while picturing the growth card that said, *Letting my daughters go.* She finally managed a good-bye with forced cheeriness in her voice. She hung up the phone and exhaled all the bluster she had held back. "I need a cup of tea."

As she put a pot on to boil, she thought back to college when she and her roommate shared their worries while they sipped and warmed their hands around their mugs. She wished she could talk to someone now, but she hadn't made that type of friend since she moved to Oregon and met Michael. Busy at first with her studies, she shared any spare time with him. Then marriage, motherhood, and work left little time for friendships.

She poured the boiling water over a teabag into her favorite teapot, rather than straight into a mug, knowing these new worries would require more than one cup to think through. The tea steeped as her mind ricocheted from Sophie's engagement to Oasis's sale, on to Colleen's study abroad and back to Sophie. When she finally poured it, she breathed in the spicy-orange aroma and then took a sip.

"Whoa!" Marjorie's mouth pursed. Nutmeg, who had been watching Marjorie with her own wrinkled brow, raised her ears.

The bitter tannic-acid flavor brought to mind the tea she had shared with Colm from the cup lid of a thermos bottle. She wished she could laugh now as they had then. She carried her cup to the computer and began a letter.

Dear Colm...

However, the words wouldn't come. How could she put on paper all the worries plaguing her? Sophie hadn't known Niko long enough to be marrying him so soon. Marjorie would miss Oasis like a member of the family, but was she being selfish? Was selling her better for Oasis?

She pushed back from the keyboard and sipped her tea. Both girls would live so far away. If Sophie moved to California, she'd leave her friends, her family, and all her support systems behind. How would a semester away affect Colleen's studies? Would she still graduate on time? Could Sophie find work in California? Marjorie had never met Niko, but what she did know, she didn't like.

At last, it occurred to Marjorie that she had one Friend who could bring peace to a troubled heart. She bowed her head.

My Friend, I raised these girls to be independent, and when they left home, I put them into Your care. Help me trust them to make good decisions and trust You to give them wisdom. I want them to be happy. I don't know why this is hitting me so hard. I just don't want to lose them. I don't want to be all alone…again…like when Michael died.

Marjorie's stomach clenched. A constriction moved up her throat and sucked in air that collided with a sob. She laid her head down onto her arms and wept, a shoulder-shaking, breath-gasping cry for help.

Nutmeg circled and whined. Trained not to jump, she lowered her ears in apology and then gently put both front paws on Marjorie's lap and tried to lick the tears from her cheeks. Smelling-salted back to the moment by doggie breath, Marjorie hugged Nutmeg and then wiped her eyes and blew her nose. "You're right, Nutmeg, I'm not alone."

You're right, too, My Friend. Not alone, but terrified of being so. She thought of Colm's latest unanswered letter and retrieved it from a paper pile on the table.

Dearest Marjorie,

Please allow me to share some words from my grandmother. A woman in my parish died, leaving her husband behind. Only six months later, our family received an invitation to his wedding. My mother seethed at the thought that he would dishonor the memory of his first wife by remarrying so soon.

I'll never forget the logic behind my grandmother's words when she asked, "Is there any doubt of that man's love for his wife when she was alive? Sure now, what man from an unhappy marriage would be wanting to commit himself again so soon?"

Marjorie, you yourself say your marriage was a happy one. Why, knowing how lovely marriage can be, are you afraid of intimacy? I know you've counseled many unhappy couples, but such experience should encourage you. You know the pitfalls of relationships and how to avoid them.

At the risk of an amateur analysis, could it be something deeper? Another reason that keeps you from reaching out?

Your friend,
Colm

Marjorie hugged the letter to her chest. She shook her head at her own folly. She had thought she was being loyal to Michael. But really she had been afraid to love, to risk a repeat of the deep hurt she'd felt when Michael died. She didn't know if she could survive that kind of pain again. However, she couldn't stand this loneliness based on fear. She was sure of that.

There was more. She had called God her Friend but blamed Him for letting Michael die. So, she kept herself from trusting Him completely. Yet, when she'd felt the most abandoned, He stood near her, offering abundance to her.

She remembered the nudges she now knew were from Him. The flashed images of Colm's card in her drawer. The advice she gave students that resounded in her heart. Exhorting Tessa to place one person into God's hands in order to be ready for the next. The feeling of release as she remembered her daughters agreeing someone out there needed her love. The chance meeting at the dance studio. Telling the lonely freshman to make the call.

Her new awareness of being cherished by God filled her soul and raised her chin. She gave one nod and walked to her nightstand. With shaking hands but a determined heart, she removed her wedding ring, planning to place it in her drawer. She reconsidered and slid it onto her right hand. Michael would always be a part of her. Marjorie's inner spirit twirled around on tiptoe.

She took Colm's card out of the drawer and picked up the phone.

Thirty-three

Thank you, Friend.

The Wednesday night before Thanksgiving, Joe and Tessa settled into their hotel room, next door to Amy and Stephen. They had driven halfway to Tessa's parents' home, where they would spend the long weekend. As Tessa came from the bathroom, rubbing lotion on her hands, she heard Joe saying good night to the children. He closed the adjoining door and locked it.

She turned to him and he smiled. *That boyish smile would have led to more in the past*, she thought sadly. But she pushed the idea aside, not willing to head down that road of hopes raised and dashed. She stopped in front of the mirror, removed her earrings and necklace, and then quickly brushed through her short curls.

She glanced at Joe, only slightly aware that he was watching her, before she was lost in thought about plans for the following day. She hadn't brought anything lacy or fun for this motel night, but wore a modest robe and nightgown, prepared for the three nights when they would share her old bedroom with their children. She wondered what worries were making Joe so quiet tonight. Usually he would read his magazines until she was ready, but she didn't hear any page turning coming from the bed behind her.

Tessa moved away from the mirror. She carefully lifted layers of clothes in her suitcase and slid out what she'd wear the next day. She felt into each corner, not finding the book she thought she had packed.

As she straightened, she felt Joe slip his arms around her waist and turned, caught completely by surprise. He looked into her eyes; their souls joined through their gaze. "Tessa, come to bed," he whispered. "Please. Now."

Tessa couldn't help but laugh. So the new antidepressant must finally be working. All the nights she had yearned for those words, and they were whispered to her when she least expected it.

Joe untied Tessa's robe and guided it down off her shoulders. His breathing was shallow, and she felt her own breath come faster. Her mind jumped ahead in anticipation. Joe's crinkled-eye smile shot joy through Tessa that sent silent praise heavenward. "I love you so much," he whispered close to her ear.

She turned her lips toward his, but before they met, a knock insisted at the inner door.

"Mom! Stephen's sick. He's throwing up."

"No!" whispered Joe, his face clearly crumpling with disappointment. Tessa slid back into her robe, touched his cheek, and went to the door while he sank to the bed with a low growl.

When Tessa entered the children's room, she grasped the situation in a quick glance. Wrappers covered Stephen's bed: Almond Joys, Cheetos, sunflower seeds, beef jerky, M & Ms, and on his nightstand, three open soda cans. She could hear Stephen paying the consequences in the bathroom and hurried in to murmur words of comfort.

Tessa heard Amy explaining to her dad, "We found this little refrigerator full of great snacks." She slipped back into the room and looked at Amy's bed: one Mounds bar, a peanut bag, and a single can on her nightstand.

A pale Stephen emerged from the bathroom and groaned when he saw the collection of evidence on his bed. "I wasn't even that sick after Halloween."

Tessa went to the mini refrigerator and checked for what remained—six tiny bottles of liquor and two beers. "Could have been worse, I guess." The price list for the snacks, obviously overlooked by the children, stood next to the beer. She handed it to Joe to read, and his moan sounded remarkably like his son's. He whistled low and pointed out that the children had gone through at least fifty dollars of what they thought were complimentary treats.

"Stephen, maybe you've learned something about self-indulgence?" she chided.

"Or gluttony?" contributed ever-supportive Amy.

Joe scowled. "Time to learn about finances, too. You two add up what you've spent, and in the morning we'll talk about how you'll pay for it. Now go to bed. We'll get you up at seven to head to your grandparents', where we'll all try not to self-indulge at Thanksgiving dinner."

Tessa thought about how much Joe loved his mother-in-law's mashed potatoes and gravy and realized it might not be easy, even for him.

She took Joe by the hand and led him back to their room. "Good night, kids. No talking," she said before she closed the door. She looked at Joe with a wink as she turned the lock. "Now, where were we?"

Joe turned the radio on quietly and took Tessa in his arms. He stepped back to untie her robe once again and laid it carefully across the chair. He lifted one hand in the air and extended the other to guide her waist toward him. Her hand reached to his.

They danced to his music.

⌘ ⌘ ⌘

The night before Thanksgiving, Siara and Mo joined Hank on his drive to the airport to pick up his grandmother. Rather than Hank traveling to Spokane to spend the holiday, he had convinced her to come share the weekend with him.

Early Thursday morning, when Hank returned to his apartment from work, he found Mo watching the parade on television and his two favorite women bustling and laughing in his small kitchen. He would have liked to stay awake and watch them get to know each other, but they sent him off to bed.

"How can we talk about you if you're here?" Siara teased. He climbed into bed to the sound of happy female voices in his home, a first for him. He listened as Siara told Esther about her reconciliation with her family, and how she looked forward to their promised visit to Portland. His mind turned to his own dad, and Hank realized he had reconciled with his memory of his father, too.

"Dad," he whispered, "I just figured out what to do with the money you gave me. I'm going to offer my bride the college education you saved for. It'll go to your new daughter-in-law instead of your son. I wish you could know her." Before falling asleep, Hank decided to ask Siara if he could buy Mo a puppy for Christmas, thinking a cairn terrier would be perfect for Mo. And a basketball hoop.

That evening, after a meal Hank rated as the best he had ever enjoyed, Hank and Siara were cleaning the kitchen together. Esther dozed in Hank's recliner while Mo read the comic books she had brought him. "A dime for your thoughts," Siara said to Hank.

"A dime?"

"Inflation."

Hank laughed. "Actually, I was thinking of the relationship paper we need to write for our class and how far I've come since the semester started when I had no real relationships. I never would have dreamed that I'd be part of a family by Thanksgiving. Now, here I am with a grandma," he lowered his voice, "and a fiancée," and then spoke normally again, "and a little buddy."

"Sounds like plenty to write." Siara spoke louder than she'd intended, and Esther jumped. She struggled out of the recliner and joined them in the kitchen to fill the teakettle.

Hank stepped aside for her. "But we're supposed to include whether we felt any benefit from praying for our relationship. I can't say I prayed about it. I'm just beginning to learn how to pray." Hank watched Esther nod approval as she turned on the burner.

"Well, I have," Siara answered in a soft voice that sounded to him like an angel's song. "I've prayed for you even before I knew you. I started as a little girl. I prayed for the boy who would grow up and marry me." At this, Esther turned and looked from one to the other. Siara nodded to Esther, but put a finger to her lips and looked over at Mo, who sat completely entranced by superheroes. "We're waiting until Christmas to tell Mo, and then I'll wear my ring."

Esther put an arm around each of them and whispered, "I'm so happy for you both. Congratulations!"

"You've been praying for me since you were small?" Hank's voice cracked as he pictured her kneeling beside her bed as a little girl.

Siara nodded. "Praying that you were growing to be the man God wanted you to become for me. And then, once I had Mo, I prayed that God would bring a man to us that would be both a good husband and a good father."

"Then I'm like those patients Dr. Gloriam mentioned who healed faster than others because people prayed for them, even though the patients didn't know." Siara smiled and nodded.

Esther said, "I've been praying for you every day since I knew my daughter was pregnant with you, Henry. I prayed all the harder once you disappeared. Praying became all I could do for you, so I did it fervently." She rested her hand on his arm. "The good Lord answered my prayer the day you showed up on my doorstep. But I think He also answered it each day by taking care of you while you grew up. With His help you've overcome a lonely childhood and become a sensitive, remarkable young man." The kettle whistled, and she lifted it, asking, "Tea anyone?"

⌘ ⌘ ⌘

Brian and Gwen spent Thanksgiving back in their hometown, eating a full turkey dinner at her parents' home at two o'clock and a second one with his family at six. "Brian," Gwen said as they watched grandparents, aunties, and cousins playing with their boys, "this is the right town for us to raise these little guys. More love surrounds them here than they'll ever realize."

Brian grinned.

"Next year let's spend a few extra days at Thanksgiving, and I'll start putting out feelers to see if I can find a counseling position when I've finished the program."

"I don't know." Brian rubbed the back of his neck. "We have friends in Portland now who would be hard to leave." Gwen looked at him with rounded eyes, and he grinned. "But I guess for the good of my boys, I could tear myself away from the big city."

She gave him a playful shove and then slid her arm around his back. "We're doing okay, aren't we?"

"Scared me there for a while. I thought our fighting could rip our family apart."

"We're not perfect yet. Forty-five dollars in our 'I'm Sorry Box,' last count. But we're feeding it less often. And Mickey seems more relaxed. For that matter, so am I. I think we're going to make it, Brian."

He curled his arm around her shoulders and nodded as his sister read Joe Pat a story, his dad played checkers with a giggling Mickey, and his nephew built a block tower with Sean.

Thirty-four

Hope and a future.

Marjorie's mind wouldn't release the misgivings that had begun when she studied herself critically before leaving home. She still wore her hair, which had been light auburn on her first date with Michael, in springy curls around her face and a bit past her shoulders, but now it had lightened almost to strawberry blonde. Her brown eyes hadn't changed color, of course, but they were framed by laugh lines when she smiled and seemed too serious when she didn't. When she met Michael, she was more slender, but he had assured her over the years that any extra pounds enhanced her shapeliness. She hoped the dark green dress she chose to honor Colm's homeland complimented those curves.

Just before five o'clock on the Saturday of Thanksgiving weekend, Marjorie walked from a parking garage to the Marina Fish House on the Willamette River. Colm McCloskey, waiting for her at the top of the wooden ramp that led down to the floating restaurant, dispelled any qualms that remained.

She inhaled sharply at the sight of him and felt young again. He wore a striking black suit with a charcoal wool vest beneath it. The suit accentuated his dark, wavy hair. As he took her hands and looked at her like he couldn't believe his luck, she noted his green eyes twinkled with a spark that hinted he had been mischievous as a boy.

"Ah, Marjorie, you look lovely. But what is this? You've changed your cologne. I don't smell that Oasis scent that so attracted me in the first place."

Marjorie had phoned ahead for early reservations so Colm could enjoy the view before the sunset. As requested, the hostess seated them

231

at a window. Marjorie looked out and tried to see the view through Colm's eyes. A sternwheeler paddled past the restaurant on this main artery through Portland's downtown. Ducks swam near the restaurant. Across the water, joggers and walkers traveled the Eastbank Esplanade walkway that flanked the river past five bridges.

After they placed their orders, Colm opened the conversation, telling her about his homeland and the many wonders there.

Marjorie sighed. "I'd love to see Ireland and know the country of my ancestors."

"You reminded me of home the first day I saw you." He paused. "When I thought of coming to America to teach, I was in a panic. I hadn't realized how small my world had become back in Ireland until the prospect of vastly enlarging it loomed ahead. I'd think about applying for my passport or choosing what to bring with me. Suddenly, I couldn't breathe, and my heart would race until I thought I'd drop dead on the spot." Colm sat erect. "Good heavens! This is hardly the kind of talk to impress a woman on a first date. Usually I am quite a competent person." He shrugged like an embarrassed teen.

"But here you are. You must be quite capable to have conquered your fears."

"I went to a good friend of mine in the psychology department who convinced me that I could relax myself out of a panic attack, and it wouldn't kill me. He pointed out that perhaps I had been avoiding for years things that made me uncomfortable. He said it was time to face my fears, in order to be released from them. Wasn't it he who recommended writing the list of all of my fears? A very humbling experience, by the way. But I began with the easiest and started facing them, one by one."

Marjorie nodded. His mention of the lists on their first meeting had led her to write her own growth cards. Though she hadn't prioritized them, the cards helped her resolve to overcome her fears, as each arose. Her thoughts jumped to her students this term: Gwen, Tessa, Hank, and the others. She thought how each step of progress they made was really a result of facing their fears and continuing to reach out.

As she imagined reaching her hand out to Colm, a waiter brought them bowls of fisherman's stew. She felt her cheeks burn at the thought of giving in to her impulse. Marjorie appreciated the soup's aroma as well as the chance to collect her emotions and her wandering attention. She pulled her focus back to his words.

"That's what I was doing the day we met at the stable. My fear of horses is one of my worst. It has been ever since a bad experience as a child. You have to understand that in Ireland everyone loves horses. We're devoted to them and take pride in them, whether a pony pulling a jaunty car or a fine thoroughbred racing at the Irish Derby. Not to love horses is to be a bit daft."

She smiled sadly. Her own affection for Oasis heightened her sympathy for someone who couldn't appreciate the special relationship that can develop with a horse.

"At University College, I managed to avoid them quite well. Here in Portland, apart from the mounted police downtown, 'tis fairly easy, too. But horses came next on my list of fears, so I forced myself to drive out to the stable that morning. My cousin's wife used to ride there and recommended me to the owner's care. I sat trying to get up the nerve to get out of the car to talk to…Melle, is it?…when you parked near me."

Marjorie cocked her head. She didn't remember seeing him before her fall.

"I was fighting down the panic when I first saw you. A beautiful woman getting out of her car next to me…"

Marjorie bobbed her appreciation of the compliment.

"…wee girls half as tall as their horses were calmly leading them past the car, and I couldn't even move."

Marjorie sighed with sympathy, and he grinned as if the good-natured brunt of a joke. "A half hour later, I had decided that simply surviving there in the car was enough progress for one day. I started the car to back out and turned to check behind me."

Colm became animated. "That's when I saw you thrown from the horse. Your head hit the fence. Running toward you before I knew what I was doing, I feared you'd broken your neck and died on the spot. Wasn't I relieved that you seemed to be uninjured?"

"Just wounded pride." Marjorie had relived that day in her mind many times and glowed with the thought that Colm remembered it so clearly as well.

"I was thinking you still shouldn't be moved, but then I saw that beastie start walking back toward us. I surely hoped you could walk because, otherwise, wouldn't I have to be carrying you?"

"But you didn't think of leaving me?"

He looked shocked. "No, not at all, at all."

Marjorie sensed her little-girl self pirouette as his words rekindled the feelings from that first meeting. "Very brave to put my welfare above your fear."

"I feel more foolish than brave." He paused. "You certainly are lovely to talk to."

Marjorie again felt her color rise. Thankfully, they were interrupted by the arrival of his pecan-topped salmon and her hazelnut-encrusted halibut. She told him about her growth cards and their part in her struggle to let go. As the conversation continued, she was delighted to see that, though Colm wrote and sometimes spoke quite formally, he didn't take himself seriously. In fact, he seemed to especially enjoy laughing at his own foibles. She had missed laughter in her life. Maybe that was part of her initial attraction to him. Well, that and his shamrock green eyes…and his smile that lifted his face so that even his hairline shifted…and the way she felt cherished when she was near him.

By dessert, their conversation turned to the spouses they had lost. He seemed unthreatened as he listened about Michael. In turn, Colm told her about Dympna. After two years of marriage, fertility testing had discovered her cancer. She fought valiantly for another year before leaving Colm all alone. The ache in her chest made Marjorie understand the expression, "Her heart went out to him." Marjorie felt a growing connection to Colm as they honored each other's lost loves by the telling of their stories.

After dinner they strolled along Waterfront Park. She described how the west side of the river had been reclaimed decades ago when a harbor road was replaced with lush grass, trendy shops, fountains, and walkways. It made a vibrant heart for the city. As they ambled, Marjorie shared her concerns about her daughters and told of her sad decision to sell Oasis.

He took her hand in silent support. His fingers didn't nestle between hers the same way Michael's had, but the strength of his hand calmed her. She reveled in the simple pleasure of it the whole time they watched a flotilla of sailboats and yachts decorated with Christmas lights parade by. Occasionally he would stroke his thumb against the back of her hand. When the last boat passed, they danced in the dark to its strains of "Silent Night." When the music and parade ended, Marjorie rested her head against his chest. Colm raised her hand to his lips and then accompanied Marjorie to her car.

They kissed gently before she opened the door, and he said, "Good night, Marjorie Gloriam. May God bless your sleep and may His angels watch over you. I'll call you tomorrow, if I might." She nodded with misty eyes, moved by his kiss and touched by his prayer.

⌘ ⌘ ⌘

The next morning, Marjorie stayed under the hot spray of the shower longer than usual as she relived the memory of the previous evening. The phone rang just after she stepped from the shower. She wrapped the towel around her and hurried to her room. "Hello?"

"*Ad majorem, dei Gloriam!*"

Marjorie chuckled. "Is that you, Colm?"

"Good morning, Marjorie! When I said, 'Good night,' I used your whole name, which all along has had such a familiar ring to it. I couldn't figure out why. Then, while I was shaving, it popped into my head, the old Latin phrase, *Ad Majorem Dei Gloriam!* I don't suppose your middle name starts with D?"

"Diane."

"Marjorie D. Gloriam, you are named for the 'greater glory of God!'"

"Yes, I realized that coincidence myself when I married Michael and took his last name. In fact, *Ad majorem, dei Gloriam* was spelled out in mosaic behind the altar of the chapel where we married. The chapel was on a Jesuit campus, and that's their motto." She had enjoyed the humor her Friend expressed when He brought her and Michael together—God's humor, and surely a sign of His blessing on their marriage, too. She never before had met someone else who caught the significance of her married name.

Marjorie didn't dare share her next thought. *Marjorie D. McCloskey. No, it doesn't have the same spark as Marjorie D. Gloriam.* She shook herself. Way too early to be thinking along those lines, anyway. He would be returning to Ireland at the end of the school year, but she wouldn't let herself dwell on that now.

"Marjorie, would you by chance be preparing to go to church?"

"Yes, Colm, that is precisely what I'm doing."

"Might you consider meeting me at St. Michael's at 10:00?"

"Could you make it in time to meet me at St. Juan Diego's for the 9:30 instead? I'm a reader there today. Afterwards, I'll make you an American Sunday breakfast."

"Grand. I'll see you there. And Marjorie," he said, "thank you for a brilliant evening."

"I'm sorry it took me so long to face my fears. I'll look forward to seeing you, Colm."

Thank You, My Friend. Thank You for bringing this interesting man into my life. Please let me be a blessing to his life, too.

Marjorie sensed a special wink from her Friend when she reviewed the reading and saw it came from the book of Jeremiah. Later, she read the words to the congregation but cherished them as words meant especially for her.

"'For I know the plans I have for you,' declares the Lord, 'plans to prosper you and not to harm you, plans to give you hope and a future.'" Her heart swelled as she continued. "'I will be found by you,' declares the Lord, 'and will bring you back from captivity.'"

He had kept His promise.

Ah, 'tis not the end.

'Tis only the Beginning.

References

Gottman, John M. & Silver, Nan (1995). *Why Marriages Succeed or Fail: and How You Can Make Yours Last.* Simon & Schuster Adult Publishing Group.

Real, Terrence (1998). *I Don't Want to Talk About It: Overcoming the Secret Legacy of Male Depression.* Simon and Shuster Adult Publishing Group.

Schnarch, David M. (1998). *Passionate Marriage: Keeping Love and Intimacy in Committed Relationships.* Henry Holt & Co.

Zilbergeld, Bernie (1999). *The New Male Sexuality.* Random House.

"I know the plans I have for you declares the Lord, plans to prosper you and not to harm you, plans to give you hope and a future.... I will be found by you,' declares the Lord, 'and will bring you back from captivity." Jeremiah 29:11, 14.

About the Author

BETTY ARRIGOTTI had finished a Master of Arts in Counseling but wanted to use her writing passion to help more couples than she could as a counselor. This story grew out of a collection of her favorite psychologists' advice for building stronger marriages. It was only after the first draft was completed that she recognized herself in each of the characters. Perhaps you will see yourself or your loved one in them, too.

Each Lent Betty sends a weekly email called "Four Minutes for Marriage" to a growing audience. Betty has added a new series called, "Four Minutes *Before* Marriage." She invites you to visit her website at **www.BettyArrigotti.com** to access the series.

www.BettyArrigotti.com
www.oaktara.com